KINGDOM'S DREAM

Her mother's death leaves Katie Cullen alone in the world. Swansea is no place for a young girl on her own. The navvies who are building the new railway look for trouble, and the outskirts are transformed into a shanty town as the silver track wends its way to the town centre. Katie meets handsome Bull Beynon, foreman of the railway builders and falls in love with him. But Bull lives with the spirited Rhiannon. Katie and Rhiannon are caught in a network of lies and deceit as their lives become intertwined with those of the women at the Mainwaring Pottery. Llinos, the still-beautiful owner, is having to live with an old scandal, while her friend Eynon endures the marriage of his daughter Jayne to the rascally Dafydd Buchan. Secrets and love affairs bring tragedy in their wake in the town now dominated by the monster they call the Great Western Railway.

KINGDOM'S DREAM

Iris Gower

CHIVERS PRESS
BATH

First published 2001
by
Bantam Press
This Large Print edition published by
Chivers Press
by arrangement with
Transworld Publishers Ltd
2001

ISBN 0 7540 1612 9

British Library Cataloguing in Publication Data available

Printed and bound in Great Britain by
BOOKCRAFT, Midsomer Norton, Somerset

To my dear friend D.L. Anne Hobbs, M. Ed.,
the real expert on the Great Western Railways,
with much love

CHAPTER ONE

It was growing dark and fog crept between the rise of Kilvey Hill and the sheltering heights of the Town Hill. It blanketed the stink from the copper works, holding it low over the houses. In Swansea, candles and lamps were being lit but the lights scarcely penetrated the gloom. A fine rain had begun to fall and Katie Cullen shivered, pushing back a curl of dark hair that had escaped from under her bonnet. She was sheltered in the porch of St Joseph and she was the last one of the twenty members of the choir left at the church, except for old Tom Walters who was locking up.

'Night, Katie!' He slammed the door with an almighty bang, startling her out of her reverie. 'I'm sorry I can't walk you home tonight, especially with those navvies from the Great Western Railway roaming the streets, but I promised my daughter I'd go round there for a bite of supper.' He hesitated. 'I did tell you, didn't I? I'm so forgetful these days.'

Tom was the mainstay of the Bethesda choir, organizer, conductor and general dogsbody. He *had* forgotten to tell her and she would miss his company.

'Not to worry, Mr Walters.' Katie brushed a raindrop from her cheek but another dripped from her bonnet and splashed on to her fingers. 'I'm big enough to see myself home.' She glanced up uncertainly at the lowering clouds.

'Found yourself lodgings yet, child?' Mr Walters said gently. 'I know you've got to get out of that

1

house by the end of the month now that your mammy's, well . . . you know.'

'Yes, I know. I'll be all right, Mr Walters,' Katie said, brushing away his sympathy, touched but embarrassed by it. 'Go on you, your daughter will be waiting for you. I'll be just fine, don't worry,' she said. 'See you next week.'

She watched the old man hobble away, leaning heavily on his stick, and suddenly felt lonely. 'Mammy,' she whispered, 'why did you have to die and leave me by myself?' She rubbed her cheeks as tears mingled with the raindrops. She was so alone now, with no one to care if she lived or died. Except, perhaps, Mr Walters who would miss having a good contralto voice in the choir. She smiled and pulled her bonnet forward to shelter her face.

Yes, Mr Walters would miss her. It was a small consolation but warming for all that. She began to hurry towards Greenhill. She was not looking forward to letting herself into a cold dark house and spending another night by a cheerless fire built with nothing but sticks and cinders—the coal had run out almost a week ago and the weather had turned spiteful, as if to punish her.

Katie felt insubstantial, as if she did not really exist, for her footsteps were muffled by the rain and fog. She chewed her lip, telling herself that tomorrow she must concentrate on finding a job where she could live in.

As she reached the higher ground on the road running up from the town, she quickened her step as she passed the bar room of the Castle from where she could hear the sound of Irish voices raised in drunken song. She smiled: the choir could

2

take some tips from the navvies, sure enough.

A gang of them was coming down the street towards her and Katie dodged into a doorway, not wanting to draw attention to herself. The railwaymen had taken over the town: they earned good money and were not shy of spending it, not on their women or their living quarters though—the navvies' homes were hastily built huts on the side of the tracks—but on beer.

Katie saw the camp women each time she ventured into town. They cooked outdoors when the weather was fine, the smoke from their fires adding to the stench of the copper works that dominated the town. Katie wondered what would happen when the railway line was finished. Would the navvies vanish from Swansea leaving a trail of broken-hearted women behind them?

Abruptly she stopped walking as the door of Tom's Tavern opened and men spilled onto the roadway. Two fell to the ground, limbs entwined, and began to punch each other with more enthusiasm than accuracy while the others cheered them on.

Katie attempted to sidestep them but as she edged past a hand shot out and caught her ankle. 'A colleen, look, a sweet young girl and she's mine!'

The men clambered to their feet, fight forgotten. The one who had hold of Katie transferred his grip to her waist.

'Let me go!' Katie tried to slap his face but he laughed, holding her away from him with ease.

'Don't be like that, lovely. Seth only wants to take care of you.' He dragged her into the doorway of Taylor's grocery store and pressed himself against her. 'You're out looking for business, aren't

3

you? Well, your search is over. Seth will pay you well for a bit o' pleasure but, for pity's sake, stop struggling.'

'I'm not one of the bad girls who roam the street so leave me alone!' Katie kicked out sharply and her booted foot caught the man's shin. He hollered with pain. 'You bad bitch!' He grabbed her by the throat and shook her.

'Right, Seth, that's enough.' The voice was low but full of suppressed anger. 'It's the likes of you get us navvies a bad name.'

The man spun round, releasing her at once. 'Right, Bull.' He stepped away from her. 'Sorry, Bull, I got carried away, like.'

'Are you all right, miss? I'm Bull Beynon, foreman of the Swansea line, and I apologize for the way my boys are behaving. They're a bit drunk, that's all.'

He towered over her, dark and strong, his shoulders broad under his jacket. He had a kind voice but Katie was not taking any chances. She pushed past him and ran as fast as she could towards the lamplight further along the street. She heard shouting behind her as she darted out onto the road, unaware of the carriage and pair thundering towards her. And then the horses were on her, eyes rolling, hoofs raised. She scarcely felt the blow as everything swirled around her head and darkness claimed her.

*   *   *

'Hell and damnation! We've hit someone! Stop the carriage, Jacob.' Eynon Morton-Edwards leaped down onto the road, his eyes straining to see the figure lying on the cobbles. He heard the roar from the navvies, and although he was one of the richest, most powerful men in Swansea he felt a dart of discomfort as he saw the crowd of men milling across the road.

'It's the Great Western navvies, sir,' his driver shouted. 'They're drunk again, and this is no place for a gentleman on a Saturday night. Get back in the coach, sir, please.' He had to raise his voice to make himself heard.

'Don't be ridiculous, Jacob. Hold the animals still—it looks like we've run into a young girl.'

Eynon Morton-Edwards bent over the slim figure on the ground. The girl looked respectable enough: she had a silver cross hanging across her small breasts and it was clear she was not one of the doxies who plied their trade along the town's streets.

'Is she all right?' A big man hurried into the roadway. 'I'm Bull Beynon, in charge of the navvies.' He knelt in the road beside the girl, lifting her head and cradling her in his arms.

'Do you know her?' Eynon asked, and when the man shook his head he said, 'All right, come on, then, man, help me get her into the carriage. I'll take charge of her now.'

Bull Beynon picked up the girl easily and waited until Eynon was in the coach, then handed her over to him.

'Turn the horses, Jacob,' Eynon said quietly to his driver. 'We'd best get the hell out of here.'

Jacob flicked the reins and the horses set off at speed. 'Those damn navvies,' he called over his shoulder. 'There's always trouble with them on pay day. Ought to be locked up,' he continued.

Eynon settled the girl on the seat beside him and ran his hand over her thin limbs. 'Nothing broken, by the look of it,' he said, 'though there's a nasty bump on the child's head.'

'Well,' Jacob said defensively, 'we're not to blame. It's the navvies. I wish they'd get out of Swansea. The place would be much safer without them.'

'Ah, but maybe they're a necessary evil, Jacob,' Eynon said. 'They're laying the track for the railway and we've got to put up with them until the job's done.' The girl's head lay against his shoulder and her eyes flickered. She stirred in his arms. 'I think she's all right,' he called, relieved. 'She's coming round. We'd better find out where she lives.'

The girl opened her eyes and looked up at him in alarm. 'Who are you?' she whispered, as she drew away from him, a frightened expression on her face.

'I'm Mr Morton-Edwards, child.' He peered at her in the gloom. She looked very pale. 'Are you feeling all right? That was a nasty tumble you took.'

'I'm all right. Could you please take me home?'

Before Eynon could speak, Jacobs turned in his seat. 'Out, my girl. If you're feeling all right you can find your own way home. You've given Mr Morton-Edwards enough trouble as it is.'

'Hush, Jacob,' Eynon said, 'and you, child, stay where you are. Tell us where you live and we'll get you safely home to your parents.'

'I got no parents, sir,' her eyes were large and beseeching, 'but if you'll take me to Greenhill I'll be all right.'

'What are you doing out at this time of night anyway?' Eynon frowned. 'You're little more than a child and yet you mix with the navvies.'

'I wasn't mixing with them.' The girl was near to tears. 'I came to town for choir practice. The Bethesda choir are singing tomorrow at Alderman Stanley's banquet.'

Eynon studied the girl. She was a few years younger than his daughter and she smelt of roses and freshness. Even though she was of the lower orders she was neatly dressed and obviously intelligent.

'What's your name?' he asked, as Jacob set the horses in a trot, disapproval clear in the line of his shoulders.

'I'm Katie Cullen, if it pleases you, sir.' Her voice was a little stronger. 'And I'm sorry to be a trouble to you.'

'Nonsense. It's I should apologize for knocking you down.'

The fog that had hugged the valley was thinning a little as the land rose towards Greenhill and Eynon sighed. It had been a wasted evening as far as he was concerned: all he'd wanted was a good night of conversation and wine with his friend Father Martin. Well, that was ruined now.

'We're nearly there, sir,' Jacob's surly voice broke into Eynon's thoughts, 'but it looks as if more navvies are up by here and they're making a nuisance of themselves too.'

But the sound of Irish voices singing into the night was sweet enough to bring tears to the eyes, and Eynon smiled. 'They seem peaceable to me.

'Is this where you live, child?' he asked, as Jacob drew the carriage to a halt. The girl nodded and got shakily to her feet. Reluctantly Jacob jumped down from the driver's box, ready to help her onto the road.

A navvy came towards the carriage. 'Evening, sir. Is this little madam free for the rest of the night?'

'I'm not a madam and I'm not free. Go away and leave me alone.' She sounded near to tears, and Eynon held up his hand to Jacob indicating that he should wait a moment.

'Ah, a little Irish girl, a fresh young beauty. Come here, colleen, it's a long time since I held a girl in me arms.' The man rested his hand on her arm and she drew away so sharply she almost slipped on the wet cobbles. 'You go, sir,' she said to Eynon. 'I'll be all right.'

'Oh, no, you won't,' Eynon said. 'Get back into the carriage.' He reached out and drew her up the steps. 'Jacob, take us home, there's a good man.'

'But, sir, that girl is no good—a doxy for the navvy, she is, and you can't get lower than that.'

'Be quiet.' Eynon spoke harshly. 'I won't have disrespect shown to my guest. Drive on, Jacob.'

Jacob clucked his tongue in annoyance and flicked the reins at the horses.

'Where are you taking me, sir?' the girl stammered. Her head was bent low and her hair, loose from its pins, hung over the soft, childlike curve of her cheek.

'I'm taking you to my house,' Eynon said. 'No one will bother you there, Katie Cullen. We'll sort things out in the morning.' He heard Jacob's cluck of disbelief. 'Just do as you're told, there's a good man, and put some pace into the horses, will you? I just want to get indoors and pour myself a stiff

8

brandy. I think I need it—it's been a bloody awful night.' He rubbed his eyes wearily, wondering what his daughter would have to say about a strange girl being brought home at this time of night. Well, it was only a temporary arrangement. Come daylight, the girl could make her way back to wherever she belonged. For now she would share the room of one of the maids. At least she would be safe there and he owed her that much.

*   *   *

The next day Eynon was up early and had long finished breakfast when his daughter put in an appearance. She said she wanted to talk to him and he knew exactly what she was going to say. She'd give him hell over Katie Cullen and then she'd forget all about it.

He could hear the impatient tap of her foot as he stood in the drawing room, gazing out over the long stretch of land that led down to the bay. The fog of the previous night had vanished and the gardens of the Big House were bright with early spring blooms. Drifts of daffodils glowed yellow among the trees and crocuses lent patches of brilliant colour to the flower-beds.

'Father, are you never going to offer me an explanation?' Jayne's voice was high-pitched, hard and angry. 'Why did you bring a harlot into my house last night? Have you no shame?'

'The child is not a harlot. What makes you think she is?' he asked. 'I spoke with her when I got up, and as she appears to be looking for work I've said I'll take her on here as a maid.'

'Well, you always were taken in by a pretty face,

9

Father.' Her tone changed. 'I suppose I shall have to put up with your little ways now you're getting older—and I realize you must have been lonely since you lost Isabelle. She was a good wife but surely you can do better than a girl of the lower orders, Papa?' She sighed then smiled at him. 'But as I love you so much I'll forgive you this time.'

'Why are you being so reasonable all of a sudden?' Eynon's daughter never did or said anything without good reason.

'Father, I've got something to tell you and I know you're not going to like it.' She did not meet his eyes. 'Now, promise you'll hear me out and you won't get angry.'

'All right, out with it. What's happened? Have you run up a bill at the milliner's, perhaps?'

'No, Father, nothing so trivial!' She looked uneasy. 'I've fallen in love and I intend to be married before too long.'

'This is all rather sudden, isn't it? Who, may I ask, is the lucky lad?'

'Stop treating me like a child, Father. This is serious.'

'Listen to me, Jayne. We all fall in love more than once in a lifetime—look as me, I've had two wives and countless ladyfriends.'

'I'm different from you, Father. I'm really in love, and the last thing I want is to fall out with you about it.'

'Why should we fall out?' Eynon was humouring her. 'It's not some chimney-sweep or an Irish navvy, is it?'

'No, Father, don't be so silly.' She played with the ribbon in her hair.

Eynon frowned. 'Very well. But who is this man

that you want to marry?'

'It's . . .' She hesitated. 'It's Dafydd Buchan.' She held up her hand. 'And please understand that I intend to marry him whatever you say.'

Eynon felt as if someone had dealt him a mortal blow. 'Buchan of all people! How could you, Jayne?'

'I told you. I've fallen in love with him.' She set her lips. 'Just think about my feelings for once.'

'But you can't marry Buchan. He's a womanizing waster.' His tone was sharp. 'Where have you been seeing him, and how long have you been deceiving me?'

'I'm not trying to deceive you, Father—I've just told you about him, haven't I?' Jayne glared at him.

He tried a softer approach. 'Come here, *cariad*,' he said.

'You won't coax me out of it, either,' she said, but came to him slowly, and he enfolded her in an embrace. Her hair was fresh-washed, soft as silk, pale as his own. She was his beloved child, his only child, and he could deny her nothing but marriage to Buchan. For God's sake, how could he stomach it?

'Sit here beside me, Jayne.' He led her to the plump sofa that faced the large windows. Beyond the bright garden, the sea rolled into the shore aglow in the sunshine. 'I want only what's best for you.' Eynon said. 'You know what a reputation Dafydd Buchan has around here, and I'm afraid you'll be hurt.'

'Please, Papa, forget about the past. Dafydd is a respectable businessman now. His pottery in Llanelli is flourishing and he owns half of Carmarthen. He's richer even than you, so I'd be

11

well cared for.'

Eynon knew she was trying not to lose her temper, but he had to make her see sense. 'The fact remains that Buchan is the father of an illegitimate son. Have you forgotten the scandal that raged throughout the town about his liaison with Llinos Mainwaring?'

Jayne looked at him mutinously.

'Even if you don't remember other people will. Can you live with the shame of people talking about you, saying you're second best to Llinos?'

His words stung, and Jayne moved away from him. 'That's over and done with now!' she snapped. 'And you forget, Father, that your own past isn't above reproach, is it? I think your own feelings for Llinos are clouding your judgement.'

'That's beside the point.' Eynon swallowed uneasily. 'I deplore Buchan's lack of moral fibre but it's his interference in the laws of our country that worries me.' He struggled to keep calm. 'Burning down gates and storming the workhouse isn't the sort of behaviour expected of a gentleman, is it?'

'Dafydd was protesting against the toll charges, as you well know.' Jayne's voice was filled with righteous indignation. 'He was trying to help people less fortunate than himself to get justice. In any case, that was a long time ago. Father, I intend to marry Dafydd whatever you say.'

She stared at Eynon challengingly. 'He's coming here tonight to speak with you, and if you don't want to lose me for good please be civil to him.'

'And what if I send him away with a flea in his ear?' But he knew what Jayne would say, even before her lips framed the words.

'I shall elope with him and bring disgrace on you.' She came to sit beside him again and snuggled her head into his shoulder. 'Please, Papa, just give Dafydd a chance.'

Eynon relented. He could never deny Jayne for long but this infatuation with Buchan was not to be borne. Still, a little diplomacy might not go amiss. 'All right. If this man is the one you really want, then what can I say? Just promise me you'll have a long engagement. You're still very young, you know.'

'Probably as old as my mother was when she married you,' Jayne said. She kissed his cheek. 'I'm going to have a bath and change into something special for tonight.' She smiled at him. 'I really must have a new wardrobe soon, Papa. My gowns are so old-fashioned, I dread to be seen in them.'

Eynon was on safer ground now and smiled in relief. 'Get the sewing woman up here any time you like, and make sure the bolts of material are from new stock or you'll be buying sun-damaged goods.' He hugged his daughter and kissed the top of her head. She was so precious to him. Jayne had been the only bright thing in his life since he lost Isabelle.

'You've gone all dreamy, Papa. You're thinking of Isabelle again, aren't you?'

He remembered the terrible events that had led to Isabelle's death. The rioting against the tolls had reached a crescendo and she had been caught in the thick of the fighting at the Carmarthen workhouse. She had been crushed beneath the hoofs of the horses ridden by the dragoons. Dafydd Buchan was to blame for it all, and now his daughter wanted to marry the man.

'I know you miss her dreadfully, even now, Papa, but I'm here. I'll always be here when you need me.'

'You're right, I still have you, my lovely child,' he said. 'Promise you'll give your father some of your time when you're a married woman.'

'Don't worry, Papa, I'll always love you—and don't forget you still have good friends.' She paused and there was an edge to her voice when she spoke again. 'You'll always have Llinos Mainwaring to keep you company, won't you? You still love her—you've always loved her, even when she disgraced herself so badly. If she hadn't been married to the foreigner you'd have married her like a shot.'

'Llinos is a good friend and I won't hear a word against her,' Eynon said sharply.

'All right, Papa. We won't talk about it any more. But you must promise you will be polite to Dafydd. I'm always nice to Llinos, aren't I?'

'Yes, Jayne, I'll grant you that.'

Suddenly they heard a carriage drive through the gates and went to the window. 'Here's Llinos now!' Eynon exclaimed.

'Talk of the devil!' Jayne had come to his side. 'Mrs Mainwaring and her bastard offspring, no less.'

Eynon caught his daughter by the shoulders. 'Jayne!' he said sharply. 'You aren't being polite about her now, are you?'

Jayne twisted out of his grip as the front-door bell echoed through the house. Eynon heard the maid's voice in the hall and his heart leaped in anticipation. Even after all these years, Llinos's presence still had the power to stir him.

She came into the room like a breath of fresh air, leading her son by the hand. She was flushed from the sunshine, her eyes were glowing and her hair, soft and silky, was shaped into a bun on her slender neck. She was still as lovely as the day he had first set eyes on her.

'Llinos! How delightful.'

'I'm sorry to arrive unannounced,' she said breathlessly. 'It's such a beautiful day that I couldn't stay in the house. I hope you don't mind.'

'Of course not. Sit down, the maid will bring us refreshments.' He glanced at his daughter. 'Take Sion into the garden, Jayne, and show him the changes we are making.' It still hurt him to look at the boy. Dark and strong-featured, the image of his father. God damn Buchan! Eynon wondered briefly how Llinos's husband coped every day with the tangible evidence of his wife's infidelity.

'Don't let him be a trouble to you.' Llinos kissed Jayne's cheek.

After a brief pause, Jayne looked at Sion and smiled. 'Come on, let's go out and leave these old dears alone.' She halted in the doorway. 'I know you want to talk about me, Father, but it won't do any good, you know. My mind is made up.' Then she left the room, and Sion followed her, anxious to be out in the sunshine.

'Forgive her forthrightness but my daughter can be a little wayward.' Eynon grimaced.

'There is no need to apologize,' Llinos said. 'A great many people are sharp with me now.'

'Oh, Llinos,' Eynon said softly, 'I can't bear anyone to hurt you, and it's time my daughter learned to be more tolerant.'

Llinos smiled. 'Jayne can wrap you around her

15

little finger with no trouble,' she said.

Eynon watched as Llinos settled her full skirts around her dainty ankles. Her waist was as trim as a girl's and her breasts rounded and womanly. Even now Eynon lusted for her. He cleared his throat. 'I have something to tell you.' This was going to be difficult. 'Jayne is talking about an engagement.' He released his breath sharply. 'She thinks she's in love with Dafydd Buchan.'

Llinos pressed her hands together and looked up at him. 'So she wants to marry Dafydd? Well, he's very rich, and a good man into the bargain. She could do worse.' Her eyes glistened with unshed tears and her soft lips trembled. 'Don't worry about my feelings, Eynon. Dafydd was bound to marry sooner or later.'

'You still care for him, then?' He could scarcely believe that after all the man had put her through she still wanted him. The idea made him feel angry and sick.

'He's the father of my child and will always have a special place in my . . .' she hesitated '. . . in my affections.'

'I'll never understand women.' Eynon shook his head. 'And I'll never understand Joe's forbearance.'

'Perhaps he has a more forgiving heart than you, Eynon,' Llinos said softly. 'Anyway, it's a case of "let he who has never sinned cast the first stone", isn't it?'

Eynon could find no answer and thrust his hands into his pockets. 'It hurts that you allowed Dafydd Buchan into your bed and always denied me,' he said at last.

'So it's your pride that's hurt, then, is it?' Llinos asked. 'Eynon, can't you see that a woman is ruled

16

by her heart while a man is ruled by lust?'

'That's not true! Llinos, my love for you has always been pure. Have I ever tried to make you betray your wedding vows?'

'No, you're a true gentleman, my dear friend.'

'And that makes Buchan anything but a gentleman, and I'm supposed to agree to him marrying my daughter.'

'Eynon!' Llinos got to her feet abruptly. 'Jayne is a woman now and she has feelings—strong feelings. She must love Dafydd very much to set herself against you.' She rested her hand on his arm and he resisted the temptation to pull her close. 'No man has an unblemished reputation. You know that from your own experiences with Jayne's mother, don't you?'

'I was a very young man when I met her.' He knew his protest was weak. 'I never loved her, but I married her when I learned she was expecting my child.'

'You were tempted by a beautiful, willing woman and you succumbed. No one would blame you for that.'

'At least I was free to marry, which was more than you were when you bedded Buchan.' He watched as she made her way to the door. 'Llinos, I'm sorry.'

'I have to go, Eynon, I have no part in any of this. It is no concern of mine who your daughter marries.'

Eynon followed her into the hall. 'Please, Llinos, don't go like this. Stay and talk, drink tea with me. I didn't mean to upset you.'

'Well, you have upset me.' Llinos was taking her gloves from the maid. 'I am upset that you still

17

choose to judge me.' She looked up in his face and Eynon felt his love for her melt his heart. 'You are my dear friend, Eynon, and no man or woman will ever take your place, but there is a limit to what I will accept from you.'

He watched helplessly as she slipped her arms into her light coat. 'I'm sorry, Llinos. I was carried away with anger against Buchan and I took it out on you. Say you forgive me.'

'I'll consider it.' Her lips were trembling.

'You'll come to see me again, soon?' he asked pleadingly.

He stood by the open front door with her and watched as she sent the maid to fetch her son. Damn Buchan! One way or another the man was ruining Eynon's life and he could not be allowed to get away with it.

CHAPTER TWO

Bull Beynon stood looking at the scene around him with frustration. The work was going too slowly—the railway line from Landore into Swansea was only half finished and the navvies were restless. If the job was to be finished in time for the grand opening next year, the supply of new equipment must be improved.

Further along the track, the navvies were setting up their temporary huts for the last leg of laying the tracks that would carry the iron monsters a few more miles into the heart of Swansea town.

Bull caught sight of a girl with bright hair and recognized her. His heartbeat quickened. 'Miss

Cullen!' he called.

She stopped walking and hitched her large bag on to her other arm. 'Mr Beynon,' she said breathlessly, and glanced around her as if she had a mind to run away.

'I don't mean to be forward, Miss Cullen, but I want to apologize again for the men. They won't bother you now, you can be sure of it.' He seemed to be rushing his words. 'Are you well again after your accident?'

'I'm very well, thank you,' she looked away shyly, 'and you were kind to stand up to them the way you did.' She glanced up at him. 'One good thing to come out of it all is that Mr Morton-Edwards gave me a job at the Big House and I'm settled there now. I've just been fetching some of my things from Greenhill.'

His eyes were a warm blue as they looked into hers. 'Can I help you with that?'

'No, thank you. I've got to get used to managing because Cook's put me in charge of the shopping.'

Bull folded his big arms across his chest. 'Mr Morton-Edwards has a fine reputation and I know he'll take care of you.'

Katie smiled then and her whole face lit up. She was like a flower touched by the sun. 'He's a good master to work for.' She seemed more at ease as she put her bag on the ground. Bull resisted the urge to pick it up—it looked far too heavy for a small girl like Katie.

'And I'm sure you will make a good maid.' He watched, enchanted, as the colour came into her cheeks. She was so pretty, so dainty, and he wanted to put a protective arm around her slim shoulders. 'I wonder if . . .' Was it too soon to ask her to come

19

out with him? 'I wonder if I can call on you sometime.'

She picked up her bag hastily, covered in confusion, and Bull cursed his clumsiness, but as Katie began to walk uphill he fell into step beside her. She glanced at him then quickly looked away. 'I'll have to see what the master thinks about gentlemen callers.' She stopped and faced him. 'I shouldn't be taking you away from your work—I don't want you to get into trouble.'

Bull was touched by her concern. 'As foreman I have some privileges,' he said, 'and I don't often abuse them. Would you mind if I walked with you a little while, then?'

'That would be nice. But you'd better not come right to the house in case Mr Morton-Edwards don't like it.'

As Bull walked along beside her he was very aware of how he towered over her. She aroused within him his protective instincts. He wanted to hold her and keep her close to him. 'Can I meet you later?' he asked humbly. He was in charge of hundreds of men yet he was behaving like a gauche child.

'I'll try to pop out into the garden round the back of the house when the master's having supper.'

Bull felt jubilant. 'I'll look out for you later, then.' He watched her walk across the stretch of muddy lawn and disappear into the Big House. Then he leaned against the wall, as excited as a boy waiting for his first love. He had made progress. He smiled and looked up at the sky: the day was brightening.

Katie stood in the kitchen of the Morton-Edwards house and gazed around her. The table was scrubbed clean and the fire burned brightly in the huge fireplace. She was lucky to get a position in such a fine house.

'Well, put the bag down, girl,' Cook said, 'and count yourself lucky that the master isn't a stickler for time. You've been an age doing that little bit of shopping. Did you fetch the carrots I asked for?'

'Yes, Cook, and some of my clothes from Greenhill as well. That's why I've been so long.'

Cook poured tea out of a brown china pot. 'Come on, then, sit down. No one's going to bite you.' She smiled wryly. 'Except perhaps Miss Jayne. She bites all of us from time to time. Right little temper on that madam.' She eased herself into her chair. 'Your mam would have jumped at the chance to get you a good place like this, wouldn't she?'

'I expect so.' Katie wondered briefly how she could bear to live in a strange household. Until her mother's death she has been spoiled: as a treasured only child born late to the Cullen family she had been kept at home and not forced into labour like so many of the Greenhill children.

'Well, you'll find things strange at first,' Cook said, 'but you look the sort of girl who'll soon settle in. You're going to be an upstairs maid, lucky girl. Got your own room, haven't you? The master must like you. He's as good as gold, bless him.' Cook refilled her cup but did not offer Katie more. 'Shows us a bit of *chwarae teg*, you know, fair play. If we do our jobs well enough, he leaves us alone.'

As Katie put down her cup Cook looked at her

impatiently. 'Right, then, we'd better get sorted out. I'm Mrs Grinter but mostly I'm just called Cook. That little scamp doing the veg is Lottie, and Becky does the floors and such.'

The other maids glanced at Katie and nodded. Cook tapped her arm. 'Go on, then, girl, and get your room sorted out, because after that you're going to do a bit of work.' She half smiled. 'Nothing too hard, mind! You'll start by dusting the lamps in the bedrooms. Go on, off with you!'

Katie made her way up the back stairs, wondering if she would be able to find her room. On the top landing she opened a door and realized at once that this was Cook's: a large nightgown was laid out on the bed and a pair of enormous slippers stood on the floor.

She found her own up another flight of stairs, high in the attic. She knew it was hers because it was bare of personal possessions. She put her bag on the floor, took out her clothes and put them in a drawer. Some time soon she would have to go back to Greenhill for the rest of her things. Then she sank onto the bed. This was to be her home now, perhaps for a long time, until she married—if she ever did get married.

Her thoughts turned to Bull and his gentle kindness. He was a giant of a man but now she knew him he did not frighten her. Did he like her— really *like* her? Surely he must think something of her to ask her to meet him again. But he might have asked out of politeness. Katie sighed. Everything in her life was changing and she could only hope it would be for the better.

*　　　*　　　*

22

'Bull, what are you standing down here by the track for? It's starting to rain. I thought you was never coming home.' The question startled him and he turned to smile at his woman. Rhiannon had been with him during the long months of work on the Great Western lines.

'Just thinking,' he said mildly. He never raised his voice to Rhiannon the way he did to the men who worked for him. Then he went on, 'Just thinking that the work on the line isn't progressing as it should. We're at least three weeks behind.'

'Well, love, you know as well as I do that some jobs always do take longer. It's the weather as much as anything and no one can blame you for that.'

'Still, it sticks in my craw that men like Seth O'Connor encourage the navvies to take time off on the lamest excuse. They claim they're sick when they're just full of beer and worn out with whoring.'

Rhiannon came closer, her eyes speaking volumes. 'Well, Bull, a bit o' that's a good thing, isn't it?'

He felt his loins begin to ache. Rhiannon had that effect on him. He stared at her, trying to analyse what it was about her that he needed. He felt affection for her, but not love. And she didn't make him feel ten feet tall the way Katie Cullen did.

Rhiannon was lovely to look at even now, in her plain gown, the fullness of her breasts emphasized by her tiny waist. But she was a camp woman. She had been a camp woman when he met her and she had never pretended to be anything else. He wondered how many men she had slept with. She was only about twenty-two, with a fine skin browned by the sun and dark hair twisted into a bun at the nape of her neck, but she had lived life to the full.

'Why are you lookin' at me like that, Bull?' Her eyes slanted up at him. 'Fancyin' a bit of lovin', are you, boy?'

'Aye, but I've got work to do.' He rested his hand on her shoulder.

'What—now? It's getting late, Bull, time you came home with me and let me look after you—like a wife would.'

Bull looked up at the dying sun, at the red seeping among the clouds that threatened more rain. More time lost, more days to spend living rough in a shed at the side of the track. 'Don't say that, Rhiannon.'

She hugged his arm. 'I don't really want to be your wife, I'm happy as I am.' But she was lying, and they both knew it.

'Go on you, make a brew and I'll get back as soon as I've finished here.' He needed to talk to the engineer: the next consignment of sleepers, bolts and screws had not been delivered, and no man could build a railway without the right tools. And later, when it was supper-time at the Big House, he would be seeing Katie again.

*   *   *

He found Cookson seated in the public bar of the Castle. The inn was crowded with navvies, and thick smoke filled the room, hanging like a pall over the heads of the drinkers.

'Something wrong?' The engineer indicated a

chair. 'Sit down and talk, man, I don't like the look on your face.'

'I need supplies.' Bull sat opposite Cookson, aware of the other's fine clothes, the crisp linen and good leather boots he wore. He rubbed his calloused hands along his moleskin trousers and vowed that one day he, too, would dress in fine clothes.

'I know, and I'm making enough noise about them to wake the dead.' Cookson smoothed his beard. 'The materials are on their way, that's all I can say.' He waved to the landlord. 'I'll get you a beer. It's time you relaxed a bit, man.'

Bull sank back in his seat. Cookson was right: he needed respite like everyone else. He closed his eyes briefly and a vision of the little Irish girl flashed into his mind.

'Evenin', sir, Bull.'

Bull looked up to see Dan O'Connor standing beside him. 'Won't take up much of your time. I jest wanted to say you did good to stop the men fussin' that little girl. She was so frightened she was run over by a carriage, wasn't she?'

Bull frowned. 'It's no thanks to your brother that she wasn't killed. Your Seth was disrespectful to her, and if he acts like that again he'll find himself out of a job.'

'I know, and that's why I'm offerin' an apology, see? Seth don't mean no harm—it's just that the drink runs away with what little sense he's got.' He touched his forelock to Cookson. 'Sorry to take up your time, sir, but I jest needed to have me say.'

When Dan had gone Cookson leaned forward in his seat. 'I don't know what he was referring to but I do know some of these navvies can't behave properly around a decent woman.'

'It was a young Irish girl, sir, Katie Cullen, sweet little thing, but no real harm done, I assure you.'

'And that's because you stepped in. You're a good man to have around, Bull. I've got a lot of respect for you, and one day I hope to get you some kind of promotion. In the meantime, see the young girl in question gets an apology from me.'

'I'll do that,' Bull said, smiling. Even if he was spotted hanging around the Big House he had the perfect excuse to do so now.

*

Katie saw him before he saw her. Bull Beynon was walking swiftly uphill and her heart lifted. She had escaped from the house without too much trouble although Cook had been more than a little suspicious when she said she needed some air.

'Air?' Mrs Grinter had sniffed. 'Everyone knows night air does more harm than good. Still, I suppose this is one of your funny Irish ways.' Mrs Grinter was never going to accept that Katie had been born and bred in Swansea.

Bull was coming nearer and Katie fell back into the shadow of the doorway. He did not see her until he was pushing open the back gate and walking up the path through the lavender bed.

As she looked at him now in the evening light she noticed that his hair was thick and springy, and his shirtsleeves were rolled up to reveal powerful arms. She felt a surge of triumph that such a man was even bothering to talk to her, but that was quickly followed by common sense: he was so good-looking, so manly, that he probably had hordes of women chasing after him.

'Evening, Miss Cullen,' he said. 'The engineer,

Mr Cookson, asked me to give you his apologies for the men's uncouth behaviour.'

'Oh, I see.' Katie felt disappointment. 'I suppose that's your only reason for coming all the way up here, is it?'

'No, of course not,' Bull said quickly, 'I told you I'd be here and I always try to keep my word.' He leaned against the wall of the house. 'But if I'm asked any awkward questions I've got a good answer. I can hardly disobey my boss's express wishes, can I?'

Katie smiled. 'No, I suppose you can't.' She looked at him, not knowing what else to say. Why was she so stupid, so tongue-tied? She really wanted to make a good impression on him.

Suddenly the back door opened and Mrs Grinter was on the step. 'What you up to, Katie Cullen?' She stared at Bull in disapproval. 'And who are you, might I ask?'

Bull smiled. 'I'm Bull Beynon, foreman on the railway,' he said easily. 'My boss Mr Cookson was worried about Miss Cullen's accident the other night and sent me up to apologize on his behalf.'

Mrs Grinter's features softened. 'Oh, I know all about the accident. Poor Katie was knocked down by Mr Morton-Edwards' horses. That's why he gave her a job, see?'

'So the apology is accepted, is it?' Bull was smiling and Katie could tell that Cook was charmed by him.

'Well, yes, I suppose it is.' Cook lingered on the doorstep. 'I think Katie better come in now, though. Don't do no good for a girl's reputation to be alone with a man when it's getting dark.'

Cook took her arm and Katie had no choice but

to go into the house with her. She turned briefly to wave to Bull and then the door was closed.

'He seems a nice man but you got to be careful of them navvies, whoever they are. Got a bad name, they have, as well you know. Now, girl, get off to your bed. You'll have to start work proper tomorrow.'

Later as Katie lay and stared at the flickering candle flame on the washstand she felt like hugging herself. Bull liked her, he really did, and she was the happiest girl in all the world.

*   *   *

Bull was striding along the line away from the site of the blasting. Thankfully the rain had ceased in the last hour and he had been able to get some work done. He heard Seth O'Connor call a warning and looked up to see Katie Cullen coming towards him. 'Damn it!' He hurried towards her and took her by the shoulders. 'Katie, what are you doing here? Don't you know this is a dangerous area? We're blasting rock any minute now, girl!'

'I'm sorry,' she said, her face white. 'This is a short-cut home. I have to collect the last of my things before the landlord lets the house to someone else. Am I really in danger?'

Bull was conscious of her sweet scent. 'Of course you are. Come on, now, let me take you back to the road. You'll have to call to the house later.'

He smiled, realizing that Katie was very aware of his hands on her shoulders: a rich colour had come into her face and she was looking at her boots.

'How often do you get a day off?' he asked abruptly.

'I don't know. I'll have to ask Cook. What if I let you know when I get time off to fetch the rest of my things from Greenhill?' She grinned. 'Mind, I know what she'll say—I've only just started work and I want days off already!'

'I'd better arrange to meet you then, if only to stop you killing yourself on the workings here.'

'I don't want to give you any trouble. Look, I'd better go, I'll see you again, I'm sure.'

Bull was disconcerted by her precipitous departure but as he watched her hurry away from him into the narrow streets of the east of the town, he knew that one day Katie Cullen would play an important part in his life.

CHAPTER THREE

Dafydd Buchan strode through the pottery yard, pushing back his unruly hair impatiently as he tried to imagine life as a married man. He paused in the vestibule of the offices and stared through the small glass window. He could see Shanni Morgan, head bent over a ledger, brow furrowed as she studied the figures on the page. Shanni had come a long way from her childhood, spent in the slums of Swansea.

Marriage suited her, he reflected. She had a bloom about her now that the rough edges had been knocked off the rebel child she once was, and the aura of a confident young woman had settled round her like a cloak. The change in the girl had been wrought by Llinos Mainwaring, who had educated Shanni and, more importantly, had told her always to hold her head high.

Llinos . . . His mind drifted to the days when he had lain in her arms, delighting in the passion he shared with her. She had been his darling then, and would always be his love. He would be with her now if he'd had the choice, but she had made her decision to return to her family and he had had to let her go.

He liked to think that she had left him and returned to her husband and child for duty rather than love. He knew that something magical was still between them, the attraction so heady, so irresistible, too strong a bond to break. The pain of her going had not left him and even now Dafydd yearned for her. Would he ever get her out of his mind, his heart?

He saw her in his dreams, smiling at him, sated and flushed with love. The thought of her brought the familiar heat to his loins, an urge to taste her sweetness, if only one more time, before he tied himself to Jayne Morton-Edwards in holy matrimony.

His eyes focused again on Shanni: tendrils of red-gold hair fell across her alabaster cheeks. As if attracted by his gaze she looked up at him and her face was illuminated with happiness. She was in love with him, had been from the time they first met. Even marriage to Pedr Morgan had not altered her feelings. She was a lovely girl with a fiery nature, but he would take Llinos Mainwaring before Shanni any day of the week.

He raised his hand in greeting and stood there for a moment, listening to the sounds of the pottery, which had brought him such satisfaction, more even than the farmlands he owned but had never worked—he had tenant farmers to do that for him.

Shanni made to rise from her chair but Dafydd was not in the mood for dalliance this morning. He had a fitting to attend and other matters to arrange so that his wedding should meet all expectations. Two of the richest families in Wales were going to be joined in marriage. It would not be a union made in heaven but Jayne was pretty enough, young, enthusiastic, and would probably be content with the outward trappings of a good marriage. And children, oh, yes, he wanted children— legitimate sons to take over his great fortune.

He was a man and he would find it easy to lie with his young bride. Besides, he needed relief from the pent-up feelings that plagued him day and night, and if that meant a darkened room and the image of Llinos behind his closed lids as he made Jayne his wife, so be it.

*

Swansea was bright with sunshine and it was market day: herds of cattle were penned behind wooden fencing in readiness for the sales that would take place later in the morning. Dafydd paused to inspect them. Some were from his own farmlands: they were well fed and strong, good animals for breeding as well as eating.

The tailor's shop was housed in a long narrow building on the edge of the market, and as Dafydd let himself in a bell chimed, summoning Mr Perkins from the dimness of the interior.

'Ah, Mr Buchan, your suit is almost ready. One more fitting and it will be finished.' This man was the finest tailor in the whole of South Wales.

Grudgingly Dafydd allowed himself to be

31

dressed in his wedding attire. He stared at his reflection in the long, speckled mirror, and saw himself as a man with an aura of youth still upon him although closer inspection would reveal lines of pain and disappointment around his eyes and mouth.

'How is your brother, sir?' Mr Perkins mumbled, through a mouthful of pins.

'Not too well, Perkins. He was never strong but he can't seem to shake off the fever he caught last winter.'

But it was more than just the fever. Ceri had not been the same since the rioting back in 'forty-three, when a crazed farmer had injured him. 'I'm afraid, Perkins, that my brother grows weaker by the day.'

'I'm sorry to hear that, sir, sorry indeed.' Mr Perkins slotted pins deftly into the turned-up cuffs of the jacket. 'I hope he's fit enough to attend your wedding, Mr Buchan. It would be a sad day if he missed such a glorious occasion.'

'He'll be there,' Dafydd said, 'but I think you'll have to take in his suit a little. He has lost a great deal of weight in the last few months.'

'Ah, poor man, and here am I with all this blubber!' Mr Perkins clutched his stomach and shook it. 'I sit all day, sir, and I love my food, and neither of those make for a trim figure.'

Dafydd wished Perkins would be quick about his business: standing in a gloomy room with the tailor fussing around him was not his idea of a good day. His thoughts turned to his meeting a few days ago with Jayne's father. He resented the way the man had spoken to him, with barely concealed hostility. It seemed he would never be accepted as a suitable husband for Morton-Edwards' precious daughter.

32

But Dafydd knew that the root of the problem was that Eynon was in love with Llinos Mainwaring and would never forgive him for having become her lover. But Jayne could always get round her father.

It was with relief that Dafydd stepped back into the street where he smelt the rich aroma of meat pie and realized he was hungry. As he walked along the high street he felt the warmth of the sun on his face, and as the street broadened out he saw that the grass flourishing at the side of the road was dotted with wild flowers. It was good to be alive— and then he remembered his wedding. The euphoria vanished. Once he was married, Llinos would be lost to him for ever. But he must look forward now: Jayne was going to be his wife and one day she would bear him fine sons to take over his business empire.

*   *   *

As Llinos stepped down from her carriage she saw him. Her breath caught in her throat as she watched Dafydd's tall figure disappear through the polished glass doors of the Mackworth Hotel. Almost in a dream, she followed him, wanting to talk to him, touch him. She was a fool—she had put her past behind her and now that she was Joe's wife again she intended to remain faithful to him. So why did her heart miss a beat whenever she caught sight of Dafydd?

The doorman doffed his hat to her and Llinos hesitated before she stepped into the foyer. She tried to spot Dafydd in the crowd of people enjoying morning coffee or a glass of tea. And then he was standing in front of her. She took in his

33

thick hair, the square cut of his jaw, and most of all the joy in his eyes as he looked down at her.

'Llinos,' his voice was a caress, 'I was just thinking about you, and how the sight of you would make this a wonderful day for me.' He took her arm and guided her across the room to a quiet corner. She breathed in his familiar scent joyfully.

'I love you so much, Llinos, my darling, but you know that, don't you?'

She resisted the urge to put her arms around his neck and hold him close. She wanted him as much as ever. 'You're getting married, then, Dafydd.' Pain crept into her voice. 'I suppose I should congratulate you.'

He took her hand. 'It's you I want—you I'll always want, Llinos—but I have to get married some time. I need children, sons to inherit my fortune.'

'You have a son,' Llinos said.

'I know that, and I'll always be there if Sion should need me, but I have to have legitimate heirs, Llinos. You must see that.'

She found herself praying that he would never have another son. Her fingers curled around his and she was just about to speak again when a shadow fell over her. She looked up sharply. 'Joe, I didn't expect to see you here.'

'Evidently,' Joe said.

'I was just congratulating Dafydd on his marriage to Jayne,' she said quickly. 'What are you doing in town? I thought you were out with Lloyd today.'

'I'll tell you when we get home,' he said. 'And I'd like to leave at once, if you don't mind.'

Llinos got to her feet. 'Joe, there's nothing

wrong, is there? Sion or Lloyd—they aren't hurt?'

'No, but I would prefer to discuss family matters in private.'

Llinos turned to look at Dafydd. 'I hope you'll be very happy.' The words were stiff, formal, and in her heart Llinos knew she did not mean any such thing. She followed Joe from the hotel and grasped his arm. 'Joe, tell me what's wrong.'

'Nothing is wrong. There's something we have to talk about but there is no need for hysteria.'

'Joe,' she said, 'how did you know where to find me?'

'It wasn't difficult. You and Buchan are still the talk of Swansea and some are eager to tell me when they see Mrs Mainwaring with her fancy man.'

She heard the anger in her husband's voice and caught his hand. 'Joe, I'm sorry. I just saw Dafydd and I had to talk to him. I didn't mean to be deceitful or to make you angry.'

'Angry? Of course I'm angry! What's a man supposed to feel when he sees his wife sitting cosily with her lover?'

Suddenly Llinos was as angry as Joe. 'He is *not* my lover! He hasn't been for a very long time.'

'And I must believe *that* when I find you with him in an hotel?'

'At this moment I don't care what you believe,' she said. 'I bumped into him and I spoke to him about his marriage, that's all.'

'So you say.'

'Look, Joe, you're no saint, are you? Were you not the first to break our marriage vows?'

'Look,' Joe said, more calmly, 'I thought we'd put this behind us, but the sight of you with him just drove me mad.'

'I can't ignore him,' Llinos said. 'He is the father of my child.' As soon as the words passed her lips she could have bitten out her tongue.

'Oh, I know that. So does half of Swansea.'

'At least I never lied to you, Joe. I never pretended it was my destiny to love Dafydd, as you did with your Indian woman.'

'Did I lie?' Joe asked.

'Well, you told me your son would one day be the head of your people, and you were wrong about that, weren't you? Your son by your squaw wasn't meant to live.' She paused. 'Admit you were wrong, Joe.'

'Was I?' Joe was quiet and Llinos stared at him in alarm. 'What do you mean?'

'It's Lloyd. He's going to America—he wants to learn the ways of the American Indian.' He paused. 'So you see, Llinos, one day my son might be ruler in my land.'

'No!' Llinos said. 'I don't want my son living among . . .' Her words trailed away and she looked up at Joe in despair.

'Go on, say it! You don't want your son to live with savages. That's what you meant, isn't it?' He bundled her into the waiting carriage and sat stiffly beside her, his face turned away. She knew she had hurt him badly, but all she wanted now was to beg Lloyd not to go away.

'I'll be glad to get home,' she said, breaking the silence.

'Aye, the pottery is your home, isn't it, Llinos? But have you ever asked me about my home?'

'Where is your home, Joe?' Llinos asked, laying her hand on his arm. 'Is it the estate in England

36

your father left you, or is it in America, or here with me?'

Joe did not answer, and they finished the journey in silence.

When Llinos alighted from the carriage she breathed in the all-pervading smell of damp clay, felt the heat shimmering from the kilns and knew that this was her world. She could not give it up to live in America, not for Joe and not for Lloyd.

'You are happy enough here, though, aren't you, Joe?' she asked. 'Swansea has become your home, hasn't it?'

He took her arm, drew her across the yard and into the house. He did not speak until they were inside the hallway. 'I'm going to America with Lloyd,' he said, 'and I want you and Sion to come with us.'

'When do you expect all this to happen, Joe? Nothing like this can be planned in a few weeks.'

'I've booked us a berth on the *Marigold*. She's sailing out of Swansea next week.'

Llinos stared at him, aghast. 'So soon? You must be mad! I can't uproot Sion and take him away from everything he knows and loves. In any case, I don't want to go to America, not at my time of life.'

She went into the drawing room where she found Lloyd. He got up at once to embrace her.

'Lloyd,' she said, 'tell me it's not true. Tell me you're not going to throw up your career for a dream.'

'But, Mother, it will be an adventure. You and Sion will enjoy living beneath the sun, breathing fresh air and seeing the stars shine at night, instead of looking up at the clouds of smoke from the copper works.'

'I can't go traipsing about the world now, Lloyd. I'm too old for that.'

'Nonsense, Mother! You're still young and beautiful.'

'I'm not going to America,' Llinos said flatly. 'This is my home. This is where I was born and this is where I will die.' She walked to the door and stood to look back at her husband and son, two men so alike yet so different.

'I'm going to lie down. I'm tired.' She went slowly up the stairs. Once in her room, she closed the door and locked it. Then she fell on the bed and muffled her sobs in the pillows.

CHAPTER FOUR

The morning sun brought light and colour to Swansea's shop windows. Spirals of steam rose from the dew-wet cobbles of the Stryd Fawr lending the high street an aura of mysticism and magic. Jayne Morton-Edwards stepped down from her carriage. Her spirits were high as she gazed around her, drinking in the sights and sounds of the town she loved. Then she glanced at the splendid ring that graced her elegant white hand, which was accustomed only to needlework and painting or playing the piano. Those were the sort of skills a woman needed if she was to make a good marriage.

She paused before the large window of Howell's Emporium and stared eagerly at the fine gloves and dainty slippers; all fit for the wedding of the year.

'Oh, look, miss. Isn't that posy lovely?'

Jayne looked at the flowers, the daffodils and the brightly coloured tulips, none of which would be available when she married at the height of summer. 'You stupid girl, Katie!' she said impatiently. 'I shan't be choosing my bouquet until much later in the year.' She resented Katie: her father had more or less insisted that the girl become her personal maid and Jayne felt that a young girl from the back-streets of Swansea was more fitted to kitchenmaid than lady's maid.

'Still,' she relented a little, 'it is very pretty.' She supposed it was natural for the girl to be excited: all this luxury must be overwhelming for a girl of her sort.

'Come along, let's go inside. The air is a little chilly out here.' Jayne swept into the shop without so much as a glance at the doorman, who doffed his cap to her. She was immediately aware of the stir her appearance caused among the shop assistants. An obsequious salesman crossed the expanse of good carpet, so anxious to serve her that he almost stumbled over one of the finely carved chairs.

'Miss Morton-Edwards, how may we help you this morning? A bolt of fine silk suitable for a wedding gown?' He looked at her archly. Jayne was gratified that he knew of her engagement and smiled, unaware of how her face was transformed: all at once, she was a happy young woman with smoky grey eyes and pale golden hair. She was in love and happiness radiated from her like perfume.

'Thank you, Frazer, but bring me something really expensive and special, because I haven't yet seen a cloth I like and time is getting short.' Not that Jayne worried about that: any seamstress worth her salt could make up a wedding dress in days.

'I think we have just the thing.' The man bowed and disappeared through a door. Jayne took a seat, relishing the feeling of being a bride. Since she was a child she had dreamed of a fine wedding to a handsome man, and hers owned acres of fine farmland as well as a flourishing pottery.

She spent a happy hour while Frazer brought out bolt after bolt of the finest silks and satins. At last she had seen enough. 'I'm tired now,' she said, 'so I'll look at the slippers and gloves another day.'

Then she felt a draught—the doors of the emporium had swung open. Looking over her shoulder she saw Shanni Morgan sweep into the store as if she owned it. Her red hair was tumbled about her face in a most disgraceful way, and even though she wore ordinary clothes there was still something about her that drew everyone's attention.

'Good morning to you, Jayne.' There was a knowing look in Shanni's eyes. 'I hear you're marrying Dafydd. Congratulations.' She spoke in the cultured voice she had learned from Llinos Mainwaring.

'Excuse *me*,' Jayne said. 'I was not aware that we were on familiar terms. It's Miss Morton-Edwards to you.'

'Ah, but you will soon be the wife of my dear friend.'

Jayne's eyes narrowed. It was impossible to guess how close Shanni had been with Dafydd— she might even have been intimate with him during the time she'd spent fighting the toll charges with him. The thought made Jayne burn with anger and jealousy and she could have slapped the pretty face that smiled at her now. Instead she used her tongue to bring the upstart down to earth. 'I hear you found your proper place in society, then?' She forced a smile. 'You married a humble potter, didn't you?'

'I might never be as rich as you,' Shanni said, 'but I'm better educated and more of a lady than you'll ever be. Now, if you'll excuse me, I've more important things to do than talk to you.'

Jayne watched as Shanni made her way towards the millinery counter. Then, anger searing her, she got up. 'Come along, Katie. I need a little air to get the smell of that woman out of my nostrils.'

Without waiting to say goodbye to the bemused salesman, Jayne hurried out of the shop. The cool breeze soothed her burning cheeks and she climbed up the carriage steps and twitched her skirts into place as she sank into the padded leather seat.

'That Shanni Morgan is nothing but a slut from the slums, yet she gives herself such airs.'

Katie lowered her head. She'd learned it was best not to interrupt when her mistress was in a bad mood. She hadn't realized when she became a lady's maid that it would mean putting up with a spoiled madam like Jayne Morton-Edwards.

'If Llinos Mainwaring hadn't taken her in, she would be in the workhouse now and that's good enough for her sort,' Jayne fumed. Why had she allowed that common little peasant to get the better of her? If only she could find out how close Shanni had been to Dafydd she might be able to deal with the situation more appropriately.

When the carriage stopped outside the pillared

41

door of her home Jayne pushed aside the driver and climbed down onto the driveway. Without a backward glance she hurried into the house and flung her coat on the floor. She went immediately to her room and slammed the door behind her. The meeting with Shanni had spoiled her day.

She sank down on the bed, trying to control the trembling in her hands, telling herself to be calm: she was the one marrying Dafydd not Shanni. And what if Dafydd had lain with her? She would have been no more than a casual diversion, quickly forgotten.

She sighed deeply and sank back on the pillows, her thoughts turning to her wedding day. She anticipated the stir it would cause in Swansea. The sun would shine on the pale satin of her gown and a gentle summer breeze would lift her veil to reveal her beauty. Dafydd was a lucky man to have her, and she would never tire of telling him so.

The men in her life, Dafydd and her father, saw her as a child but she had brains in her head and one day she would surprise them. She slipped off the bed, opened a drawer in a chest that smelt of beeswax and camphor and took out the crackling documents nestling beneath her night clothes. 'Great Western Railways.' She waved the papers in the air. 'Now that I own part of you I'll bring a great deal more to the marriage than Dafydd ever dreamed of.'

Carefully she folded the papers away again, smiling to herself as she covered them with a soft cambric gown. They might call the enterprise the South Wales Railway for the moment, but everyone knew that the much-respected Isambard Kingdom Brunel had set his stamp on the venture and what he touched always turned to gold.

She returned to her bed, sank back once again into the pillows and turned her mind to more important matters: her gown, the headdress of real pearls, and the golden band that would tie her and Dafydd together in a bond that would never be broken.

*   *   *

Shanni was pleased that she had triumphed over Jayne Morton-Edwards. Now she would shop to her heart's content, secure in the knowledge that she had got the better of the other woman. As well as being intelligent, Shanni was also quick to hear any gossip and what she had overheard had come from the horse's mouth.

She had been about to leave her small room at the pottery when she heard voices in the office across the passageway. Dafydd had been talking to his brother. Shanni peeped round the door and saw that Ceri Buchan looked so pale and thin that a puff of wind might have blown him away. At first the talk was about business and she had been about to leave when she heard the word 'marriage'.

'I think you're doing the right thing in marrying Miss Morton-Edwards.' Ceri spoke as if it was an effort to get the words out of his mouth. 'I know you think she's a spoiled brat but marriage will tame her, especially when children are on the way.'

'Well,' Dafydd replied, 'you know how I feel about Llinos, and that will never change.'

'You've accepted that Llinos will never be yours and we must all compromise a little in life.'

Shanni had returned to her chair to think over

what she had heard. So Dafydd was not head over heels in love with his bride. Somehow that gave her a fleeting sense of satisfaction.

Now Shanni chose a frivolous hat, decked with feathers and hand-stitched roses, and a pair of lace gloves. It pleased her that she could shop in the same emporium as Jayne Morton-Edwards. Perhaps her purchases were small, but although Pedr was only a potter he was skilled and earned a generous salary.

Later Shanni took a hansom cab home. She wondered briefly what Pedr would say about the money she'd spent. He was a practical man who did not believe in fripperies, as he called them. On the other hand he loved her to distraction, and Shanni could always coax him out of a bad mood with soft words and passionate kisses.

He was waiting for her in their small neat cottage. Beads of perspiration glistened on his forehead and the flames of the cooking fire roared up the chimney.

'Hello, husband.' Shanni kissed him soundly. 'I've bought a new hat,' she said. 'Guess who I saw in the emporium?'

'Well,' Pedr sighed—a sigh of exasperation, Shanni knew, 'who did you see? Surprise me.'

'I saw Jayne Morton-Edwards and I ruffled her feathers, I can tell you. When I'd finished with her, she flounced out of the place in a fine temper.' She sat on his knee and put her arm around his neck. 'You're not cross with me, are you, Pedr? I didn't spend much.'

'What do you need a new bonnet for, love? You're not going to get an invitation to the wedding of the year, are you?'

'No, I'm not, but as an employee you'll have to turn up to watch Dafydd tie the knot and of course I'll come with you.'

'You're right as usual, girl. Come here and give me a proper kiss.'

Shanni responded to him eagerly. She might not love Pedr as she should but she enjoyed the intimacies they shared, and Pedr was a wonderful lover. When his fingers brushed her breast, she pushed them away teasingly. 'Not when I'm wearing my best going-to-town clothes,' she said softly.

'To hell with your town clothes! I want you, and I want you now.'

'No, no!' Shanni laughed. 'You won't have your wicked way with me, you naughty man.'

It was a game they often played, when Pedr was the hunter and she the hunted, he would chase her upstairs and throw her on the bed.

'Now, Mrs Morgan, I've got you where I want you.' He looked so fierce, his eyes gleaming, his touch on her shoulders urgent, that Shanni found she wanted him as much as he wanted her.

Quickly he took off his clothes, fell across her, undid her bodice and pressed his hot mouth to her nipple. Shanni moaned with pleasure. As he took her to the heights of passion she cried out his name, knowing that if this was not love it was the nearest she was ever going to get.

CHAPTER FIVE

Katie was still shy with Bull because he seemed so strong, so self-assured, and she still couldn't believe he might be interested in her. It was too early to say that they were walking out together but Katie knew that she was falling in love with the big, gentle man.

It began to rain but Katie didn't mind: she was with Bull, which took away all thought of the weather.

'How is work going? Do you like being a lady's' maid?' Bull looked down at her from his great height and she resisted the temptation to take his hand.

'I think I'd rather scrub floors than dress Miss Jayne, but as long as I pretend to be stupid I get on with her.'

Bull stopped walking and put his finger under her chin, forcing her to look at him. 'You're so lovely, Katie, funny and warm as well as beautiful. I can't believe my luck that you're here with me.'

The words thrilled Katie. Bull was telling her that she was his girl and colour flooded her face. He was a perfect gentleman: when she'd told him she was picking up the last of her belongings today from the house in Greenhill he had insisted on coming with her. When they reached the house she knocked timidly on the door, feeling a flutter of apprehension. What if the new tenant had thrown her things out into the backyard?

A large florid-faced woman opened the door. She stared suspiciously at Katie. 'If you're beggin' I 'aven't got nothing so go away.'

'No, it's not that—' Katie began but the woman was closing the door.

Bull leaned forward and held it open. 'Miss Cullen has come to collect her belongings. I'm sure that's all right with you, Mrs . . .?' He smiled and the woman was transformed.

'You're Bull Beynon from the railways. I've heard about you and all good. Come in, don't stand in the doorway there and catch a chill.' She shuffled backwards to let them pass. 'I'm Maeve O'Connor, got some kin working on the railways, see? Do you know Seth and Dan O'Connor?'

Bull smiled easily. 'I certainly do. We won't disturb you for too long, Mrs O'Connor, we'll pick up everything now and then we won't have to bother you again.'

Katie followed him into the house, admiring the ease with which he had handled the awkward woman. No wonder they'd made him foreman on the line—he had such a way with people. She put her bits and pieces into a bag—there wasn't much, just the pair of china dogs her mother had loved, and a few clothes she had not been able to carry last time.

As soon as she and Bull left the house she sighed with relief. 'Thank goodness that's over,' she said. 'It was kind of you to come with me. I don't think I'd have got past that dragon if I'd been on my own.'

Bull grinned. 'Well, even I was a bit afraid of her sharp tongue. Give me a tough navvy in drink before a woman in a bad mood any day. Look,' he continued, 'I'll come with you to the Big House, drop these things off and then perhaps I could take

47

you for a walk along the beach?'

Katie glanced up at the sky. A breeze had sprung up and was chasing away the rainclouds. 'That sounds lovely . . . Bull.' She said his name shyly.

'Lovely and safe?' Bull teased. 'I can hardly take advantage of you outdoors with the rest of Swansea looking on, can I?'

Not that he ever would take advantage of her. Bull had such fine manners and she loved him for it. She longed to tell him how she felt about him, but she didn't want him to think her forward.

'Right, then, Miss Cullen, let's get you back to the Big House, drop off these things and spend the afternoon doing just as we please.'

*　　　*　　　*

Llinos felt at a loose end. Without Joe the house was strangely empty and she missed him badly. She missed Lloyd, too, with his arcane wisdom and his ability to laugh at small things. Even though she had grown used to their son's absences while he was at college, it unsettled her to know that he was in America.

She was troubled: would Lloyd really give up all he had worked for to live with a Native American tribe? Would he exchange a secure future for a dream? It certainly seemed that way.

From upstairs Llinos heard the sound of her younger son laughing, and her features softened. Sion was a joy. He was not too old to hug and kiss her, and when he wound his arms around her neck she felt she held the whole world in her grasp.

The laughter stopped, and the only sound now was the rain. It had been pouring off and on for the best part of a week and the gardens looked dispirited. Standing at the window, looking beyond the garden to where the kilns steamed as the heat inside met the day's chill, Llinos felt as though she had been abandoned by the whole world. And Dafydd would soon be married, lost to her for ever.

She frowned. What could Dafydd have in common with such a selfish girl? Jayne needed to grow up before she was ready for marriage. As for herself, perhaps she was too old for love—at least of the passionate kind. Would she never again know the starburst of sensation that had been so thrilling, so rejuvenating?

She sank into a chair and covered her eyes with her hands. Dafydd. She could picture him now, well built, muscular, with a fine white skin.

The jangling of the doorbell startled her and Llinos looked up and towards the window. Who was visiting her at such an early hour? Her heart leaped as she saw the carriage standing outside the front door. The monogram, gleaming gold in a sudden shaft of sunshine, told her that it belonged to Dafydd Buchan.

The maid looked into the room and spoke in a hushed voice. Ever since Joe had gone away she was acting as though there had been a death in the household. 'Mr Buchan to see you, Mrs Mainwaring. Shall I show him in?'

Llinos's first instinct was to say no but, heart fluttering inside her like a trapped bird, she nodded. The maid disappeared, and then Dafydd was in the room, filling it with his presence.

'Dafydd,' her voice was faint, 'what are you doing here?' She pulled herself up sharply. 'Please, sit down.' He looked no different from when he had been her lover.

Instead of sitting down, he crossed the room and then she was in his arms. 'My love, don't talk to me as if I was a stranger.' His hair brushed her cheek and she was filled with an overwhelming longing to lie with him just one more time, to feel his hands on her, to have him move within her and bring her such joy.

It was madness to think like that, and Llinos disentangled herself. 'Dafydd, please, don't touch me. I can't bear it.'

He took her hands and led her to the sofa, his fingers entwined with hers. 'Llinos, listen to me,' he said gently. 'If I could have you I would never look at another woman. As it is,' he shrugged, 'I'm going to marry Jayne. You must see that I need a marriage and children to take over from me some day. But I will always care for you and Sion, you know that.'

'I will look after Sion,' Llinos said stiffly. 'You know I can provide for him so don't trouble yourself.'

Dafydd looked into her eyes. 'I still love you, Llinos, and, God help me, I still want you as much as I ever did.'

He touched her shoulder and instantly she was aflame. She rose quickly and put as much distance between them as she could. 'Dafydd, please don't torment me like this. You are going to be Jayne's husband, and you must be faithful to her or you will destroy her. She is young, she has dreams, and those dreams include a husband who loves her.'

'But I don't love her,' Dafydd said quietly. 'Believe me when I tell you that this is a marriage of convenience, nothing more or less. Of course I will try to make her happy, that goes without saying.'

'I can't bear it!' Llinos said brokenly. 'I keep picturing her in your arms, as you make love to her in the way you made love to me.'

'It will never be like that.' Dafydd came towards her. 'You will always be first in my heart.' He took her in his arms and, with his hand behind her head, forced her to look up at him. He kissed her then, and she melted against him. 'How could I give her my body in the way I gave it to you when I can't give her my heart or soul? You already have them, my sweet girl.' He kissed her again, and Llinos prolonged it, wanting more of him.

At last she moved away. 'Please go, Dafydd. I can't bear to be with you, now that you belong to someone else.'

'I want you so much,' Dafydd said, breathlessly. 'Please, Llinos, can't we . . .'

His words trailed away as Llinos held up her hand. 'No, we can't!' Tears burned her eyes. 'It's over between us, my love.'

'Are you saying you don't want me? Because if you are then I know you're lying.'

She shook her head. 'I want you as much as you want me, but we can't be together, not now, not ever.'

'Ever is a long time.'

Dafydd moved to the door and Llinos almost begged him to come back to her but she straightened her shoulders. 'I can't be the one to hurt Jayne,' she whispered. 'I've known her from the day she was born.' She fought for control. 'She is an innocent and doesn't know yet that infidelity and betrayal are part of every marriage.'

51

'Llinos, it's not like you to be so cynical,' Dafydd said. 'You are so sad, and if I could save you pain I would, you know that. But I can't lead my life like a monk. Please, though, Llinos, say you'll let me see Sion sometimes.'

'Sion knows only one father and he is Joe,' Llinos said firmly. 'He must never know the truth.'

'But he's bound to find out one day, Llinos. You must see that.'

She sank into a chair. 'You may be right, but now he's too young to understand the ways of the world. Let him enjoy his childhood.'

'I sometimes think children know more of what's going on than we give them credit for,' Dafydd said gently.

'Please, you must go, Dafydd. We have nothing more we can say to each other.'

'Goodbye then, my love.' He kissed her hand. 'And remember, I'll never stop loving you.'

She stood in the window and watched him walk round the house towards the stables, then returned to her chair and once more covered her face with her hands. She felt even more alone than ever.

*   *   *

'What do you think, Dafydd? The oyster or the virginal white?' Sunlight splashed in through the windows of Howell's Emporium as Jayne held up the scraps of fabric.

He scarcely glanced at them as he thought of her naïvety. She was a virgin in every sense of the word, the sort of girl any man longed for, chaste and wealthy, but Dafydd had drunk of a more mature wine and had no taste for novelty. 'Pristine white

52

for you, Jayne,' he said smoothly, 'to reflect your purity.' He searched her face for any sign that she had understood the irony in his words. She had not. Indeed, she was flushed with what he took to be pleasure.

'Then white it will be.' She included the salesman in her beatific smile. 'Send a bolt of the satin to my father, will you, Frazer?' She took Dafydd's arm and led him towards the door. He smiled down at her indulgently. She was a pretty thing and so easy to please: Jayne would make him an excellent wife, not too demanding, not too bright, and certainly with no ambition except to have a gold band on her finger. 'You're such a sweet girl,' he said, and Jayne smiled up at him, her small teeth white and even, her pale skin tinged with pink.

'Do you think so, Dafydd?' There was an edge to her tone and Dafydd wondered if she was more perceptive than he gave her credit for. 'You do really care for me, don't you?' she said. 'You never say much so I don't know what you're thinking or feeling.'

Dafydd patted her hand without speaking. It was a good thing she did not know that his thoughts were too often of Llinos. Poor Jayne: she would never fathom him. There was only one woman who understood him and that was Llinos Mainwaring.

They left the hurry and bustle of the main streets and sat close together in Dafydd's carriage. He stared out at the sun-dappled hedgerows and speculated on his life and loves. He had done well in both. He had loved Llinos for years, and he would not have missed those times for anything. Now he had Jayne, who adored him and would give

53

him healthy children. Financially he would always be secure by virtue of his father's enterprise in the early years of the century, and in fact he was one of the richest men in Wales.

He would have liked to buy into the new railway line but he had made his move too late: the shares had been sold. It was an opportunity missed because soon there would be a station in Swansea. Some time ago he had stood on the hill and looked down at the work in progress on the track, knowing that this was the future, that this railway would reap a great harvest in a few years' time.

Still, Dafydd was never one to shed tears over investments he *might* have made. He had his own pottery, his extensive farmlands in Carmarthen, and now his shares in the big Swansea Pottery. He had no need to worry about the future: he and his brother and their families would live well for the rest of their lives.

Ceri. The thought of his brother sent Dafydd's spirits spiralling downwards. It would be a miracle if he lived to see Dafydd married. Whatever ailed Ceri, it was sapping the strength from him and lately he had lost even the hope that had been so much a part of him. He had one comfort, his belief in a just God, and he prayed devoutly.

'You're very deep in thought, Dafydd. Look! We're home! Wake up, my darling, and shake off that gloomy expression.'

'Sorry.' He covered her hand with his. 'I was thinking of my brother, wondering if he will be well enough to come to the wedding.'

'Of course he will. It's only a few weeks away.'

He was tempted to snap at her, to tell her that not every story had a fairy-tale ending, but the look on her face of admiration and love stopped the words in his throat.

He alighted from the carriage and helped Jayne down onto the gravel of the drive that led to her father's house. He wondered how he would be received this time: Eynon Morton-Edwards' feelings fluctuated between acceptance of the situation and open hostility.

Eynon was in a genial mood, and as Jayne took Dafydd's arm and followed her father into the drawing room he could see why. Llinos was sitting there, her skirts spread around her dainty feet, and at her side was Sion, the image of himself. He saw her glance at his hand holding Jayne's, and though she struggled for composure it was clear from her eyes that she was unhappy.

'You know Mrs Mainwaring, of course,' Eynon said, his voice edged with sarcasm, and glowered at Dafydd.

'Yes.' Dafydd spoke just as tersely and moved to sit beside her. 'How are you, young fellow?' He looked into the face of his son, caught between love and anger. They could all be together, if only Llinos would come to him, damn it! They belonged together, but Llinos moved into the furthest corner of the sofa so that Sion was seated between her and Dafydd. He felt almost as though they *were* a family, visiting friends, that soon they would go home together, he, Llinos and their son.

'Come with me, Dafydd, darling.' Jayne took command of the situation in her usual girlish manner. 'I want you to see the flowers I have chosen for my bridal bouquet.'

Dafydd could not shake off a vision of Llinos in his arms. The feel of her and the scent of her haunted him.

'Dafydd!' Jayne took his hand and drew him to his feet. 'Come, you're daydreaming. What am I to do with you?' She looked back at Llinos. 'I know you'll excuse us,' she said. 'You and Papa will be free to talk about the past with we young ones out of the way.'

She smiled at Sion. 'Would you like to come with us? You can see the gardens and choose some flowers for your mother.'

Poor silly Jayne—she did not detect the strained atmosphere. Dafydd looked back at Llinos, who was staring doggedly at her hands.

Tentatively he took his son's hand and allowed Jayne to lead them outside into the freshness of the garden. His son's fingers curled around his and Dafydd felt tears behind his eyes. Why could a man not just take what he wanted from life?

Jayne was fussing among the flower-beds, disturbing the gardeners without a thought for the inconvenience she was causing. Well, this woman was to be his bride, Dafydd thought, and if he was to make an amicable marriage he must stop criticizing her every move.

'What do you think of these yellow roses for my bouquet, Dafydd? Will they look pretty?'

He took a deep breath. 'No, I think the pink. With your fair colouring the pink will look best.'

'You're right, of course.' Jayne dimpled up at him, her hand resting possessively on his arm. 'But you are always right, my darling. That's why I love you.'

Dafydd became aware that his son was looking up at him. 'I want to go back indoors,' the boy said, bored with this talk of flowers and weddings.

Dafydd sympathized with him.

'I'll walk with you to the door of the orangery and you can go through to the sitting room. I'll not be long, Jayne.' He was reluctant to let his son go and savoured the moments as he walked past the green lawns towards the house. 'You're a fine boy, Sion, and I hope we will see more of each other,' he said gently.

The boy looked up at him, his face bright, his eyes intelligent. 'But you're going to marry Jayne. I don't suppose you'll have time for us then.' He slipped his hand out of Dafydd's.

'Oh, I'll have time,' Dafydd said, his throat constricted. 'I'll always have time for you.'

He watched as Sion disappeared into the orangery, and the sun, glimmering on the windows, obscured him. A moment later, Dafydd turned and made his way slowly back through the gardens to where Jayne was waiting.

CHAPTER SIX

Bull stood in the work hut staring out at the clouds hanging over the diggings. Behind him the brazier burned briskly, the only warmth in the chill of the dismal day. He was angry that the work on the line was facing yet another delay. Outside, the engineer was pacing the ground, staring up as if he wished he could command the rain to cease.

Bull knew that Cookson, too, felt the frustration of constant delays as much as he did, but while the inclement weather caused them irritation and worry, the navvies were glad of the time off and

57

were doubtless making a nuisance of themselves now at the public bar in the nearest alehouse.

'Damned weather, Bull. Do you think it's ever going to clear?' Cookson called to him.

'It's in for the day, sir. Come inside for a bit—you're getting soaked to the skin.'

Cookson came into the hut and held out his hands to the warmth of the brazier, rubbing them impatiently. 'Bloody bone-ache! It's driving me mad—this damp weather worsens it.'

Bull watched as Cookson's clothes steamed in the heat and the smell of wet serge permeated the small hut.

'Want a smoke, Bull?' he asked affably. He took out his pipe and rubbed it sensuously as if it was a beautiful woman.

'No, thank you, sir.' Bull did not indulge in the almost universal habit of smoking: he had seen his father die coughing, his teeth stained brown from the tobacco, his moustache turned yellow.

'You're not like your run-of-the-mill navvy, Bull.' Cookson took his time lighting his pipe. 'I'd say you're a cut above the rest.' He regarded Bull steadily. 'Had any education, man?'

Bull almost smiled. His education had consisted of a few hours a day spent at his mother's side, but she had taught him to read and write and do his figures. She had been a woman of distinction who had married beneath her, in her family's eyes, but she had been in love with Donald Beynon until the day she died.

'My mother was an educated lady, sir.' His brief reply forestalled further questions.

'I see.' Cookson cleared his throat. 'Well, no good hanging around here in this weather. Why not

58

take a bit of time off? Get down the Castle with the other men—a break will do you good.'

'Aye, you might be right, sir. It looks as if it's coming down even harder.' He watched as the engineer took a flask out of his pocket and drank from it, then offered it to him.

'Thanks.' Bull took the flask out of politeness rather than because he enjoyed the taste of rich dark rum, which was the engineer's habitual drink. It was fiery in his throat and he instantly felt warmed by it.

'How's that woman of yours, Bull?' Cookson pushed back his hat. 'She's a fine, comely girl.'

'She's a good enough woman to share a hut with, sir.'

'Good enough to bed but not the sort you'd want for a wife, eh?'

'That's about the length and breadth of it, sir.' Bull felt disloyal to Rhiannon but he would never marry her. He knew it and so did she.

'Well, I'll be off now and we'll meet again bright and early in the morning.' Cookson walked out of the hut, took the reins of his horse from the hitching post and mounted. He touched his whip to his hat and rode away. Bull envied the man his breeding, education and money, but he had determined that he would not be a navvy for the rest of his life. One day, and soon, he would be a respectable, if not wealthy, member of the community.

*   *   *

Rhiannon sat in the rough shanty staring out at the waterlogged landscape, which was grey and miserable in the pouring rain. She wished Bull would come home. Once he took her in his arms the world would be full of colour again. She sometimes dreamed of being married to Bull, walking down the aisle of a sun-filled church wearing a pretty gown and carrying a bunch of wild flowers—they were the only ones she liked. In fact, they were the only ones she knew, unless she spotted a rose in the garden of a grand house.

Rhiannon picked up the speckled mirror Bull used for shaving and studied her reflection. She was quite pretty, she supposed, her skin browned by the weather and her hair hanging loose to her shoulders, not swept up in curls like the styles of the gentry. Once, when her father had been alive, she had worn good boots and pretty bonnets, but that had been another life, in the northern part of Wales. Even later, before her mother's death, she had been happy. But from the age of thirteen she had been alone. 'You're not a bad-looking girl,' she told herself, 'considerin' what you've been through.' She remembered the pangs of hunger even now. She had been a thin, bedraggled scrap of humanity when she had given herself in desperation to a labourer in exchange for some food. That had started her on the downward road to whoredom.

Looking at her fresh face no one would have known she was a harlot, but she had lost count of the men with whom she had lain. They had all been the same, pushing and thrusting, then walking off and leaving her feeling like dirt beneath their feet. Until she had met Bull. Her expression softened. She loved Bull, had loved him from the moment they met. It had been in a public bar and she had

60

been dressed in good flannel petticoats bought from the market in Swansea. She looked almost respectable but if Bull had had any illusions about her they were quickly dispelled by some of the other men in the bar.

She flushed as she recalled their meeting. Bull had sat opposite her and they had begun to talk in a leisurely way at first, and then she had relaxed: she was in the company of a real man, who did not scorn her for what she was.

'Watch you don't catch something nasty from that wench,' a man had shouted across to Bull, and the crowd at the bar burst into raucous laughter.

'I bedded her last night—not bad too.' Another had guffawed heartily.

Bull had walked over to the navvies and stood, arms folded across his chest, staring at them angrily. 'If the girl is good enough to bed, she's good enough to treat with a bit of respect, right?'

'Oh, yes, Bull, if you says so. No harm meant, see. Didn't know you was taken with her.'

That night, Bull had brought her to his shanty. Outside it was like the rest of the huts along the line, but inside it was cosy with a small slope at the back that held a neatly made bed. They had spent the night together, and she had been with him ever since.

Now Rhiannon looked up eagerly as she heard his familiar step. Hurriedly, she moved to the fire in the corner and pushed the kettle onto the flames. Bull was not a demanding man and he would be content with soup warmed up from yesterday, but he liked a jug of hot tea when he came in.

'Hello, then, girl. What you been up to?' Bull

61

smelt of rain and droplets sparkled in his dark hair, but Rhiannon put her arms around him, ignoring the dampness of his clothes, and kissed him fiercely.

'I'm glad you're home.' She rested her cheek against his shoulder. One day, she knew, he would meet a decent, respectable girl and would want to settle down and raise a family. But please, God, not while he worked on the railway. 'There's a mug of tea coming up, love, so get out of those wet clothes and I'll dry them by the fire for you.'

Bull planted a kiss on her forehead. 'Hey! You're not my mother.' He pulled her hair teasingly. 'I think today the tea can wait—there's something I need more than that.'

She went with him eagerly to the bed in the slope, threw off her clothes and watched him undress, admiring his big muscles, his strong forearms.

He held her close, kissing her neck, her shoulders, her breasts. He made love to her with a tenderness that was unusual in a man taking a whore. He treated her as if she was a fine lady and it was no wonder she loved him. She breathed in raggedly, wanting him with an urgency fuelled by fear. Fear that one day he would be gone from her for ever.

CHAPTER SEVEN

Summer sunshine flooded the church of St Paul's with a dazzling luminosity. The leaves on the trees lining the pathway that led to the arched doorway fluttered in the light breeze, and the stained glass in the windows gleamed liked jewels.

Jayne, alighting from the carriage decked with roses, felt the bright sunlight was confirmation of her love for Dafydd and his for her. Not even the sight of Llinos Mainwaring could dampen her spirits because today she was marrying the man she loved and nothing would ever separate them.

The music swelled as Jayne, on her father's arm, entered the dimness of the church. Dafydd was there, waiting at the altar, his face turned to watch her.

She knew she looked beautiful, everyone kept telling her so, and Dafydd was a worthy suitor: he looked so fine and noble, his clothes cut from the finest cloth, his hair neatly trimmed and lying close to his head. And then she was beside him. She saw him smile but the warmth was not reflected in his eyes, and for a moment she doubted the wisdom of marrying a man she did not understand.

The vicar of St Paul's, known to the parish as Father Martin, smiled down at the pair, his prayer book open in his sun-browned hands. Vicar he might be, but sometimes his task included tending the churchyard. He began to intone the words of the marriage service, its resonance ringing up into the rafters of the building, and in her mind Jayne said, Thank you, God, for giving me this man. I will never betray him, and I will love him until the day I die.

*   *   *

To Llinos the service seemed interminable and she felt the strongest urge to run away: it hurt her so much to see Dafydd married to Jayne. She glanced at Eynon: he stood at his daughter's side, tall and elegant as always, his fair hair flopping over his brow in a touchingly familiar way. If she had fallen in love with Eynon, her life would never had been so tempestuous: she would have passed her days in tranquillity and peace. But then, a small voice said, she would have missed the love of two wonderful men.

The music surged, the ceremony was over. Jayne walked along the aisle on the arm of her husband, her face wreathed in smiles. As she looked up at Dafydd, it was apparent to everyone that she was truly in love with him. Llinos searched Dafydd's face and realized that he was at ease with the situation, smiling and nodding pleasantly to the congregation.

Then he caught her eye and she saw her own regret reflected in his guarded look. 'Good luck, my love!' she whispered, and the woman beside her glared at her. That in itself was nothing new—Llinos was used to being regarded as an outcast, a woman who had openly taken a lover.

She became aware that people around her were whispering and staring at her, some were even pointing, and the blood rushed to her face as she filed out of the church behind the rest of the congregation.

Outside, Jayne was surrounded, being kissed and congratulated. She looked so sweet, innocent, that Llinos felt like the wicked witch who cast a blight on marriages.

For several minutes she stood alone, wondering whether to get into her carriage and miss the wedding feast; perhaps she could plead a headache—anything to get out of watching Dafydd with his new bride. Then it was too late. Eynon was at her side.

'You're looking as lovely as ever, Llinos,' he said softly, taking her hand, and she was grateful to him for realizing what an ordeal today was for her. He kissed her cheek. 'Hold up your head, my love,' he said softly. 'Ignore the stupid, narrow-minded people who talk about you. How many of them would come out lily white if their lives were looked into closely?' He tucked her arm through his. 'As for Buchan, forget you were ever associated with him.' Eynon already bore a grudge against Dafydd, Llinos knew, because of his affair with her and now he must accept the man at his home because he was his daughter's husband.

The wedding feast was held at Eynon's house, the grand gallery set with a long table laden with food and great jugs of wine. As she looked around the room, Llinos wondered at how the social scene had changed in Swansea. New families had moved in and scarcely anyone was left of the old crowd. She was aware of the curious glances thrown her way and she knew how her affair with Dafydd must appear: she was an older woman who had led Dafydd astray. She was glad that Joe and Lloyd were not here.

Jayne bustled up to her, skirts swaying around dainty ankles, Dafydd behind her. Llinos could tell he was acutely embarrassed by his new wife's exuberance.

'Aunt Llinos, aren't you going to wish me well?'

Llinos heard the emphasis on 'Aunt' and knew it was for Dafydd's benefit. 'I wish you very well, Jayne,' she said. 'I hope you will both be very happy.' She avoided looking at Dafydd and thought guiltily of their last meeting, and of the shameless way they had kissed behind the closed doors of the drawing room. Colour flooded her face and she wanted nothing more than to get away.

It was Eynon again who rescued her. 'Llinos, come and sit at my side.' He took her arm. 'As I have no lady wife, will you be my companion at the table?'

'Gladly.' She kissed Jayne's cheek. 'Be happy,' she said, and allowed Eynon to lead her away.

'It's as much as I can do to look at that man,' he said. 'How can I trust him, Llinos?' He drew her close to his side. 'He took you, a married woman, to his bed, so how do I know he won't seduce you again?'

'Believe this, Eynon, my dear friend,' Llinos said, with some asperity, 'I will not allow him to, now that he's married to Jayne.'

'Have I your word on that?' Eynon asked.

'I swear it.'

Eynon nodded. 'Good.' He gestured to the chairs set alongside those of the bride and groom. 'Please sit here next to me, Llinos. The day will pass easier with you at my side.'

Llinos looked at the huge chargers heaped with pheasant, duck and guinea-fowl. The sight of so much rich fare turned her stomach. Wherever she looked, she saw food. She picked up a glass and sipped some wine. 'I'm not very hungry,' she said, 'so don't be offended if I eat little.'

Eynon nodded abstractedly and Llinos saw that he was watching Dafydd talking to his brother, Ceri, who looked as though he had climbed out of his deathbed. His face was pale, his cheeks were hollow. Llinos's heart contracted with pity. Ceri's wife hovered nervously at his side.

Jayne hurried over to her father. 'Please, Papa, come and say goodbye to Ceri. He's not well enough to stay for the feast.'

Llinos watched Eynon cross the room and rest his hand on Ceri Buchan's thin shoulder. Eynon had no quarrel with him: it was Dafydd he hated. She sank back in her chair, feeling that this was one of the worst days of her life. Suddenly she longed for Joe, his familiar body, the way he read her thoughts before she formed them. Tears stood in her eyes and she rubbed them away. She might be suffering the tortures of the damned but not one person here would be allowed to know it.

*　　　*　　　*

'Oh, Dafydd, this has been the most wonderful day of my life!' Jayne sat up against the pillows, her pristine nightgown buttoned to her throat. Katie had gone now and she was alone with her husband. She watched him cross the room towards her, strong and lean, a man of the world, and for a moment she was frightened. What if she did not like him touching her? She was so inexperienced in the ways of men. The only man she had ever kissed, apart from her father, was Lloyd Mainwaring and he was like an elder brother.

Dafydd put his arms round her and drew her close to him. She shivered in apprehension: from overheard kitchen talk she had gathered that love-making was a painful process.

'You're so tense,' Dafydd said softly, his breath blowing the curls away from her face. 'I promise I

67

won't do anything to frighten you.' He touched her breasts gently with his forefinger and she felt a strange sensation in her stomach. He kissed her, then his lips moved to her throat and he unbuttoned her soft cambric nightgown. When his mouth moved to her breast, Jayne felt fire inside her. Now her fear was tinged with pleasure—and not a little curiosity. She had to become a woman and now, with the husband she loved, was the right time.

She ran her hands over his shoulders, feeling the strong muscles beneath his skin. 'I love you, Dafydd,' she whispered.

'I know you do, little darling,' he said. His hands were gentle as they removed her nightgown, and she felt strangely vulnerable for she had never lain naked in her bed before. Was it immodest to undress in this way? She did not know. She had no close women confidantes.

She thought of Shanni, with her tumbled red hair and knowing eyes. If a girl from the slums could be a successful wife then surely Jayne, with her breeding and upbringing, could do better?

When Dafydd slid his hand over her flat stomach, she flinched. His hand moved lower touching her delicately and she began to relax against him. He knew how to treat a woman—there was nothing to be frightened of.

It was over quickly. The pain was minimal but somehow Jayne felt incomplete, as though she had started a feast and left it half-way. It was not a sensation she could explain or understand.

Dafydd kissed her brow, almost like a brother. 'Go to sleep now, Jayne,' he said softly. 'This has been a long day for you.'

68

He turned over and Jayne listened to his even breathing, wondering why she felt disappointed. Surely love for a bride and groom should be more than a quick coupling. But then, she reasoned, Dafydd did not want to hurt or frighten her. He was a gentleman and she was a lady. Surely a lady was not supposed to enjoy the things her husband did to her in the privacy of the bedroom. It was only the lower orders, the maids, women like Shanni Morgan, who could mate like animals in the stables.

She swallowed her disappointment and turned on her side, feeling Dafydd's naked back against her breast. Should she get up and put on her nightgown? Should she wash away the signs of intimacy? She felt lost and alone. The only woman from whom she might have asked advice was Llinos Mainwaring, but she would never speak to Llinos about Dafydd, or about her marriage.

It came to her then that Dafydd had done those things to Llinos, and she an old woman! He had kissed her breasts, entered her and even made her with child. For the first time Jayne understood jealousy. How could he? How could Dafydd have done such things to another woman?

She turned her back to him and tried to force herself to sleep but it was not until the dawn crept in through the windows that she succeeded.

*   *   *

The railway line was making progress at last. Tracks laid like a silver ribbon curved towards Swansea and the high street where the station was being built. Bull rested on his pick, wiping the sweat from his eyes. He looked up and saw Cookson riding towards him. 'Morning, sir,' he said affably, knowing the engineer was pleased that the work was going well.

'Bull—just the man I wanted to see.' Cookson held the reins of his horse taut and the animal's head lifted in protest. 'I've spoken to the board of governors and they agree with me that you'll make an excellent manager.' He paused and grinned. 'You don't seem impressed but it means more money and a house.'

'I'm pleased, sir, that my work on the dig has been recognized.' Bull's tone was dry.

'I know you've been running the team anyway but at least you'll be better off now.'

'Thank you, sir. I appreciate your confidence in me.'

'Well, Bull, you're a man who inspires confidence. Have you any interest in the engineering side of all this?'

'I certainly have, sir.' Bull knew quite a bit about it—he had worked on enough railways to have gained an insight into what was needed. 'I admire Mr Brunel's viaduct—he must be a genius to have built a structure that straddles road, river and canal.'

'You may even meet him when you're a manager. Come and see me tonight down at the Castle and we'll talk.'

When Cookson rode away Bull thrust his fist at the sky in a gesture of victory. He felt elated: he could never become an engineer without training but the next best thing was to be a manager. He wanted to shout the news to the world, to tell everyone that he, Bull Beynon, was on his way up.

*　　*　　*

He told Katie first. 'I'm being promoted, Katie. What do you think of that?' She had been to choir practice and Bull was walking her back to her new post at Caswell House where she was maid now to Mrs Dafydd Buchan. He wondered whether she would object if he took her hand.

She turned to him, her face aglow. 'It's what you deserve, Bull. You're a fine, honest worker and so well respected.' Tentatively she slipped her hand through his arm and he swallowed hard. She was so lovely, so innocent, different from any woman he had ever known.

'Katie, I know we haven't been walking out long but you do feel that we are special together, don't you?'

'Of course I do, Bull!' She smiled up at him. 'I'm so lucky to have met you.'

'Not as lucky as me.' He turned her to face him. 'Could I just give you one little kiss?'

'Not here in the outdoors, Bull, where anyone might see us.'

'You're right, of course. I don't know what I was thinking about.' He squeezed her hand. 'Come on, we're very nearly there and I'd better not keep you out too long. I don't want anyone gossiping about you.'

He saw the quick upturn of her eyes and smiled. 'You're a lady, Katie, and I respect and admire you for it.'

Suddenly he remembered Rhiannon sitting at home waiting for him, and felt a pang of guilt. Soon, very soon, he must tell Katie about

71

Rhiannon, and he knew in his heart it would not be easy.

CHAPTER EIGHT

Shanni stared with distaste into the windows of Howell's Emporium at the fur cape draped over a piece of carved wood designed to look like a seat. One thing she would never own was a fur. The thought of wearing some creature's skin repelled her. She turned away abruptly and cannoned into a slim young girl coming in the opposite direction. 'Oh, sorry, love,' Shanni said, as the girl's basket fell to the ground, spilling its contents across the road. 'I'm so clumsy! Here, let me pick up some of the fruit for you.'

'Sure there's no need of that.' The girl was already stuffing the apples back into her basket. 'Once they're washed I doubt Miss Jayne will notice any difference.'

'You work for Jayne Morton-Edwards?' Shanni asked, suddenly interested.

'Mrs Buchan she is now.' The girl smiled. 'And aren't I tired of hearing about the wonderful wedding and all the gifts the couple got and how fine she looked?' She glanced warily at Shanni. 'But I shouldn't be talking about my mistress like that. It's not very nice of me, is it?'

'Well, I'm no friend of Jayne, stuck-up madam that she is.' They began to walk along the street and Shanni glanced at the girl, liking her on sight. 'Been in service long?'

'No, but I'm getting used to it. My name's Katie

Cullen. What's yours?'

'I'm Shanni Morgan, Mrs Pedr Morgan.' She smiled. 'Best of luck with your position in the Buchan household. I've a feeling you're going to need it.' She looked at Katie thoughtfully. 'Hold on a minute, what about us having a drink in Bendle's coffee shop? My treat,' she added, as the girl hesitated.

'Well, I don't know.' Katie looked around nervously. Evidently she'd had more than one taste of Jayne's sharp tongue, if Shanni was any judge.

'Come on, no one will know. Tell Madam you had to queue for the best fruit in the market.'

Katie smiled and her face lit up. She was so pretty when she smiled: her hair was dark yet her complexion was so fair that it was almost translucent. She was dressed in plain but good clothes, and the cut of her gown was excellent. Obviously Jayne's snobbery extended to her maid's outfit. Clearly she intended to have the best-dressed servants in Swansea.

'Right,' Katie said. 'Let's go. I'm late already but I might as well be hung for a sheep as a lamb.'

When they were seated in a corner of the coffee shop Shanni said, 'Look, you don't want to be a slave to these people. Remember, we're every bit as good as they are. It's just that we haven't got their money.'

'But you're married so you don't have to work.' Katie pushed the basket of fruit under the table, glad to be rid of the burden.

'Don't you believe it! I'd go mad if I stayed in the house all day, cleaning and polishing. I work in the office of the Llanelli Pottery for Mr Dafydd Buchan.'

73

'Well, isn't that a coincidence, then?' Katie's eyebrows rose. 'Me a maid to the Buchans and you working for the master. It's a small world like everyone says.'

'Smaller than you think.' Shanni smiled. 'I've known Jayne since she was a girl.'

The waiter hovered close by and Shanni gave her order in her best cultured voice. She knew it impressed folk more than any fine outfit. She noticed that Katie was looking at her strangely. 'What is it?' she asked.

'Well, I can't place you.' Katie's face was creased with bewilderment. 'You talk in a posh voice yet you seem like one of us.'

'If by "us" you mean the downtrodden workers, then I am one of "us".' Shanni laughed. 'I was given the benefit of a good education, taught my manners and how to act like a lady, but no one can change what's inside a person. I grew up in the slums of Swansea.'

The waiter put steaming jugs of coffee and milk on the table before Shanni.

'Tell me, Katie, how did you come to be working for Jayne?'

'It was by accident,' Katie said. 'I ran into the path of Mr Morton-Edwards' coach and pair. He took me home and I ended up working for him. I wish I could have stayed at the Big House but Mrs Buchan wanted me to go with her.'

'And Mrs Buchan gets what she wants.' It irked Shanni to think of Jayne as Mrs Buchan: Dafydd had been Shanni's hero, they had worked side by side, and she had to admit she was jealous of Jayne. 'And how is Dafydd enjoying married life? Is he happy?'

74

'He seems well enough. Very even-tempered, nice enough master. He does his best to see that the staff are fairly treated.'

'Sounds like Dafydd. We were friends once and, of course, I still work for him, as I said.' But at work she had little chance to talk to him, and even if she did how could she ask him if he was happy in his marriage? He would probably tell her to mind her own business. 'I expect Jayne twists him around her little finger.' There was an edge of sarcasm to Shanni's voice.

'I don't know about that. Mrs Buchan seems thrilled and happy when the master's around. I don't think she'd believe he'd spend time chasing other women, though the gossips say different.'

Shanni was sceptical: Jayne was the sort who loved herself first, but although she might seem empty-headed there was more to her. 'I don't think anyone would put anything over on Jayne,' she said, 'she's not half as *twp* as she looks.'

'Well, I'm sure no one would ever want to fool her. She's very popular,' Katie said.

'Aye—but not among the servants, I'll bet! Still, people like her seem to have all the luck,' Shanni said. 'There's Jayne with her rich papa, married to one of the most eligible men in the neighbourhood and here am I married to a potter.'

'I'm sure you love your husband. Is he handsome?' Katie was looking at Shanni's wedding band.

'Oh, yes, Pedr's handsome.' Shanni smiled to herself. He would come home smelling of clay and paint and he would hug her to him and kiss her passionately as he always did. 'He's a good husband,' she added. 'I'm lucky to have him, I suppose.'

'And you live here in Swansea?' Katie asked.

'On the outskirts of town on the Carmarthen road. Pedr sometimes works here in Swansea but mostly he does his pot throwing in Llanelli.'

'I don't think I'll ever get married.' Katie said wistfully, 'Though I'd like to, mind, but then I'd have to leave service, find a house and all sorts of things.'

'A good man would see to all that for you.' Shanni's mind was working swiftly. 'Why don't you come to supper with me and Pedr one evening? I'm sure it would do you good to get out a bit.'

'I don't know if I can get time off,' Katie said. 'Even when the mistress is out visiting she leaves me jobs to do.'

'Well, she has to let you go out sometime. Tell me, is it true that Mr Morton-Edwards saved you from a crowd of railway navvies?' Shanni leaned across the table. 'There was a lot of talk about it among the pottery workers.' She studied Katie: she was not much younger in years than Shanni but in the ways of the world she was a baby.

'Yes,' Katie agreed. 'He was wonderful—he just put me in his carriage and drove off with me. A real gent is Mr Morton-Edwards.' She drained her cup. 'I'd better get back.' She rescued her basket from under the table. 'I'll be in for a row if I stay longer.'

'Will you ask about your day off?' Shanni asked. 'I really would love you to have a bit of supper with us.'

'I don't know. I'll have to ask Mrs Buchan.' Katie looked worried at the prospect.

'A bit of advice, ask Mr Buchan. Anyway, when

are you coming to shop in town again?'

'I'll be down on market day for sure,' Katie said. 'Mrs Buchan always sends me to fetch the best farm vegetables.' She got to her feet. 'I don't think she likes me very much—she gets me out of her way most of the time, although I'm supposed to be her personal maid.'

'All the better for you, if you ask me!' Shanni averred. 'See you in the coffee shop this time next week, then.'

'I'll do my best.'

Shanni watched as the girl made her way out. Poor Katie, to be at the mercy of a selfish wretch like Jayne. Ah, well, she would do all she could to make her life a little more pleasant, and if she succeeded Katie would be released from service for ever.

*   *   *

Katie hurried along the street—she could imagine her mistress's tantrum if she had been kept waiting for her fruit. When she let herself in through the back door of the large house she breathed a sigh of relief. It seemed that visitors had arrived for Mrs Buchan was happily engaged in entertaining.

In the kitchen, Cook looked at her with narrowed eyes. 'Where have you been, Katie Cullen?' Mrs Williams asked. 'You've been gone long enough to grow them apples.'

Cook's word was law in the kitchen but Mrs Williams was more of a martinet than ever Mrs Grinter at the Big House had been. But, Katie reminded herself, she was not a kitchenmaid, she was personal maid to Mrs Buchan. All the same, it

77

was as well to stay in Mrs Williams's good book. 'I had to wait a while in the market,' she said. 'I don't think the mistress would thank me for getting anything but the best.'

'Aye, well, I suppose you're right there. She can be right fussy about her food.'

Katie went into the yard and washed the apples under the pump. Strictly speaking, it was not her job but she hadn't forgotten the tumble they had taken. A smile turned up the corners of her lips. Thank heaven Mrs Buchan would never know that her apples had rolled all over the high street.

'Give the apples to Susie there to cut up for the pie, then help yourself to some tea—it's just been brewed,' Cook said, when Katie came back indoors. 'You look as if you need to sit down a bit.'

Katie was doubtful about lingering in the kitchen. 'Has Mrs Buchan been calling for me?' she asked.

'*Duw, duw*, girl!' Cook shook her head. 'I think the mistress has more to worry about than you. She's got her father and that Mrs Mainwaring visiting. Now, sit down and put your feet up while you've got the chance.'

Katie was grateful to slip her feet out of her shoes. It had been a long walk back from town.

'Did you hear any gossip about Mrs Mainwaring when you were out?' Cook leaned closer, not wanting the kitchenmaids to hear. 'Rumour has it she's still seeing our Mr Buchan.'

'Sorry, Mrs Williams, I didn't talk to anyone.' Katie changed the subject. 'Are the visitors staying for lunch?'

'Aye, it looks like they're staying quite a while.' Cook thumped a piece of dough on the table,

78

sending a spray of flour over her apron. 'I don't know how that Mrs Mainwaring has the nerve to go about in polite society. I know for a fact that the mistress can't abide her, and we don't have to think very hard to know why, do we?'

'Mrs Mainwaring and Mr Morton-Edwards are good friends, though, aren't they?'

Cook looked at her curiously. 'You're not thinking there's something going on between those two, are you? 'Cos there's not. It's true Mr Mainwaring has gone off to America with the elder boy but that don't mean Mr Morton-Edwards would take advantage.'

'I'm sure he wouldn't. I wasn't meaning anything like that, Cook.'

'Well, all right, then, but I wouldn't be surprised if Mr Mainwaring stayed out there in America for good rather than face the scandal of his wife's brazen ways.'

Katie concentrated on her tea, not wanting to involve herself in kitchen gossip, which spread like wildfire even if there was no truth in it. 'He's a lovely gentleman, is Mr Morton-Edwards,' she said at last. 'I can't see him doing anything wrong, can you, Cook?'

'We all like to think that,' Mrs Williams cut the dough into circles large enough to fill a pie dish, 'but he's a man for all that and likes his comforts.' She placed apple slices on top of the pastry. 'Aye, fair play, mind, you fetched a lovely bit of fruit.'

Katie wanted to smile. If Mrs Williams knew the truth she'd throw a fit. 'I'm glad they're not bruised or anything. I picked them out very carefully,' she said quietly.

'Taught by your mammy, I 'spects,' Mrs Williams

said, eyeing her curiously. 'You're from a respectable family, Katie. The Cullens were well thought of round these parts. Irish they may be but they were good honest souls for all that.'

Cook had no idea she was being patronizing: she spoke genially and meant well.

'Thank you, Mrs Williams. My mam would have been so pleased to hear you speak so kindly about us. By the way, Mrs Williams, when do I have a day off? I'd like to visit some of my friends up in Greenhill sometime.'

'Good heavens, you only just got here, girl, and you talking about a day off! You'll 'ave to wait till the mistress tells you, like the rest of us do.'

Katie put down her cup. It was time she went upstairs and made herself useful by sorting out fresh clothes for her mistress. The duties of a personal maid were not onerous but Katie was at Mrs Buchan's beck and call.

'I'd better get on. Thank you, Cook, for the tea. It was most welcome.'

'I should think so. Not many servants get the privilege of real tea like we do. No one can complain that the master's penny-pinching.'

'No indeed,' Katie agreed.

It was a relief to slip up the wide, curving stairs to the bedroom occupied by her mistress. It seemed strange to her that the master and mistress had separate rooms: her own parents had slept in the same bed.

It was peaceful in the bedroom, with the bright sun shining in through the windows, splashing the silk covers with vibrant colour. Katie saw that the dressing-table was littered with an array of bottles and boxes; it was easy to see that Mrs Buchan had been forced to get herself ready to meet her guests. Katie made a wry face. Would she pay for her absence later?

She began to clear up the clutter, putting perfumes and creams away in the small drawers of the dressing-table. This was the part of the job she enjoyed. She did not mind mopping up after Mrs Buchan when she had used all the water in the jug and spilt most of it over the washstand and she did not mind gathering up discarded clothes and taking them down to the laundry room. What did bother her was listening to Jayne talk about her husband, and how that witch Llinos Mainwaring had got her claws into him.

Suddenly the door opened and Jayne swept into the room. She sat on the bed and kicked off her shoes. 'Thank heavens that's over. It was the longest lunch I've ever had to endure. I do wish Father wouldn't bring that woman over here. He knows how I feel about her.'

Katie thought it politic to remain silent. She saw that the fire was getting low and picked up the tongs to place coals strategically over the dying embers.

'And what did you do with yourself this morning?' Jayne asked, with unusual curiosity.

'I just did the shopping, Mrs Buchan.'

'But did you speak to anyone? For heaven's sake, girl, talk to me. You're not dumb, are you?'

Katie mulled it over in her mind. Should she tell the mistress about her meeting with Shanni Morgan? Surely it could do no harm.

'I bumped into Shanni Morgan. She's married to one of the potters.'

'Oh, did you, indeed? And did she have any

gossip to impart?'

Everyone was obsessed with gossip, Katie thought, from the mistress down to the servants in the kitchen.

'Not really, but she did ask me if I'd like to visit her on my day off.'

Jayne digested this in silence and, to Katie's relief, she did not seem to be angry about her maid talking to one of the potters' wives.

'Did she speak about Mr Buchan?' Jayne did not look at Katie: she drew her legs up onto the bed and sat with them crossed, careless that her good silk dress was being creased.

'Only to say that she worked for him.' Katie thought that innocent enough. She watched as Jayne pulled the combs from her hair allowing it to fall in pale waves down her back.

'I've quite got a headache now,' she said. 'Fetch some rosewater and bathe my forehead for me, Katie, there's a good girl. Oh, and Katie, I would like you to accept Shanni Morgan's invitation but you must keep your ears open for anything she might say about me or about my husband. Do you understand?'

'Yes, Mrs Buchan.' As Katie left the room she was frowning. If her mistress thought she would act like a gossipmonger, she was mistaken. Still, it would be nice to make new friends, and somehow Katie felt that in Shanni she might have found a good friend indeed.

CHAPTER NINE

Llinos sat in the drawing room of Caswell House staring unseeingly into the fire. She had been so foolish to accept Eynon's invitation to visit his daughter. True to form, Jayne was keeping her guests waiting and Llinos was imagining her and Dafydd together. Jayne would watch him dress and shave, see how beautiful he was in sleep, all the intimate things she remembered so well. It hurt.

'When will Joe be home?' Eynon broke the silence. 'It seems so long since he went off to America.'

'I don't know,' Llinos said. 'He hasn't paid me the courtesy of telling me that yet.' As soon as the words left her lips she felt guilty. After all, it had been her choice to stay in Swansea.

'I wish he *would* come home,' she said. Without him she felt vulnerable.

Before Eynon could reply the drawing-room door opened and Llinos sat back in her seat, expecting to see Jayne make her entrance. But it was Dafydd who came into the room, his eyes searching for hers. She bit her lip and looked away, as if to distance herself from him but his presence dominated the room.

Almost directly behind him was Jayne, her face flushed, her hair less than neat. 'So sorry to keep you waiting, Papa,' she said, 'but my husband has been busy telling me how beautiful I look, haven't you, darling?' She reached for Dafydd and as Llinos watched her kiss his cheek she felt her heart shrink.

Dafydd came towards her and she held out her hand almost without thinking. He took it, and the touch of his fingers, the way his eyes bored into hers, made her feel almost ill with regret for what might have been.

'It's so good to see you, Llinos. Tell me how life is treating you?' He sat close to her, and she was very aware of the warmth of his body. Her heart was pounding so hard that she wondered if he would hear it.

'My darling's had a bad day,' Jayne said.

'There's been a bit of trouble down at the Llanelli pottery,' Dafydd explained, 'but nothing that can't be handled by Pedr Morgan.' He addressed himself to Llinos. 'Seems some of the men want to leave the pottery and join the railway navvies. The fools can't see that the work on the line is almost finished.'

Llinos had still not composed herself so Eynon filled the uncomfortable gap. 'Talking of the railways, I've managed to buy some shares.' He avoided Dafydd's eye. 'I was lucky to get them— some old man fell sick and wanted to get out of the business world. I took just a few. The rest went to an unknown buyer.'

'I've tried my best to get hold of some Great Western shares,' Dafydd said. 'They'll be worth a goldmine in a very short time.'

Llinos swallowed hard, wondering how soon she could make her excuses and leave. Everyone was keeping up the façade that this was a meeting of friends but she could tell from Eynon's expression that he was only too aware that Dafydd could not take his eyes off her.

'Have you managed to buy some of the shares,

Llinos?' Dafydd asked.

She shook her head, unable to speak. It alarmed her that Dafydd could still move her in this way and she wished she could leave their affair in the past.

She glanced at Jayne, who was looking smug: she had something up her sleeve, some secret. Could she be expecting Dafydd's child?

'I must be going,' Llinos said quickly. 'I didn't realize how quickly time was passing. My son will be wondering where I am.'

'How is the boy?' Dafydd asked.

Llinos was afraid to look at him. 'He's very bright, learning his lessons with no trouble. He will have to go away to school soon.'

'It's no wonder he's bright—he has such a brilliant mother.' Dafydd spoke in a low voice, but both Jayne and Eynon heard him. 'If you can get your hands on some railway shares, they would stand him in good stead later in life.'

'Don't bore them with talk of railways and shares, Dafydd,' Jayne said waspily. 'I'm sure Aunt Llinos has no interest in such things.'

Llinos rose. She had heard the hostility in Jayne's voice and wanted to escape. Good thing she'd insisted on bringing her own carriage. 'Eynon, will you come to the door with me?' she asked, but Dafydd was already on his feet.

'I'll see you out,' he said decisively. 'I'm on my way to a meeting anyway.' He towered over her, but she kept her eyes turned away from his face.

'I'll come too, darling.' Jayne slipped her hand through her husband's arm in a proprietary way. Dafydd could not hide his displeasure.

'Let's make a party of it—I'll come too.' Eynon sounded disgruntled, and Dafydd glanced at him.

'There's no need for all this fuss. You and Jayne stay here near the fire and keep warm. It's rather cold outside for the time of year.' He untangled his arm from Jayne's grasp and led Llinos into the hall.

The maid brought her coat, and Llinos slipped her arms into the sleeves. Dafydd opened the door and stepped out into the pale sunlight of early winter. He looked so virile, so alive . . . so dear.

'That was foolish,' she said, as he led her to her carriage. 'You'll give yourself away if you keep acting like that.'

He smiled. 'I'm merely seeing a guest out. No harm in that, is there?' He took her arm to help her in. Llinos felt the warmth of his fingers and shivered—she wanted him so much. Even now, with grey hairs appearing, she still felt the urge to lie with Dafydd, experience his vigour, his love.

'I want you so much,' Dafydd said. 'I want to take you to bed, to make love to you until we're both exhausted. Will I never stop wanting you, Llinos?'

'It's torture, I know.' She averted her eyes. 'I want you just as much but it's impossible.'

'Nothing is impossible,' Dafydd said. 'Llinos, we both want this so much, why deny ourselves?'

She struggled to find an answer. Her mind told her that Dafydd was forbidden to her, but her body had no care for honour or truth or fidelity. She looked up at the branches of the trees, stripped now by chill winds. Overhead ominous dark clouds threatened rain.

'You are married, Dafydd,' she said slowly. 'I can't forget that you belong to Jayne.' But she had made love with him when she was a married woman. She had not kept her own vows.

Dafydd echoed her thoughts: 'But you did not care about your vows when you came to me, Llinos, so why should mine be any different?'

'Dafydd, I can't hurt Jayne in the way I was hurt.' She paused, trying not to cry. 'I felt justified in being with you because Joe had been unfaithful to me.' She hesitated. 'But in spite of that, I always felt the betrayal keenly, both mine and his.'

'Joe's away. He's chosen to go off without you, which I would never do.' He sighed. 'When I walked away from our love it was to give you and Joe a chance to restore your life together. Well, you are not together, are you?'

He looked up into her face, holding her hands while the carriage rocked as the horses shifted uneasily between the shafts. 'Please, Llinos, just say you'll meet me tomorrow. We'll walk in the park, if that's what you want, but I need to be with you at least for a while.'

She tried to draw away her hands—Eynon was probably watching from the window. 'All right, then. Tomorrow in Victoria Park, the early afternoon. Now I must go.'

The driveway from Caswell House seemed to stretch to infinity, and Llinos pressed herself into a corner of the carriage as though she could make herself invisible. But she could not escape her conscience. Why was she agreeing to meet Dafydd? She knew the temptations of being alone with him. She would not go, she decided, and Dafydd would have to accept that there was nothing he could do.

Then she heard the sound of hoofs pounding along behind her and wondered if he had come after her.

'Stop, driver!' Eynon appeared at the side of the

carriage. He was holding his horse on a tight rein and his face was white with anger. 'Llinos, don't do this to Jayne.'

'I don't know what you mean,' Llinos said. 'Do what, Eynon? I have done nothing but talk to Dafydd. What else could I do outside in the drive?'

'You know exactly what I mean,' Eynon said. 'You can't hide the longing in your eyes whenever that man is near you. Are you ever going to behave like a responsible woman, Llinos?'

'How dare you speak to me like that?' Llinos knew her anger was driven by guilt. 'Since Dafydd took his vows we have done nothing to be ashamed of.'

'I don't believe you! That man makes love to you with his every gesture.' Eynon's face was white. 'I could kill the bastard for the way he disregards my daughter's feelings.'

'Are you sure it's not jealousy that is clouding your judgement, Eynon?' Llinos's voice rose. 'You are wrong about us! We have done nothing to be ashamed of.'

'Tell me you don't care for him any more, then,' Eynon said angrily. 'Just tell me that, Llinos, and I'll leave you alone.'

'My feelings are nothing to do with you, Eynon!' Llinos was as angry as he was. 'Nothing gives you the right to tell me what I can and can't do.'

'I've been your friend for as long as I can remember. Doesn't that give me some rights, Llinos?'

'And can you tell me *you*'ve never done anything wrong, Eynon? Have you never given way to your feelings?' She looked into his anguished eyes and remorse built inside her. She was about to make a conciliatory gesture when Eynon wheeled his horse away.

'When will I see you again, Eynon?' Llinos called, but he was already riding away. She shrugged. She was hurt by his attitude but she knew that as soon as he'd thought things over they would be friends again.

*   *   *

'Well, Katie, are you getting used to being lady's maid to Mrs Dafydd Buchan?'

Katie heaved her basket on to her other arm. 'Well, when she's in a good mood I enjoy my work.'

'And that's not very often, is it?' Shanni fell into step beside her. 'You know Sarah, one of the maids at Caswell House, don't you? She's a good girl, talkative, too, and not above a bit of gossip. She says she'd heard Jayne and Dafydd quarrelling.'

A carriage pulled up sharply alongside her.

'Katie Cullen, what do you think you're doing, girl?'

Katie bit her lip as she saw Mrs Buchan lean out of her carriage. 'Get in at once. You know I don't like my servants talking to the likes of Shanni Morgan!'

Katie was confused. 'I'm sorry, Mrs Buchan, but I am doing my job, that's all.'

'And gossiping the day away by the look of it. Now, get in at once if you value your position in my household, and you are never to talk to her again.'

Katie was angry now: maid she might be, but she deserved to be treated with courtesy. 'I think it's my business who I talk to when I'm out on the street—and didn't you tell me yourself that it was all right to talk to Shanni?'

'I said no such thing!'

Katie stared at her in dismay. 'But you did, Mrs—'

'Don't answer back, girl! How dare you call me a liar? I've got a terrible headache and you're making it worse. Oh, I've had enough of you. You can collect your belongings and leave my house. Get out of my sight for good!'

Katie stared open-mouthed as the carriage disappeared along the road. 'Well!' she said. 'I don't want to work for the likes of her anyway.' But for all her brave words she was upset. Where would she go? What could she do?

Shanni took her arm. 'Look, let's go and fetch your things. I'll come and help you and then we'll ask Dafydd to find you a place somewhere else, right?'

Katie nodded and quickened her step. 'Let's just get it over and done with,' she said.

Shanni touched her arm. 'You spoke up well for yourself there. I'm glad to see you're not afraid to talk back to the gentry.'

'Well, they're no better than us, they just have more money,' Katie said, with a grin.

'Apart from which,' Shanni began to laugh, 'she has to pee the same as the rest of us.'

The walk to Caswell House passed more quickly than Katie expected, mainly because she was listening to Shanni's strange views on women's place in society. 'You see, Katie, women can pull themselves up by their bootlaces if they want to. We don't have to be maidservants and wait on the rich. Many of the women who are successful now were poor like us, once upon a time.'

'Who, for instance?' Katie looked at Shanni's red hair blown in tendrils across her pale skin. She was so lucky to be such a beauty.

'Well, there's Llinos Mainwaring. Her father fought with the Duke of Wellington and was injured badly, so they say, and she was left as poor as a church mouse when the pottery got run down. It was only because she had courage and talent that she could pull everything together and make a success of her life. Except in love, though. She made a right mess there.'

Katie was intrigued. 'What do you mean?'

'Don't you know anything, Katie? Well, perhaps you've lived a sheltered life up there on Greenhill. You had a strict mam and dad to take care of you, didn't you?'

'Maybe so, but that doesn't make me stupid.'

'I'm not saying it does! *Duw, duw*, no need to be so jumpy. I only meant you were brought up in a respectable household.'

'I'm sorry,' Katie said, 'but because my family were Irish some folk treat me like a fool. Anyway, are you going to tell me more about Mrs Mainwaring?'

'She married a foreigner, didn't she?'

'What's wrong with that?' A glimmer of a smile lit Katie's face. 'I suppose you could say I'm a foreigner, too, my mam and dad coming from across the sea an' all.'

'Well, not so foreign as Mr Mainwaring. He was an American Indian and he took a squaw woman as his mistress and gave her a baby too, so all the old women say.'

'Mrs Mainwaring can't help that, though, can she?' Katie frowned. 'Quite a few men go funny

91

over women, don't they?' She thought of her father, the way he used to eye up the young Catholic girls in church then go to the alehouse and get drunk.

'Ah, but Llinos Mainwaring took her revenge.'

'How?'

'She had an affair with Dafydd Buchan—surely you heard about it? She's got a child by him too—you can see the likeness a mile off.'

Katie heard a touch of bitterness in Shanni's voice and realized there was more to the story than met the eye. Still, it was shocking that a woman could openly flaunt the child of a man who was not her husband.

'Mr Buchan is as bad as she is, then,' she said aloud. 'You can't always blame the woman, can you?'

'And you a good Catholic girl?' Shanni laughed. 'You're like me. We both have spirit, and we both think a man is as much to blame as the woman in these affairs.'

Katie looked at her closely. 'You might say that but I can tell you're angry with Mrs Mainwaring.'

'No! Well, yes, I suppose I am. As far as I can see the affair is still going on, and that's not fair to Jayne. She might be a spoiled madam but she doesn't deserve a husband who strays.'

Caswell House loomed on the horizon and Katie quickened her steps, wondering what sort of reception she would get. She led the way to the back of the house and let herself into the scullery.

Susie was laying a tray with dainty cups and an elegant silver pot from which the fragrance of coffee emanated. 'You're out of a job, then, Katie,' she said. 'So sorry, love.'

Katie put down her basket and looked at Shanni. 'Come upstairs and help me collect my things, will you?'

Shanni pushed ahead of her and, to Katie's surprise, made her way across the hall towards the drawing room. 'We'll see what Dafydd has to say first, shall we?'

She knocked at the door in a peremptory manner and pushed it open. Jayne was sitting on the large sofa, her feet neatly crossed, and Dafydd was flicking through a sheaf of papers.

'Shanni!' He looked up at her in surprise. 'What are you doing here? I thought it was your day off. Is there more trouble down at the pottery?'

'No, Dafydd, Pedr has sorted it out. I've come to talk to you about Katie here. She's been sacked and she doesn't know where to go.'

Jayne prickled visibly. 'Yes, she has been dismissed and rightly so! And how dare you, Shanni Morgan, come into my house as if you own it? You'll be the next one out of a job, if you aren't careful.'

'Calm down,' Dafydd said. 'Tell me, Shanni, what's happened?'

'Katie was shopping for Mrs Buchan and we were walking down the street talking. Jayne—Mrs Buchan didn't like it so she told Katie her job was finished.'

'That's not all of it, Dafydd!' Jayne interrupted. 'The girl answered me back. She was insolent to me and I will not tolerate it.'

With a sigh Dafydd put down the papers. 'Go and get your things, Katie, and I'll drive you over to Mr Morton-Edwards' house. I'm sure he'll have a place for you.'

'But, Dafydd,' Jayne protested, 'you must let the girl find her own situation. Why should my father take her in?' She spun to face Shanni. 'And trust you to be involved in all this! You can't keep away from my husband, can you?'

'Jayne! Control yourself and act like a lady, not a fishwife.'

Katie watched the colour recede from Mrs Buchan's face, and felt almost sorry for her.

'A fishwife, is it?' Jayne asked, her voice low with anger. 'And I suppose you have always acted like a perfect gentleman, have you?'

'Jayne,' his voice held a warning, 'don't say something you might regret.'

Katie backed towards the door. If man and wife needed to argue, it should be done in private. Shanni, however, stood her ground, apparently enjoying every minute of the confrontation.

'Oh, no, you must appear faultless, mustn't you, Dafydd? No one dares to speak of your shameful liaison with Llinos Mainwaring, do they? But everyone talks about you behind your back, Dafydd, and you know what they say?' She did not wait for a reply. 'They say it is still going on now, husband. What have you to say about that?'

Dafydd ignored his wife and opened the door of the drawing room. 'Ladies,' he said, 'after you.' Katie almost ran from the room. 'Get your belongings, Katie.' He spoke kindly. 'As I said, I'll take you over to Mr Morton-Edwards' house as soon as the carriage is ready.'

Katie went upstairs with Shanni, who looked around her with shining eyes. 'Well, that put Mrs High and Mighty in her place!' she said. 'And even with all this wealth and luxury she doesn't know

94

how to keep her husband happy.'

'Hush!' Katie warned. 'You don't want any of the other servants to hear, do you?'

'I don't give a fig,' Shanni retorted. 'Come on, now, let's get your things and join Dafydd, shall we?'

The ways of some folks were a mystery to Katie, and she wished she was back at Greenhill, living quietly at home with her parents. But they were dead and she was on her own now. She glanced at Shanni. No, not quite on her own, she had Shanni as a friend and—her heart missed a beat—she was walking out with Bull Beynon, the handsomest man in Swansea.

CHAPTER TEN

Bull ran his hands around the collar of his one good shirt, feeling hot in spite of the cold weather. He sat in the plush room of Government Buildings aware that he was being judged by the man seated before him. On him rested his future as a manager on the Great Western Railway.

'So, Mr Beynon, you wish to become a manager?' Mr Morton-Edwards looked closely at him, sizing him up.

'Yes, sir,' Bull replied. 'I'm used to the railways, well versed in the stresses and strains of steel, and I know how to check the rolling stock and make sure the tracks are in good condition.'

'But only in the way a navvy would be familiar with the workings of a railway, is that right?'

'Not quite, sir. I read and write, I have studied

95

plans with the engineers. I think I know a great deal more than a navvy.' Bull's fate might have been in the hands of the man seated opposite him, but he had no intention of crawling to him.

'Beynon is a remarkable man, Eynon,' Mr Cookson, who was also at the meeting, said slowly. 'I have the utmost faith in his ability or I would not have raised the matter. He knows all about Mr Brunel and his work on the Landore Viaduct.'

Bull remained silent, studying Morton-Edwards, knowing how shrewd a businessman he was. The talk on the line was that he had acquired railway shares when they were scarcer than hen's teeth. As he was wealthy and influential it had not been long before he was asked to join the board of governors of the South Wales line.

'Very good.' Morton-Edwards looked at Cookson. 'Well, I'm satisfied that the cost of training Mr Beynon would be well worthwhile, but I'd like to know what the other board members have to say about it. We'll be in touch, Beynon, and thank you for your time.'

Bull got to his feet. 'Thank you, sir,' he nodded to Morton-Edwards, 'and thank you for your faith in me, Mr Cookson.'

Outside, the air was cold on his face. He turned to look at the large building, grand and imposing in the fading light. Men like Eynon Morton-Edwards were used to such finery, and one day, Bull vowed, he would be too.

He mounted the horse lent to him by Mr Cookson and turned it towards home, which was still just a shanty on the edge of the muddy workings. One day, home would mean something very different.

'He's a fine young man,' Eynon said later, at his house. 'I liked the cut of his jib, though he's an independent sod.'

'The thing about Bull Beynon,' Cookson said, 'is that he's his own man, not open to coercion or bribery, a man of intelligence and a man to trust.'

'So, perhaps we should look to getting him trained properly.'

'I'm glad you agree, but I would prefer to wait until the line to Swansea is opened. At the moment he's too useful to part with.'

'I'll leave it with you, then, but in the meantime I'll bring it up with the other governors. I don't anticipate any problems there.' Eynon was more than happy to propose the young man and with Cookson seconding him, Bull would have his promotion. 'Now, will you take a glass of my new Madeira?' Eynon liked Cookson: the man was talented—honest into the bargain. 'It's not everyone I'd share my wine with,' he said, 'but I think we both deserve a drink in celebration of setting a young man on the road to better things. Apart from that, the Madeira is rich and fruity and slides down a dry throat like silk.'

'Just what the doctor ordered.' Cookson loosened his waistcoat buttons and settled more comfortably in his chair. 'Do you mind if I smoke my pipe?' He held it up.

'Please do and I think I'll join you.' Not having a woman about the place certainly had its advantages, Eynon reflected. 'My house has been a haven of peace since my daughter married,' he mused. 'I never thought I'd say it but I'm glad to be on my own again.'

'And I'd give anything to have a good woman around,' Cookson sounded wistful, 'but being an engineer's wife is no life for a woman. She either travels with her husband or waits at home alone. No, I'm better off as a bachelor, at least for now.'

'Don't say that! A young man like you needs a wife and children. You've a great deal to offer so don't sell yourself short, Cookson.' He rang the bell, and shortly afterwards he heard a light tap at the door. 'Ah, Katie.' He smiled. The girl had fitted into his household again with little trouble—relieved, it seemed, to be away from Jayne's iron rule. 'Will you fetch me my best Madeira, Katie, and two glasses?'

She bobbed a curtsey and hurried away to do his bidding.

'I think my daughter was too strict with the girl,' Eynon observed. 'Jayne gave her quite a time of it before she dispensed with Katie's services because she caught her gossiping when she was supposed to be at market. Women! Will we ever understand them?'

Cookson smiled. 'Well, if you, a twice married man, can't, I have no chance!'

'Aye, twice married and none the wiser.' Eynon shook his head. 'Give me plain honest business and I know where I am—and I'm more than happy to help Beynon.' He smiled wryly. 'But he'll have to dress in respectable clothes before I introduce him to the rest of the board. It's surprising how men of education and wealth will judge a man by his dress not his intelligence.' There was another tap at the door and Katie appeared with a tray, the glasses

98

and a decanter of the rich brown wine. Eynon poured it and handed Cookson a glass. They sipped silently for a few moments. Then Eynon took out his pocket watch and stared down at it, screwing up his eyes in an effort to see the hands. 'Got the time, Cookson? My eyes are not what they were.'

'It's sixteen minutes past six and I really should be going.'

Eynon nodded. 'Thank you for introducing me to your prodigy. He's a fine young man and worthy of your interest.' He stood up and opened the door to let Cookson into the hall. Katie was there at once with the man's coat and hat. She bobbed another curtsey and waited in silence until Cookson had gone and the front door was closed behind him.

'Why are you hovering, Katie? Did you want to speak to me?'

'I did, sir. I wondered if I may have a few hours off this evening.' She smiled, and Eynon's face softened: she really was a pleasant child.

'What's the occasion?' he asked. 'It looks as though you might have found a sweetheart—you seem excited.'

The lace on the edge of her cap cast shadows over her eyes so that he could not read her expression as she said, 'I've been invited to supper, sir, with Shanni Morgan. I hope you don't mind, sir.'

'Why should I mind?' Eynon asked. 'If you've made friends with the girl, that's your business and no one else's. Go with my blessing.'

He returned to the sitting room, amazed at how easy it was to make some people happy. Little

Katie was thrilled with such simple treats—her choir practice and now her new friends. Poor child, she must have had such a sheltered background. It was to be hoped that her innocence was not spoiled by some unscrupulous young man. Still, that was none of his business.

He poured himself another glass of Madeira and sat in his favourite chair. The fire glowed in the hearth, and outside the rain had begun to fall. He would be content if only Llinos were seated opposite him as his wife. But that would never be. Llinos was his friend, and that was all she could ever be so he might as well accept the situation.

*   *   *

Katie hesitated before she knocked at the door of the cottage. She could see a lamp burning inside and the sound of voices made her heart flutter. It was childish to be so excited by an invitation to supper with her new friends, but she couldn't help it. In any case, Shanni had invited Bull too, and that was enough to bring the colour to Katie's cheeks.

The door opened and Shanni was there smiling. Her red hair was swept up in curls at each side of her face, she was dressed in a good gown of heavy velvet and she looked every inch the grand lady. Katie felt dowdy in her heavy dark skirt and plain turnover.

'Come in and sit by the fire, Katie, love. You must be frozen, but at least the rain has stopped.' Shanni drew her into the room and closed the door on the misty night. 'Come and meet my husband, Pedr. You already know his friend, Bull Beynon,

100

don't you?' She linked arms with Katie and drew her into the warmth of the parlour, where the fire blazed brightly. 'Pedr, come and meet Katie.'

Pedr was dark and well built but when Bull Beynon came to stand beside him he towered a full six inches over him.

'Nice to meet you, Mr Morgan.' Katie said. She glanced up at Bull, who smiled encouragingly.

'Hello, Katie,' he said. 'It's lovely to see you again and I didn't think it would be so soon.' He grinned wickedly. 'I think this is some sort of matchmaking plan, don't you?' His look was meaningful and Katie smiled: she could hardly have expected Shanni to know that she and Bull were already walking out together.

'What do you mean by "so soon"?' Shanni asked. 'What have you two been up to? Come, sit down and tell us all about it.' She nudged Katie's arm. 'Are you a bit of a dark horse, then?'

'Well, Bull and me have been out together a few times now, haven't we, Bull?'

'Well,' Shanni put her hands on her hips, 'and there's me thinking you a shy little girl! You do surprise me.' She laughed. 'I'm only teasing—don't look so worried.'

Bull took a seat near Katie and she felt his magnetism. So did Shanni.

'Saints alive,' Shanni said, 'I think you're the luckiest girl alive, walking out with a man like Bull Beynon.' She touched her husband's arm. 'If I wasn't married to this one here I'd be setting my cap at Bull and no mistake.' She got to her feet. 'Well, supper won't make itself so I'll go and see if the meat is done.'

'I'll come and help you, love.' Pedr paused in the

doorway and looked back. 'Be good now, you two, because I'll be keeping an eye on you.' He winked to show he was just joking but the colour rose to Katie's cheeks.

'They mean well,' Bull said easily. 'It's just their way of throwing us together. Have you noticed that married folk can't wait for the rest of us to tie the knot?'

Katie wondered if he was annoyed. 'Shanni and I have met in town a few times and I never told her anything about us, I promise.'

'Don't worry, I'm proud and happy that you're my girl. I want the whole world to know so talk away and I won't mind one bit.' He put his hand over hers. 'Perhaps I haven't told you this but I do love you very much indeed, Katie Cullen.'

She felt a flutter of her heart as he spoke her name—she had always thought it plain but it wasn't when he said it. His words thrilled her and she looked up at him shyly, wanting to kiss him.

He leaned forward. 'Isn't it nice being together like this? I could almost imagine we were sitting together in our own little house. Once I'm manager, Katie, we can start to make plans.' He was so in charge of himself, so at ease with the situation that Katie felt like a lost little girl. Why couldn't she think of something clever to say or, better still, make a tender remark? Her mouth was suddenly dry.

'In the meantime, you're well placed working for Mr Morton-Edwards, aren't you?' Bull went on.

'Yes, I'm happy up at the Big House,' Katie said. 'Mrs Buchan could be very difficult.'

That, she thought, was putting it mildly. Strange that a nice man like Mr Morton-Edwards had fathered a girl like her.

Bull sat back in his chair. 'I'm hoping Mr Morton-Edwards will speak soon to the board of governors of the railway. I want to know if I've got the job.'

Katie would have liked to ask Bull about his plans for the future. Would he have to go away once the line was finished?

He glanced at her and smiled. 'I'll have to travel wherever the work takes me,' he seemed to know what she was thinking, 'but I won't be going away until the line into Swansea is open and by then I hope we'll be . . .' His words trailed away as Shanni came back into the room. 'Come on, you two turtle-doves,' she said playfully. 'I've been slaving over the fire making a good meal for you so come and eat it and don't dare to leave a morsel.'

Katie got to her feet, her heart fluttering. Had Bull been about to mention marriage?

'We'll talk more when I walk you home afterwards.'

Bull had spoken quietly but Shanni heard him. 'Of course you must walk her home. An innocent like Katie needs a strong man at her side.' She laughed as Katie blushed. 'Don't be shy, girl, and don't be slow! You've got a catch there that any girl in Swansea would give a month's wages to have.'

Katie walked into the kitchen beside Bull, her heart full of happiness. She was in love and it was the most wonderful feeling on earth.

CHAPTER ELEVEN

'Oh, but darling, you know how much I was looking forward to this evening. Do you have to work tonight?' Jayne was aware that she sounded pettish but this was the third time Dafydd had gone back on his promise to be in for supper with her father.

'I'm sorry, my dear, but it's something I can't put off.'

'Well, you do realize that Papa will be upset, don't you? He'll think you're doing this on purpose, that you're afraid to face him.'

Dafydd frowned. 'I've never hidden from anything or anyone in my life and I don't intend to start now, but I have a business to run, or have you forgotten? Your father has the luxury of being retired—oh, I know he dabbles in the railway but otherwise he has all the time in the world, which I do not.'

Jayne tried a different tack. 'Please, darling, just for me, just this once.' She put her arms round him. 'Please, Dafydd, I don't ask much, do I?'

'Jayne, be told, I can't come tonight.' Clearly he was in no mood to be coaxed.

'Oh, go to your stupid meeting or whatever it is,' she snapped, and drew away from him. She wondered why he was avoiding her eyes. 'You wouldn't be seeing Llinos Mainwaring by any chance, would you?'

A strange expression flitted across his face, and suddenly she was frightened. 'You surely haven't taken up with that old woman again?' Her voice was shrill, and fear clawed at her—fear and jealousy that her husband had made love to another woman. 'You're still in love with her, aren't you?'

'Don't be silly, Jayne!' His voice was sharp. 'You don't know what you're talking about.'

Jayne clenched her hands, feeling her nails cut into the palms. 'I've hit on the truth, haven't I? You don't love me, you love her.' Her anger dissolved and she sank into a chair, her hands over her face.

Dafydd's silence spelt out his guilt. Jayne raised her head and studied his face for any sign of tenderness, but all she saw was discomfort.

'Why did you marry me if you didn't love me?' Tears welled in her eyes and ran down her face. 'Am I to be a brood mare to give you legitimate sons? Why are you torturing me like this when I love you as I never loved anyone in my life?'

He sighed. 'Come here.' He drew her to her feet and put his arms round her. 'Hush, now. Of course I love you, you are my wife. I made my vows to you and I mean to keep them.'

'Oh, Dafydd, please tell me you're not seeing Llinos any more—tell me she's not your mistress, please!'

'I have not laid a finger on Llinos since you and I were married,' he said. 'Don't forget that she has principles and she would never do anything to hurt you. Try to understand that. She's a good woman.'

It was as if he was turning a knife in her heart: he was defending Llinos, pointing out her virtues as if his wife should be grateful to her. She exploded with rage. 'Get away from me! You're not denying you love that woman, not for one minute! All you do is defend her. I think I hate you!' She paused for breath. 'You do still love her or you wouldn't

105

talk about her like that, telling me how good she is. Well, perhaps it's time I told you a few home truths.' She was past thought now. All she could feel was pain. She seemed overtaken with the desire to hurt him as he had hurt her. 'You have never given yourself to me wholeheartedly. I can tell that by the way you make love to me. I have always felt disappointed when you leave my bed and now I know why.'

He didn't speak and her anger boiled over. 'That woman is the talk of the town, don't you know that? She will never be allowed into polite society ever again, and all because of her affair with my husband. She is a harlot, and you are just as bad for getting involved with a woman of such low morals.'

'Be careful, Jayne. Don't overstep the mark or you will do more damage to our marriage than you realize.'

She wanted to beat him with her fists. He had stood beside her in the church, vowed to care for her and honour her. He had renounced all other women, but now she knew that those had been just words, and he had not meant them.

'Is that a threat, Dafydd?' She was frightened but her pride would not let her stop taunting him. 'Do you really think you can make a fool of Eynon Morton-Edwards's daughter and get away with it?'

'And who is issuing threats now?' He moved to the door. 'I'll leave you to calm down, and then you must think rationally about our marriage. If you want us to have a reasonable life together, you will learn to hold your tongue.'

He left her abruptly and she sank into a chair, tears flowing unchecked now that she knew the truth: he did not love her, had never loved her.

106

Dafydd was her husband; he made love to her from time to time out of duty. All he hoped for from their union was 'a reasonable life together'.

What was she to do? Speak to Papa? But that would confirm what he had thought all along, that the marriage had been made out of expediency not love.

She could talk to Papa's friend, though: Father Martin had always been in Jayne's life. He was a good man, a man of the cloth, and very wise. What a pity she had no women friends. Had Papa's second wife lived she might have made a good confidante. Or would she? Even before Isabelle died she and Jayne had scarcely talked. Isabelle had been of the lower orders, and Jayne had never thought her good enough for her father.

She stood up and walked to the mirror hanging over the fireplace. She was young and pretty enough, with her pale hair and fine complexion, so any flaws Dafydd found in her must be in her character.

On impulse she rang the bell for the maid and almost at once Becky came in from the hallway, a duster still in her hand. 'You wanted me, ma'am?'

'Come along in, Becky, and close the door.' For the first time Jayne heard her tone: she sounded haughty, as if she thought her maid a lesser being put on earth just to serve her. 'I expect you're busy getting ready for my father's visit so I won't take up much of your time.'

The girl's face was tense: it was as if she was waiting for a rebuke from her mistress.

'Don't look so worried, you haven't done anything wrong. I just wanted to talk to you.' Jayne rubbed her wrists as if the cold had entered her bones, but it was her heart that was chilled, with pain and humiliation.

'It's my husband—' She stopped. This was ridiculous—how could a maid, an unmarried girl, help her in her grief? She looked at Becky and knew it would be absurd to confide in her. 'Be careful you marry for the right reasons,' she said. The maid was looking at her as if she had grown two heads. 'I mean, don't marry in haste. You know what the old wives say about that, don't you, Becky?'

'I don't want to seem cheeky or anything,' Becky said humbly, 'but I don't want to marry anyone, not for a long time.' She hesitated then rushed on. 'I mean, it takes time to get to know each other— look at my mam and dad! They quarrelled all the time but it don't mean they didn't love each other, though.'

Jayne realized, for the first time, that servants were human beings, with thoughts and feelings. Still, she'd said enough. Becky had evidently heard her argue with Dafydd and there was little point in feeding the servants' gossip even more.

'Well,' she spoke more briskly, 'I just wanted to tell you that there is no need to put out fresh linen for the master. He will be dining out tonight.'

Becky nodded. The news was not unexpected: the servants had noticed that Mr Buchan was absent whenever Mr Morton-Edwards came to call.

When the door closed behind the girl, Jayne stood at the window, staring out over the gardens, the fields and the hills that rolled away into the distance. She was Dafydd's wife. One day, God willing, she would have his children and they would bind him closer to her than any gold wedding band.

'So there was an accident up at Pyle.' Bull was sitting in front of the fire in his shack, his feet up on a stool. 'Seems the line broke, and with the high winds and poor conditions, the engine toppled over. No harm done, though, no one hurt.'

Rhiannon was not paying much attention: she was hanging his clothes to dry on the makeshift line stretched across the narrow confines of the hut. He frowned, wondering how to break the news that he would be leaving her.

'I'm going to be given a house.'

She glanced over her shoulder at him, her full breasts straining against the rough cloth of her gown. 'Oh, aye, and who is going to give *us* a house, Bull? I'm not daft, mind. Nobody gives us anything for nothing, not folks like us.'

'Well, it's Mr Cookson's doing.'

'So, a manager gets a house instead of a shack, is that what you're telling me, Bull?'

'Yes, but there's more I need to say, so come and sit here and stop fiddling with the clothes.'

Rhiannon sat cross-legged on the floor beside him. 'All right, go on, I'm listening.' She smiled up at him, as if humouring a child.

'Things will have to change when I'm a manager.' He knew suddenly that he should have talked to her a long time ago.

'Well, I expect you will have to go away sometimes.' Rhiannon sounded fearful, and Bull grasped now what he was about to do to her.

'I expect I will, sometimes.' He cursed himself for being a thoughtless fool.

109

'It will mean the end of us, won't it?' Her voice was calm but her hands were shaking. 'Bull, answer me, will I be coming with you to this house you've been given?'

He tried to imagine Rhiannon surrounded by respectable neighbours who knew she was a camp woman. 'Look,' he said, 'it might all be a pipe-dream. I'm supposed to be loaned one of the houses on the Neath road but nothing is sure yet.'

'Bull,' she gazed up at him yearningly, 'I'm going to lose you, I know it. You'll need a good woman to marry when you're a respected manager, won't you?'

He got to his feet. 'We're talking about something that might not happen. I'm going down to the Castle now because I need to talk to some of the boys about the work on the line tomorrow.' He smiled down at her. 'We've got all the time in the world to work things out.'

He left the shanty beside the half-constructed line and made his way onto the road. Rhiannon had been right: she would have no place in his future when he became a manager. Then he thought of Katie, and of how the way he led his life would affect her. She had no idea he was living with Rhiannon, and he knew she would be upset when she discovered that he was keeping a woman.

He should have been truthful with Katie from the beginning, he thought, and he should have made Rhiannon understand that he could never take her as a wife. But he did not want to think of Rhiannon alone in the hut waiting for a man who would never come home.

He heard the laughter, saw the welcoming light spilling from the Castle, and quickened his pace.

He would drink with the men and forget everything except that he, Bull Beynon, was going up in the world.

*   *   *

Rhiannon stared into the hot coals of the fire, which glowed so fiercely that even the bars of the brazier seemed alight. So it was over. Bull was going to leave her and live on his own in a posh house.

She looked behind her towards the bed they shared. She had lain beside Bull for many months now, close as two people could be. He had been such a tender lover, so kind and respectful even though he knew of her past. She loved him as she would never love any other man.

The tears came then, running down her cheeks and splashing on to her work-roughened hands. How could she bear to be separated from him, to lie in bed alone or, worse, to be passed from man to man? That life was over for her now, she could never go back to being a harlot as the price of a bed for the night.

If only she had borne Bull a child he would never have left her: he was too much of a gentleman for that. He would have married her and brought up their baby as respectably as he knew how.

Rhiannon went to the door and looked out at the chilly night. There were no stars and the skies were overcast, not even a hint of the moon showing in the darkness. The tears would not stop flowing and she wiped then away impatiently. What good would crying do her? It would not make Bull love

111

her in the way a man should love a woman.

She strained to see in the darkness but there was no sign of him. Perhaps he would not come home tonight. She was frozen when she closed the door of the shack and crawled into bed to lie there shivering. This was how her life would be from now on, as a woman alone in the world with no one to care if she lived or died.

'Bull, my love,' she sobbed, 'come home and love me just one more time.' But the only answer was the wind sighing through the trees behind the track.

*   *   *

'I know this will remain between us, Father.' Jayne looked at the vicar's plump, jovial face and smiled: even as he grew older Father Martin still managed to look like an overgrown baby.

'Of course, my dear Jayne. Whatever you tell me is kept here.' He tapped his broad forehead and then his heart. 'I'm a man of the cloth, and it is my duty to keep confidences.' He smiled and took her hand. 'Now, tell me what bothers you.'

'You mustn't say anything to Papa. I know you are his oldest friend but I don't want him interfering in my life.'

'Jayne, my lips are sealed, I promise.' He sat opposite her, his arms resting on his sturdy legs; he looked so wholesome, so reassuring that Jayne relaxed.

'It's my marriage, Martin.' She spoke in a low voice. 'I don't think Dafydd loves me. I think he married me because it was in his best interest to do so.'

'What has made you feel like this?'

'What do you mean?'

'Well, has Dafydd been unfaithful to you, has he been unkind in any way, is he neglecting you? What is it?'

Jayne shrugged. 'I don't know. It's just that I have a feeling that things are not right between us.'

Martin leaned forward and took her hand. 'Feelings come and go like the tide, Jayne, especially in women.'

Jayne smiled. Martin was not married so his experience of womanly behaviour was limited.

'Ah, I can see you smiling but remember, Jayne, someone on the outside, like me, sees more than those who are in the midst of trouble.'

'I wouldn't say I'm in trouble and Dafydd doesn't ill-treat me, and I don't think he's unfaithful to me, except perhaps in his mind.'

Martin held her hand more tightly. He was trying to be serious but she could see the laughter lines around his eyes.

'Why are you laughing?'

'I'm not laughing—but tell me, Jayne, what man on God's earth has not been unfaithful in his mind? Even I, Jayne, sometimes lust after a woman. It's only human nature for a man to look at women and think carnal thoughts from time to time.'

'Is it?' Jayne was surprised by his answer. 'I thought the Bible tells us that even carnal thoughts are wrong.'

Martin kissed her fingers playfully, his large belly quivering on his lap.

'Well,' Jayne continued, 'perhaps I'm being silly but Dafydd does go out every time my father visits us and it makes me suspicious.'

'Rubbish! It just means your husband is not comfortable with Eynon.'

'So you think I'm being fanciful?'

'You are a young girl, Jayne, and you know little of the ways of the world, but you must realize that a wife is everything to a man. He might have a mistress but if he is discreet no one blinks an eyelid. You must understand that it means nothing—a mistress never takes the place of a wife.'

Jayne did not like the idea that a man was almost expected to keep a mistress. She felt more confused than ever. Did Dafydd ever have the opportunity to be unfaithful? She supposed he did every day of the week—so why would he choose the evenings on which her father visited to go to another woman? He was more intelligent than that.

'I *am* being silly, aren't I? It's just that I know Dafydd and Llinos Mainwaring . . . Well,' she shrugged, 'you know as much as I do about that.'

'That's in the past, Jayne.' Father Martin was serious now. 'I know Llinos, and I believe she would do nothing to hurt you.'

'Do you really think that?'

'Llinos is a complex woman who has done things that I can't condone, but she is an honest soul. Believe me, now that Dafydd is married she will keep away from him.'

'Thank you, Father Martin.' Jayne hugged him. 'I feel so much better for talking to you.' She kissed his plump cheek.

He pinched her chin. 'Now, get on home to your husband and next time I see you I want to know you're happy.'

When Jayne left the manse, all her doubts about

114

Dafydd and Llinos had vanished. If Father Martin was right, she had nothing to fear: Dafydd was her man and, as the vicar had pointed out, she was the one he had married.

She smoothed her hand over her stomach. Soon, very soon, she would be carrying Dafydd's son, and when that day came, he would be bound to her for ever.

CHAPTER TWELVE

In the office Shanni glanced up and saw that the light was going. She was alone in the building but she did not feel lonely: from outside she could hear the voices of the men working on the kilns, which needed to be kept at a constant heat until the pots were baked: the fires around the perimeter of the walls had to be kept burning throughout the night.

Shanni closed the account books and placed them on the shelf behind her with a sigh of satisfaction. She was proud of her work: she had come a long way from the pathetic young girl living in the slums of Swansea. She accepted that her climb up the ladder had been due largely to Llinos Mainwaring's kindness, and she was grateful for all Llinos had done, but Shanni had made most progress through her own intelligence and effort.

Llinos had been given everything in life but had thrown it away to have a sordid liaison with Dafydd. It was true that Dafydd was handsome, and Shanni was attracted to him although she had never made love with him. But would she if he asked her? She pushed away the uncomfortable thoughts and put the rest of the papers in the desk drawer.

A sound in the outer office brought her to her feet. Who could be in the building at this late hour? The door opened.

'Shanni?' Dafydd's voice was a shock, and Shanni felt his presence as warmly as if he had taken her into his arms. He stood in the doorway, bringing with him a breath of cold air from outside. 'Why aren't you at home with your husband?'

'And why aren't you home with your wife?' The minute she spoke she knew she had said the wrong thing.

'As your employer I don't explain myself to you, Shanni,' he said curtly, and she bit her lip, cursing herself for a stupid, tactless fool.

'I'm sorry,' she said at once. 'I was being facetious and I apologize.'

He smiled. 'Llinos did a good job on you, Shanni!'

'She helped me, of course, but I had the brains to learn my lessons well,' Shanni protested.

'Well,' Dafydd came into the room, 'I should tell you not to lose your temper, but with your red hair and sparks flying from your lovely eyes you look good enough to eat.'

Shanni opened her mouth then closed it again abruptly. He was flirting with her. Dafydd, the man she had loved for so long, was noticing her as a woman not just as an employee. Her nerves were tingling, and she was aware of his scent as he stood close to her.

He sat down on the edge of her desk. 'I might as well confess that I get bored with my wife sometimes,' he said. 'I came down to the pottery

116

for something to do that did not involve domestic things.' He smiled. 'That's my excuse for being here. What's yours?'

'Pedr is away on pottery business, as you well know, and I didn't feel like going back to an empty house just yet.'

He looked at her seriously. 'We never have been reduced to talking about domestic issues, have we? You and I were too involved in fighting the injustice of the toll gates while all my wife thinks of is the next supper party and which of her rich, spoiled friends to invite.' He made a gesture of dismissal. 'I'm being disloyal to Jayne. I'm not saying she's brainless, not at all, but she concentrates on the trivialities of life.'

'She's been brought up that way.' Why was she defending Jayne, Shanni wondered. She did not even like the girl. 'I'm afraid her father indulged her too much. She'll grow up, given time, I'm sure.'

Dafydd took her hand. 'You're a wise owl for one still so young, but you had to fight for survival, didn't you?'

'I certainly did.' She thought of the slum where she had been born, Fennel Court: a lovely name for a dreadful, poverty-ridden place. 'And you're right, I should be grateful to Llinos Mainwaring. I'd still be living in squalor if it wasn't for her.'

'Come here, you look so sorry for yourself.' Dafydd drew her slowly towards him. 'You're a bright girl and you'd have got out of the slums one way or another, I'm sure.'

He bent forward as if to kiss her but Shanni jerked away from him. 'I know you're flattering me but you shouldn't, Dafydd. What are you trying to prove to me?'

117

'I'm not trying to prove anything.' He pulled her into his arms. 'I'm just trying to kiss a beautiful woman.'

His mouth was hot and urgent on hers and Shanni's resistance melted. She leaned against him, wanting the moment to go on for ever. She knew it was wrong, but a kiss was not really a betrayal, was it?

His arms encircled her and he pressed her closer to him. She knew he was aroused, and disentangled herself from his arms. 'We shouldn't be doing this, Dafydd.'

His arms dropped to his sides. 'You're right, but you look so desirable. And you want me so why fight it?'

He had read her correctly and, anyway, what harm would it do? He was touching her again, his hands slipping from her shoulders to her breasts. Her breathing became ragged, and she stopped thinking about anything except how wonderful it was to be in Dafydd's arms. This was what she had wanted for years.

They did not undress. He drew her onto the floor of the office and Shanni knew there was no turning back, not now. He took her quickly, with finesse, his touch gentle, but Shanni was disappointed: she found herself yearning for her husband's vigorous love-making.

When Dafydd rolled away from her, she began to cry. He cradled her in his arms and smoothed back her tangled hair. 'What's wrong, little Shanni? Didn't I please you?' He kissed away her tears. 'I was too eager for you but we can easily put that right.' He touched her breast but Shanni pushed him away.

'You're playing with me. You've always known I thought myself in love with you.'

'And now you know different? Aren't you still in love with me just a little bit?'

'I don't think so.' Now that she had lived her dream and been possessed by him, she was not sure that she had ever loved him. She straightened her clothes. 'That was the first and the last time, Dafydd. This must never happen again.'

'But it was so wonderful—how can it be wrong?' He touched her hot face. 'Don't feel guilty about it, Shanni. What we did was natural and it was what we *both* wanted, wasn't it?'

'What we did was wrong, Dafydd. We're both married. How can I face Pedr when he comes home?' She pushed him away. 'Oh, it's all right for you! A man is easily forgiven when he beds another woman, but the womenfolk suffer every time.'

Shanni remembered her mother, poor Dora, victim of an affair with a married man and reviled for it. And Llinos, people talked about her: she was no longer fit company for the respectable matrons of the town. By giving in to her lust for Dafydd, Shanni had become just like them: a harlot. 'I'll be an outcast in Swansea.' Shanni tried to gulp back her tears. 'Folk will say "like mother like daughter" and I'll be spat on in the street.'

'No, Shanni, we won't tell anyone what's happened here tonight. No one need ever know about it.'

Shanni swallowed hard. Could she live with Pedr, knowing that she had been unfaithful to him? She thought of him, dear reliable Pedr. He loved her so much that if he knew she had lain with another man his life would be ruined. Dafydd was

119

talking sense. It was best to keep their indiscretion between themselves.

'I'd better go home,' she said dully. She needed to bathe, wash away her guilt and cleanse herself for her husband. 'How could I do it?' Her head rested in her hands. She could not look Dafydd in the face.

'I'm sorry, Shanni,' he said gently. 'I'm so sorry. Had I known you would feel like this I would never have touched you.'

Suddenly she was angry. Dafydd had used her to end his boredom and she, like a silly gullible fool, had let him.

'Do you think me a whore?'

'Of course not! If I wanted a whore I could buy one for a few pennies down the Strand. I think of you as a beautiful, intelligent young woman and I wanted to make love to you. Is that so wrong?'

'I'm going home.' She picked up her jacket. 'I'm taking a couple of days off work while I decide what to do. Perhaps I can find my self-respect again if I don't see you.'

'I'll walk home with you.'

'No. Just stay here or go home to your wife— anything. Just leave me alone.'

The air was cold on her cheeks as she set off uphill away from the pottery buildings. She still could not believe what she had done. Then she became aware that her name was being called and turned to look back over her shoulder.

'Shanni, wait.' Katie Cullen was waving to her. 'We'll walk with you.' Bull Beynon was with her, his arms protectively round her waist. There was such a sweet innocence about the couple that Shanni felt even more ashamed of her own behaviour. She waited for them to catch up—she could hardly run away from them even though that was what she wanted to do.

'What are you doing out alone at this time of night?' Katie said.

'I was in the office. I had some bookwork to finish,' Shanni mumbled, envying Katie her uncomplicated life. The girl was radiant with the first flush of love, and Shanni felt sullied in comparison.

'Well, Pedr should have come to fetch you, then. Bull met me from choir practice. He wouldn't let me walk home alone. Still, you have us for company now.'

'I'm all right,' Shanni insisted. 'Pedr is away, and I'm not afraid of the dark. I can walk back on my own.'

'We won't hear of it, will we, Bull?' Katie slipped her arm through Shanni's. 'You must remember how I was accosted by the railway navvies. Do you want the same thing to happen to you?'

Suddenly Shanni felt weary: all she wanted was to get home and crawl into bed.

'You're very quiet,' Katie said. 'You're missing your Pedr, aren't you? I can tell by the expression on your face. You two are so happy together it's a pleasure to be in your company.'

It was as if Katie was rubbing salt into her wounds but, of course, she had no idea of what had just happened. Shanni changed the subject. 'How's the work on the railway going, Bull? I hear there's a bit of trouble on the tracks, is that right?'

'Some people are objecting to the width of the gauge but Mr Brunel is a brilliant engineer and everything will be sorted out in time,' Bull said.

'And Bull has some wonderful news.' Katie's face was rosy with pride. 'Go on, Bull, tell her.'

'It's just that when my stint on this job is done, and the line is open to Swansea, I'm going to train to be a manager.'

'That's wonderful, Bull,' Shanni said, trying to sound enthusiastic. 'You're too good for navvying, I'd say.'

'Well, nothing wrong with a bit of honest toil.' Bull's eyes gleamed in the moonlight. 'But I'd rather toil with my brain than with brawn.'

The journey to Shanni's house seemed interminable but at last it came into sight. 'Here we are, then. You've seen me home safely now. Hadn't you better be getting back to the Morton-Edwards place before you're dismissed?'

Katie laughed. 'Mr Morton-Edwards is a real gentleman to work for. In any case, he's met Bull and he approves of our . . . our friendship.'

Shanni could not face Katie and Bull any longer. She wanted to get indoors and shut out the world. 'Thanks for keeping me company, both of you.' She forced a smile. 'I'll see you again soon, I'm sure.'

'Shall we come in with you for a while?'

Shanni touched Katie's arm. 'Thank you but no. I'm not a little girl, I'm an old married woman, remember?'

She watched as Katie and Bull walked away arm in arm along the cobbled road. Then she went inside the warm darkness of the house she shared with Pedr, her haven, her home.

She lit the lamp and the light illuminated the room, throwing the shadowy corners into relief. The fire was almost out but with a little effort Shanni coaxed it back to life. Once the flames were

122

licking up into the chimney, she put the kettle on to boil before dragging the tin bath in from the backyard.

The water just covered the ridged bottom of the tub but Shanni washed scrupulously, trying to flush away the scent of Dafydd that seemed to cling to her. When she had finished she crouched before the fire and closed her eyes. 'Dear Lord, forgive me for my sins because I don't know if I'll ever forgive myself.' She sank back on her heels and tears filled her eyes. She had judged Llinos Mainwaring and found her lacking, but now she was as bad. For the first time she understood what Llinos must have gone through, especially when she knew she was having a child.

'Oh, no!' She put her hands over her face. What if she found herself with child over the next few weeks? She would not know who was the father.

She emptied the bathwater into the yard and looked up to see a cold moon glaring down at her. She felt that her guilt must be in her face as well as in her heart, that others would see it as plainly as she felt it. She closed the back door and turned wearily towards the stairs. She wanted to sleep, forget what she had done.

The bed was cold without Pedr's reassuring body beside her, and she knew now how much she loved her husband. She had loved him all along.

'Oh, Pedr, my love, what have I done to you?' Deep, painful sobs racked her body. She wanted Pedr to take her in his arms and tell her he loved her. She wanted to put back the clock to change all that had happened tonight. Lying there in the darkness she wondered if she would ever feel clean again.

CHAPTER THIRTEEN

'Now, Dafydd, I will not accept a refusal from you this time. You are coming to see Papa with me and no excuses.'

Dafydd sighed. His wife could be such a child sometimes—she thought she only had to say the word and he would agree to everything she suggested. Still, it was about time he made an effort to get on with Eynon. 'Very well, I'll come with you, but if your father starts to look down his nose at me I'll just walk out.'

'I've talked to Papa and he will be pleasant, so you must be too.' Jayne smiled coyly. 'I told him that his grandchildren would not take kindly to a rift between the two of you.'

She had Dafydd's full attention now. 'Jayne, are you trying to tell me you are with child?' His spirits lifted. A son would make his marriage almost happy.

'No, silly!' Jayne shook her head, and curls bobbed around her face. 'We haven't been in bed together since I last saw my . . .' She looked at him from under her lashes. 'But I will leave my bedroom door open for you tonight, shall I?'

'Yes, of course, darling.' He kissed her cheek, wishing he could summon some enthusiasm but he found Jayne a bore in bed. She acted like an immature girl, lying quiescent beneath him. Even Shanni Morgan had shown more imagination.

At the thought of Shanni, Dafydd pulled himself up short. He should be ashamed of himself. He had taken advantage of the girl's infatuation with him.

124

He had no excuse. She was a married woman in love with her husband, and he had been wrong to coax her into betraying her vows.

'Pay attention, Dafydd, I'm asking your opinion.'

'What were you saying?'

'I want you to help me decide what clothes to take over to Papa's house.'

'How long are we staying there, for goodness' sake?' Dafydd spoke impatiently.

'We'll be having tea and I'll need a day-time gown for that, and then I will have to dress for dinner because Papa is inviting guests. I can't let you down, Dafydd—what would people think if Dafydd Buchan's wife was improperly dressed?'

Dafydd did not give a damn what people thought—he had never pandered to public opinion and had no intention of starting now. Still, the proprieties were important to his wife and he forced himself to give her his attention.

'I like you in all your gowns, Jayne. I know you have impeccable taste so I'll leave the matter in your hands.' He paused. 'I particularly like you in blue, though. It complements your fair complexion.'

He had said the right thing. Jayne dimpled at him, her eyes shining, and suddenly he felt guilty. It took so little effort to make his wife happy so why didn't he try a little harder? Once he had been caring, considerate of the feelings of others, but as he had grown older he had become more cynical. Just look at the way he'd used Shanni to relieve his boredom.

But life had dealt him some hard knocks: the one woman he wanted was out of his reach, and he could not even acknowledge his young son. He

125

cursed Joe Mainwaring. The man had taken Llinos back but now he had gone off to America, expecting Llinos to live like a nun, a prisoner in her own house.

'You've gone all quiet on me again, Dafydd,' Jayne said. 'Is there something on your mind?'

He shook his head. 'I was wondering how I could get my hands on some railway shares. I wish I'd bought them when I had the chance.'

The look on his wife's face was a little smug. 'What?' he asked. 'Have you heard anything about the shares—anyone selling out, perhaps?'

'No, nothing like that. Now, come along, Dafydd, go and get ready or we'll be late for tea with Papa.'

Perhaps he had underestimated Jayne, Dafydd thought. She was up to something, but what was it?'

'All right, I'll be an obedient husband and do as you say.' He took her in his arms. 'And I shall look forward to seeing your bedroom door open tonight.' He kissed her hair. If there was a time to learn any of Jayne's secrets it would be after love-making. She always seemed quiet, almost subservient, then.

Jayne snuggled into his shoulder and Dafydd felt a rare moment of tenderness for his bride, which pleased him because one day, Jayne, scatterbrained Jayne, would be the mother of his children.

*   *   *

Llinos looked out of the carriage window at the mellow old house belonging to Eynon Morton-Edwards. They had been friends for as long as she could remember and in many ways she loved him,

126

but it was only because of their friendship that she had agreed to join Eynon and his guests at the lavish dinner party this evening.

She felt a tinge of unease in knowing that Dafydd would be there, but it was inevitable that they would continue to meet for he was Eynon's son-in-law. How comfortable life would be if she could just shut herself away from the world.

As she alighted from her carriage, she saw Father Martin, as plump and angelic as always, standing in the doorway of the large house. 'I just pipped you to the post, Llinos, my dear.' He took her hand and kissed it. 'I must say you look charming as ever. I shall insist that I sit next to you when we eat, and any morsel you leave I shall gobble up. You know what an appetite I have.'

Llinos admired Martin. He might be a clergyman but he was never judgemental: he took people as they were, sins and all.

'Why are you so kind to me, an outcast among the gentry of Swansea?' she asked quietly.

'Well, my dear, if Jesus Christ could make a friend of Mary Magdalene then I can certainly be friends with a lady who has made a few mistakes in life, can't I?'

Together they went indoors to where two maids were waiting to take their coats. A babble of voices from the drawing room told them of the earlier arrival of other guests, and Llinos froze. Martin put his hand under her elbow and propelled her into the room. The assembled company fell silent, but Eynon broke the spell. He moved towards her, eyes shining with pleasure. 'Welcome, to two of my favourite people. Come and sit down—we were just going to listen to Jayne play the pianoforte.'

127

Llinos felt eyes resting on her as she took a seat on the sofa beside one of Eynon's guests. The man moved closer to her, and Llinos knew what he was thinking: that she was a woman without scruples, an easy target for his dishonourable intentions. She was pleased when Martin squeezed between them, forcing him to move away.

She looked up to see that Dafydd was watching her. He nodded briefly as his eyes met hers, and she pretended not to notice his gesture of recognition.

Jayne seated herself at the pianoforte and as her fingers ran lightly along the keys the soft, haunting strains of Beethoven's 'Moonlight Sonata' filled the room.

Llinos glanced at Dafydd and saw, with a pang of pain, that he was watching his wife as though amazed. Jayne's fingers flew across the keys, now softly and then more boldly, as she played an expressive passage. She really was talented.

When Jayne finished the sonata Dafydd began the clapping and Llinos bit her lip, feeling the sting of jealousy as she dutifully joined in with the applause.

Eynon went to his daughter and kissed her cheek. 'You see what a talented daughter I have?' His face showed his pride in Jayne's accomplishment. 'We are to go into dinner now but I will try to persuade Jayne to favour us with some more of her playing later.'

Llinos had been seated next to Eynon and Martin was at her other side. His eyes were already resting on the laden table. 'This looks good enough to eat!' he quipped. 'But, first, let us pray.'

As he said grace Llinos closed her eyes, wishing

herself a million miles away. She was getting too old for all this emotion.

Having said grace, Martin was the first to pick up his napkin. His eyes gleamed with unashamed relish as the mutton soup was served, steaming hot and rich with meat and vegetables. 'Delicious. Do try to eat some, Llinos, it will do you good.' Then he leaned closer and whispered, 'You must keep up your strength, my dear Llinos. Don't let the glares of the old biddies here spoil your appetite.'

Llinos dipped her spoon dutifully into her dish and began to eat. Martin was right: going hungry would not solve anything. Yet she had little appetite: she could not forget that seated opposite her was the man who had been her lover, had fathered her son, and was now with his wife, apparently besotted with her.

She saw Eynon watching her, and when he caught her eye he smiled encouragingly. Eynon and Martin were true friends, and she must learn not to care about the spiteful gossip of other people who meant nothing to her.

'Martin,' Eynon said, 'have you heard that the railway is on course to come into Swansea next summer?'

'I have indeed.' Martin popped a slice of pork into his mouth and began to chew industriously. Food was far more important to Father Martin than railways.

'The station is only half built.' Dafydd leaned forward in his chair. 'I can't see it being ready in time.' His eyes shone with interest. 'I understand Brunel himself will be on the first train into Swansea. Now, there's a man I admire.'

'A fine engineer,' Eynon nodded, 'but the broad-gauge line will never take off. The narrow tracks will win through.'

'Enough of this, gentlemen!' Jayne rapped her knife on the table. 'Just wait until the ladies have withdrawn before you talk business, if you please.'

Dafydd seemed amused at his wife's air of authority and made her a mock bow. 'Quite right, Jayne. We are being very rude and I, for one, offer my heartfelt apology.'

Llinos attempted to enter into the good-natured laughter that followed. Jayne was smiling at her husband and then, tenderly, she touched his hair, smoothing it down over his collar.

Llinos knew she was wrong to covet another woman's husband, but Dafydd had been *her* love in the past. Under the table she pressed her hands together to stop them shaking.

At last, the meal was over and Jayne rose, which was the signal for the ladies to retire to the drawing room. Llinos seated herself near the windows, an outsider in the room full of gossiping women. She listened half-heartedly to the trivial discussion about hats and gowns and the dreadful cost of hiring servants. What narrow lives these women led.

'Aunt Llinos,' Jayne's voice roused her from her thoughts, 'why are you so quiet? Do you miss your husband and son?'

Every eye turned in her direction and Llinos tried to speak lightly. 'Of course I do, but they are in the great plains of America having a fine adventure.'

'Well, you can't begrudge them that, can you?' Jayne's eyes were fixed on her.

'Of course I don't. I like to see them both

130

happy.'

'I think you keep quite a few people happy.' Jayne's words rang with spite. 'Especially the menfolk.'

Laughter rippled through the room and colour rose in Llinos's cheeks. She stared at Jayne, and the girl had the grace to look away.

'Other women's husbands.' The whisper from one lady was loud enough to be heard by everyone in the room. Llinos stood up and smiled at them disdainfully.

'When men have such dull wives who can only talk about servants and other trivia, it's no wonder their husbands seek diversion in more amusing company.'

Jayne sat back in her chair in command of herself. 'You might once have enjoyed these men you talk about but your time is past now, Llinos. You are an old woman.'

'Is that why your husband sought me out only the other day, Jayne?' As soon as the words were spoken Llinos regretted them. Jayne had drunk a little too much wine but she did not deserve to be shamed in front of her guests.

She moved towards the door, but Jayne was there before her, barring her way. 'You're lying, admit it! You're making it up about Dafydd wanting you, aren't you?'

The uncertainty in the girl's voice touched a chord in Llinos. 'I might have misunderstood his intentions,' she said slowly.'Perhaps Dafydd was merely being kind to an old lady.' Her voice was edged with sarcasm in spite of her pity for the wretched look on Jayne's face.

'I hate you, Llinos!' Jayne said. Her voice rose.

'You're a harlot and you should not be allowed to mix in polite society. I think it's time you left. Don't come back here.' She was shouting now. Suddenly the door opened and Eynon was standing there, his face white. 'Is this a meeting of fishwives?'

Llinos wanted to hide. 'I'm sorry, Eynon. It was a mistake for me to come here tonight.'

'Llinos, what has happened? What was all the shouting about?' Dafydd, followed by the other men, came into the room.

Jayne turned on him. 'This—this harlot tells me you've been making improper advances to her. Is it true, Dafydd?'

He looked at Llinos, his eyes guarded. 'I'm sure there has been some misunderstanding. Llinos is not a lady to throw about such accusations lightly.'

'Ask the other ladies, if you don't believe me.' Jayne was beside herself. 'There is no misunderstanding, Dafydd. You have slept with her and you still want her.'

'I married you, Jayne,' Dafydd said sternly, 'and I have been faithful to my marriage vows. Now, enough of this gossip. I'm ashamed to hear it in front of your father's guests and I will not tolerate it any longer.'

He turned to Eynon. 'I'm sorry there has been a scene, but you brought together the wrong people this evening.'

Eynon nodded slowly. 'You're right. Perhaps you will all collect your belongings, all of you, and leave. No, not you, Martin, or you, Llinos. I want you to stay.' He looked at the other guests. 'These people,' he gestured at Llinos and Martin, 'are my true friends, and I want to be alone with them. Jayne, you must sort out your problems with your

132

husband in private, like a lady.'

Dafydd cast one last look at Llinos before he led his wife through the large ornate doors into the darkness. When the room had cleared, Llinos sank on to the sofa. 'I'm sorry, Eynon. I shouldn't have allowed matters to get out of hand.' She felt the hot tears slip between her fingers. 'Jayne was rude and the other women thought it funny, but I was equally to blame because I'm older and should be wiser.'

'There, there, Llinos, cry it all out.' Martin put his arm around her. 'Let the old gossips have their day. Not one of them is fit to clean your boots so forget their spiteful remarks.'

'You must stay here tonight,' Eynon said. 'I'm going to have the maid put a hot stone in one of the beds. You can't go home like this.'

'No,' Llinos said. 'I must go home—I have a young son and I want to be with him.'

'Very well. Martin and I will take you in my carriage and your groom can follow us. I want to see you safely indoors or I won't rest tonight.'

'Thank you for being so kind.' Llinos dabbed at her eyes with a scrap of lace handkerchief. 'I'm sorry I offended your daughter.'

Eynon took her hands and drew her to her feet. 'I know what a shrew Jayne can be, and I know you well enough to understand your anger. She must have hurt you badly. Come, now, let's get you home.'

As she sat in the carriage with Eynon at one side of her and Martin at the other, Llinos thought over the events of the past hours. She should have kept her anger and jealousy to herself. She had hurt Jayne, and what about Dafydd? What did he think of it all? She had not made his life any easier. Well, she was too bone weary to worry about any of it now when all she wanted to do was climb into bed and sleep. Tomorrow she would write a letter apologizing to Jayne but now she must try to put the incident out of her mind. That was hard to do, though, and the morning light was creeping into the room when at last Llinos fell asleep.

CHAPTER FOURTEEN

Rhiannon was waiting for Bull to come home. That was all she seemed to do these days. It was only a matter of time before he left her but she hoped he would stay until the work on the line into Swansea was finished. Then she would have a few more months to think about her future.

She parted the faded curtains and stared out through the aperture that served as a window. A light drizzle of rain was misting the hills that rose above the tracks, which gleamed like silver ribbons running away into the distance. Soon the iron monster they called a train would race through the cut in the hills, carrying dignitaries from town to town. Rhiannon had seen it all before: she had been a camp follower since she was fifteen.

She let the curtains drop and returned to sit near the fire, shivering as the damp seemed to penetrate her bones. How wonderful it must be to live in a house with strong stone walls and a proper roof to keep out the rain.

Once, she had lived in a house. She had had a mother then, a widow who had lost her husband to

134

the Liverpool and Manchester line. Rhiannon's home was not much, just two rented rooms, but it had seemed perfect to her. A tenant lived downstairs and kept chickens in the tiny back garden. If the landlord knew he turned a blind eye, and Rhiannon woke every morning to the raucous crowing of the cockerel.

Once the lodger, who was called Mr Crow, tried to explain to Rhiannon how the chickens' eggs were fertilized but Rhiannon thought that when the noisy cockerel fluttered onto the back of one of the hens he was intent on hurting her, judging by the screeching that ensued.

Then, one day, Mr Crow demonstrated to Rhiannon how humankind produced young, and she lost her virginity among the stench of feathers and potato peelings. When her mother died soon afterwards Rhiannon, alone in the world, could scarcely imagine how she might live. She left the town, sure that soon she must produce a child. That did not happen, but by the time she knew she was not expecting one, Rhiannon was too far into the trade of prostitution to go home. She had kind men and she had wasters, but all of them wanted only one thing of her: that she be willing to accommodate them when they came home drunk on pay day. For that she was fed and clothed, albeit haphazardly, and given a roof of sorts over her head.

It was when Rhiannon followed the railway camps into South Wales that she met Bull Beynon. The first time she set eyes on him she knew that he was a man of quality. It was Bull who had stood up for her against the O'Connor boys: he had taken her into his own hut and looked after her ever since. She owed Bull Beynon a great deal, and he was the only man with whom she had ever fallen in love.

Now she sat up, listening. He was coming—she would recognize his step anywhere. She heard his voice outside, close to the open window of the hut. There was another voice too, Seth O'Connor's, and they were talking about a woman, Katie Cullen. Rhiannon moved closer to the window.

'So, you've got two women on the go now, then.' Seth sounded amused. 'The lovely respectable Katie Cullen and your doxy to warm your bed at night. Lucky sod.'

There was a pain in Rhiannon's chest. Bull was talking now and she held her breath, wondering if he would deny it. 'Keep your nose out of my business, Seth, do you understand?'

'Aye—but if a man can't bed an innocent virgin like Katie I suppose Rhiannon would come in handy.'

Bull came in, his hair glistening with tiny beads of moisture. He was so clean, so handsome. How could she ever live without him?

'Bull, you're late, you must be starved.' She forced a note of cheeriness into her voice as she pushed the pot of stew over the fire. The smell of mutton filled the small hut and Bull sniffed appreciatively. He took off his topcoat, and Rhiannon felt him watching her as she broke large chunks off the loaf.

'Know me next time?' she said lightly.

He raised his eyebrows and drew up his chair to the rickety table. 'Can't a man look at a comely wench these days, then?'

'I hope you're going to do a deal more than look,

136

laddie.' She felt warmed inside with the knowledge that Bull desired her. 'I'm ready for a tumble myself.'

She began to unbutton her bodice but Bull held up his hand. 'Let's eat first, love.'

She hid her disappointment and ladled out the stew. 'Good bit of mutton, this,' she said. 'Got it this morning from the market, and the veg was all fresh in from the farms. Didn't cost a fortune either.'

'You're a thrifty girl, Rhiannon, I'll give you that.'

'Compliments are all fine and good, but I hope you're going to give me more than words when we finish our food.' It was the one hold she had over him, his desire for her, and that was still there: she could see it in his eyes.

'I have to go out later.' Bull dipped bread into the stew. 'There's a meeting in town tonight—there's talk about the work not coming up to scratch so I'll have to be there to speak up for the navvies. They can't afford to be laid off.'

'Can I come?' She heard the entreaty in her own voice and hated herself for her weakness, but Bull was slipping away from her.

'It wouldn't be right. Lots of ladies from town are going along, hoping for a look at the great man himself.'

'And the good women would object to a slut like me being there, is that it, Bull?'

'You know as well as I do what they have to say about the likes of us. There's no good to come of flouting our ways under their noses, you must see that.'

'I suppose Katie Cullen will be there?' The lash

of jealousy was so painful that Rhiannon could hardly breathe.

'What's that to do with you?' His voice was hostile, and Rhiannon knew she had gone too far.

'I heard you talking to Seth O'Connor and her name spoken, that's all.'

'Look, Rhiannon,' there was a warning in his voice, 'we have an understanding, don't we? You're not my wife, you don't tell me when I can come and go.'

'Well,' she softened her tone, 'I'm only asking to come with you because I'm curious about the railway. It's natural enough, isn't it? After all, my father was a railwayman, and even before that I remember the old folk talking about Mr Trevithick who came from Cornwall to show off the iron monster he called a steam locomotive. Railways have been in my blood for as long as I can remember.'

'Well, you can't come to this meeting, love, sorry.' His mind was made up and Rhiannon conceded defeat.

'Right, but I'll be ready for you when you come home, then.' She ruffled his hair playfully, but her heart ached as she looked at his dear face, the familiar line of his shoulders and the strength in his thighs. Lord above, she wanted him. She wanted Bull inside her, owning her, making her feel clean and good, helping her to forget her sordid past. But he was slipping away from her.

'I might be late so don't go waiting up for me.'

'Right.' She pushed away her bowl: she was no longer hungry—at least, not for food. Hungry for love, yes, hungry for a man to put a wedding ring on her finger, most certainly, but she would never

138

have either.

Later, she watched from the door as Bull strode off into the darkness of the night, feeling as if she was saying goodbye to him for ever.

*   *   *

Katie dressed quickly for the meeting. She pulled on her striped shawl then brushed back her hair so that most of it was hidden beneath her bonnet. She would see Bull tonight and though it was only two days since she had been with him she felt shy all over again. Her heart was fluttering like a butterfly inside her as she imagined being with him in a public place. This would be the first time they were seen together by Bull's workmates and the bosses.

Katie paused to look at herself in the mirror hanging over her bed. Her cheeks were flushed and her eyes bright with anticipation, but all Katie saw was a girl with an old-fashioned bonnet and a cape passed down from her mother. Would Bull be ashamed of her?

He was waiting for her at the back gate of the Big House, and she felt a thrill as she looked at him standing in the moonlight. 'Evening, Bull,' she said softly. 'I've missed you these past days, mind.'

He smiled. 'I'm glad about that because I've missed you too.' He took her hand and tucked it under his arm. 'Well, my lovely, let's get to this meeting.'

The town hall was packed with people, all hoping that the great Mr Brunel would put in an appearance. In the lamplight Katie's heart almost burst with pride: Bull had on his best suit, and his unruly hair was neatly combed. He was a handsome

139

devil, and she was the lucky girl who was with him.

At first she scarcely listened to the discussion about the railway—a few days' work had been lost, what did that matter?—but it seemed as though the meeting would go on for ever while the city fathers were questioning the safety of the viaduct.

When Bull got up to address the meeting, Katie sat straight in her chair, staring at him in astonishment: she had not known he was to speak.

'The Landore Viaduct is a work of monumental importance to Swansea,' he said. 'We who work on the railway have ensured the structure is as sound as Mr Brunel intended it to be. Remember, it must be strong enough to carry a laden locomotive across river, road and canal. And this is no time to lay men off. We must keep up with the work on the track now, whatever the weather.' He paused, and everyone waited for him to continue. 'This railway is a vital link in the line from Chepstow to Swansea. Swansea needs it, so if we all put our efforts and our enthusiasm into it we'll be celebrating when summer comes and the line is in place.'

As Bull sat down a cheer went up from the men and Katie found herself holding back tears of pride. He was a real man, honest, strong but never looking for a fight the way some navvies did. She slipped her arm through his, as if to tell the world he was hers.

One or two of the ladies raised objections to the viaduct being built at all and then Jayne Buchan got to her feet. 'Listen, ladies,' she said, in a clear voice, 'we must tolerate this railway—no, we must welcome it.' Heads turned to look at her. 'Don't you realize the benefits it will bring?'

'What benefits?' another woman called.

140

'We will not need to take the coach along pitted roadways when we want to travel to Cardiff, for example. We will sit in comfort on a proper seat. There will be no more waiting while horses are changed, no more delays when an animal goes lame.' She smiled. 'Just think, we can go shopping in Cardiff whenever we want a change from Swansea. Isn't that worth putting up with a few minor inconveniences?'

'It was clever of Mrs Buchan to get the women on the side of the railways,' Bull whispered. 'She takes after her father in matters of business.'

Shanni Morgan stood up, her red hair tumbled around her face. 'It's all well and good for the grand folks,' she began, 'but what about the people who are to live around this monster? The viaduct might be a danger to us. What if it should collapse with the weight of these locomotives? And what about the dust and grime that will shower down on the heads of unsuspecting passers-by?'

For a moment the room was in uproar, and it was Bull who stood up and called for order. 'Please, ladies and gentlemen, there will certainly be a little inconvenience to the people living near the railway, but think of the financial advantages. Men will be needed to work constantly on the line, and local men will be employed here when we railway workers move on.' He spread his hands in a gesture that encompassed everyone in the hall. 'We will all benefit from the railway in one way or another and the town will be revolutionized with it creating opportunities for work and travel.'

When Bull sat down Jayne Buchan began to clap and soon everyone in the hall followed suit. Bull's fervour had persuaded them that the railway would

141

indeed be an asset to Swansea.

When the meeting was over Katie remained in her seat while Bull talked to several of the well-dressed gentlemen of the town. She was so proud of him that she couldn't keep the smile off her face.

Later, she held her breath as Bull took her arm in his and led her out into the night. The rain had stopped and the clouds had cleared to reveal a sliver of moonlight. Katie felt as though she was walking through a magic world filled with breathless beauty. It was the world as she had never seen it before. Love was wonderful.

As they began the steep walk towards Eynon Morton-Edwards' house Bull took her hand. His grip was strong, and thrills of joy spiralled through Katie's veins so that her senses were tinglingly alive.

He led her through the large gates and skirted the drive, making for the back of the house. All was in darkness there, but Katie knew the kitchen would be a hub of activity with Cook and the maids preparing food for the next day. She was not sure what to expect when Bull stopped walking and swung her to face him. Was he going to kiss her? She had never kissed any man and she was afraid. Her heart was pounding and she turned her face up to his as he leaned towards her, but he did not kiss her. Instead he touched her cheek lightly with his forefinger.

'I'm so proud of you, Bull,' she said, 'the way you handled the meeting.'

'And you'll be even prouder once I'm a manager with my own house,' he said teasingly.

'I like you just as you are, Bull.' Katie was breathless—would he think her too forward?

'That's all that matters, then.' He cupped her face with his hands then kissed her so lightly that she had no time to be afraid. 'I know you're a good girl, Katie, and I wouldn't do anything to hurt you so I'd better go while I can still resist temptation.'

Then he was walking away from her, a tall broad-shouldered man, and even as he disappeared from sight she began to miss him.

As she had thought, the kitchen was a hive of activity. The new maid, Dolly, was washing up pots and pans. 'It's nice for some to have so much time off, in't it, Cook?' she said spitefully. Cook was just taking freshly baked bread from the oven and didn't reply. She put it on a tray to cool then slumped into a chair, wiping the sweat from her brow with the sleeve of her dress. Her eyes were sharp, though.

'What you been up to, Katie?' she asked. 'Courting, by the look on your face.'

'You know where I've been. At a meeting in town. It was about the railway line, and Mr Morton-Edwards gave me his permission so long as I told him all about it when I got back.'

Mrs Grinter sniffed. 'The master isn't very well. He's gone to bed early so whatever you got to tell him will keep until morning.'

'I knew he wasn't feeling good,' Katie said, 'or he'd have gone to the meeting himself.'

'Well, that's as maybe, but who walked you home, girl? Was it that man of yours? I'm sure as eggs are eggs you didn't come home by yourself.'

'No need to ask who walked her home,' Dolly sounded triumphant. 'It was that man they call Bull—built like one too, I'll bet.'

'Don't be vulgar, Dolly.' Cook pretended to be

143

affronted but her eyes were gleaming. 'He's real nice, isn't he, Katie? A gent.'

'He's wonderful.' Katie pulled off her shawl and bonnet and sank into a chair. 'I'm so lucky to have him.'

'So that's what you think!' The maid shook the water off her hands and dried them on her apron. 'He's no gentleman, isn't Bull Beynon. He's got a woman on the go in one of them shanties at the side of the railway track—Rhiannon, she's called.'

Katie felt the colour drain from her face and Mrs Grinter looked at her shrewdly. 'Didn't you know, Katie? I thought everyone did. Oh, you poor little thing.' She flapped her hand at the maid. 'Make a brew, Dolly, there's a good girl. Katie looks as if she could do with a pick-me-up.' She eased off her shoes. 'See, Katie, them navvies, they all have women to cook for them and to follow them from camp to camp; cheap women they are who will go wherever their man is working. It don't mean nothing, not really.'

Katie felt cold. Surely Bull would have told her if he had another woman. But, then, what did she know about him? What on earth made her think he really cared about her?

'Are you sure?' Katie clung to a thread of hope, but Dolly's next words dashed it.

'Oh, aye, I've seen her myself—a beauty she is too. Seems at one time she was a harlot, like, went with the men, lots of them, for what they could give her, but Bull rescued her, see. He must like her a lot to do that, don't you think?'

Dolly made the tea and Cook pushed a cup towards Katie. 'Go on, girl, a hot drink will do you good. You look like you seen a ghost.'

144

Katie stared at her cup, feeling numb. How could she have been such a fool? She had heard the stories about the navvies so why had she thought Bull was any different from the rest? 'I think I'll go to bed.' She got up and hurried to her room at the top of the house. When she closed the door she sat on the bed in the darkness, too upset even to light a candle. She thought about Bull, about his strength, the feel of his hand holding hers, and the butterfly touch of his lips, and tears brimmed in her eyes. She cried for a long time but at last, exhausted, she lay dry-eyed in the darkness, vowing never to trust any man ever again.

CHAPTER FIFTEEN

Jayne stared at her reflection in the ornate mirror hanging in the hall. She was on her way out to town, but not for a shopping spree. Today she had an important meeting with a man at her bank. She smiled at her image and saw that her eyes were shining with anticipation. She was going to acquire even more shares in the Great Western Railway, thanks to Mr Prentice.

Jayne congratulated herself that Jason Prentice was not only a damn fine manager of money but her devoted slave. She had only to smile at him and he would give her anything she asked for. Dafydd would be so jealous if he knew, but she had no intention of telling him about her business interests, not yet. She would surprise him when the time was right. But when would it be right?

Her spirits sank a little. It was becoming more

and more difficult to get her husband to pay her any attention at all. Jayne bit her lip. No one need tell her that Dafydd still believed himself in love with Llinos Mainwaring. She twisted the gold band on her finger. Dafydd was *her* husband, and one day, when they had a family, he would see where his real interests lay.

A pale shaft of sunshine washed the morning streets of Swansea as Jayne's carriage negotiated the plethora of traffic into the centre of the town. She breathed deeply: she felt she was a woman in charge of her own destiny, a businesswoman. If Dafydd knew the real Jayne he would be more than a little surprised. She knew he saw her as empty-headed, a pretty acquisition to dangle on his arm— and, what was more, a rich one. The two families together owned more property and had more business interests than anyone else in the county. And yet if she could not make Dafydd love her just a little, what good was all their wealth?

Jason Prentice was waiting for her with obvious anticipation. He was a great improvement on the old man her father employed to do his business. Jason was young, eager, hungry for success, and he was willing to go just that little bit further for Jayne Buchan.

'Good morning, Mrs Buchan. Please, let me show you through to my room where we can be more private.'

As Jayne swept past him she was aware of the admiration in his eyes, and breathed in the heady sense of power it gave her: she felt that Jayne Buchan was a force to be reckoned with. The pity was that her husband did not know it.

Jason closed the door behind him and held a

chair for her with a reverence that made her smile. 'I've taken the liberty of ordering a pot of tea. I hope I did the right thing?'

'Of course, Mr Prentice, but when did you ever do the wrong thing?' She smiled at him with what she hoped was the right degree of warmth, not too familiar.

When she held a cup of tea in her gloved hands, she leaned back in her chair and gave him the benefit of her smile. 'The shares, Mr Prentice, do tell me how you came by them.'

He looked doubtful, but Jayne's smile widened. 'Please, Mr Prentice, you can trust me to be the soul of discretion, I promise you.'

'Oh, I know, Mrs Buchan. It's just that we here at the office are not at liberty to disclose the business of some of our other clients. However,' he added, as Jayne's smile became a frown, 'in your case I can make an exception.'

He leaned forward. 'A Mr Coals, an old client of ours, has just passed away.' He paused, then continued as though the words were being dragged out of him. 'It seems his daughter, herself an elderly lady, wants nothing to do with shares. She says she does not understand them—but, then, does any gentle lady understand matters of money?'

This was an opening for flattery and Jayne took it. 'Oh, I know, Mr Prentice, that I would be lost without your advice and guidance. Please go on.'

'Well, Mr Coals held a fair amount of shares, and though you are not obliged to take them all I think it would be a good move because then you would be one of the biggest single shareholders in the South Wales area.' He smiled, well pleased with himself for handing Jayne such a bargain. He put his elbows on the desk and leaned even closer to her. 'You will also be a powerful force in the business of the railway.'

Jayne agreed with him. She, too, had understood that one day the Great Western would run across most of the South West. 'I can't thank you enough, Mr Prentice.' She leaned forward to put her cup on the desk and saw the solicitor's eyes widen as he breathed in her perfume. She smiled her most dazzling smile and put her hand over his. 'Go ahead with the deal. Just tell me where to sign the papers and I will be so grateful.'

As Jayne left the office, she reflected that men would believe anything that fell from the lips of a woman they desired. She had signed the relevant papers but had taken care to read every word, pretending to be slow. She was now the proud owner of twenty per cent of the entire share stock; most of the rest of the shares were held by a consortium of businessmen. Somehow, she would have to find out just where she stood and once she knew how strong her position was she would present the news to her husband.

When she got home she found Dafydd there. 'Hello, darling.' He bent to kiss her cheek almost absently. 'What are we having for luncheon?'

'Cook is doing saddle of lamb. But why are you home in the middle of the day? Usually I don't see you until the evening, just before you pop out to your club.'

If he heard the reproach in her voice he chose to ignore it. 'I want to see Ceri. I feel I've been neglecting him the last few weeks.'

'Then perhaps you'll take me with you?'

'Yes, why not? You can talk to his wife while I go over their business affairs.'

Jayne sighed. 'Dafydd, come and sit down. We never talk to each other now.' But when had he ever talked to her?

'What is it?' he asked indulgently. 'You need new tea-gowns, is that it?'

'No!' Her tone made him look at her properly for the first time since she had come in.

'You are not with child, are you, Jayne?'

She heard the note of hope in his voice and took a deep breath. 'No, I am not.' She forced herself to speak calmly. 'I just wanted to talk to you about business. You never include me in anything important, do you?'

'I've said you can come with me to my brother's house, haven't I?'

'Yes, so I can keep your sister-in-law occupied while you amuse yourself looking through Ceri's papers.'

'We're not quarrelling, are we, Jayne?' There was a note in his voice that boded ill, but Jayne was angry already.

'Yes, we are.' She wanted to put her hands on her hips and rail at him. But she capitulated. 'I'm sorry, Dafydd,' she said softly, remembering the effect her smile had had on Jason Prentice. Perhaps she should tease him a little, coax him into a better frame of mind. Confrontation was not the way to deal with Dafydd—she had learned that much already. 'Sit with me for a while. I'm lonely.' She took his hand and drew him to sit beside her on the sofa. She snuggled close to him and looked into his eyes. 'If you want a baby, my darling, you will have to love me a little more.' She put her arms

149

around him and caressed his shoulders, then kissed his cheeks, his mouth.

'Why, little Jayne,' he held her away for a moment and looked into her face, 'I do believe you're awakening into womanhood.'

How could she tell him she longed for his touch? When he lay with her she felt he was hers—at least for that moment. 'Come upstairs,' she whispered. 'Please, Dafydd, I want you to hold me close.'

He took her hand, led her into the hall and up the curving staircase to her bedroom. He undressed her swiftly, expertly, and she wondered how many women he'd undressed before he met her.

They lay together on the bed, limbs entwined. Surely this, the most intimate act, would make him love her more. She ran her hands over his shoulders and, greatly daring, allowed her fingers to trace a pattern across his strong buttocks. He was a fine figure of a man and it was no wonder that other women wanted him. But she was the one he had married, she reminded herself, and it was she who, one day, would bear him legitimate sons.

He took longer with his love-making than usual but somehow, when he fell away from her, Jayne still felt unfulfilled. She knew something was missing from their union, but what was it? She loved him so much and she wanted him so much, but after love-making she felt more lost and alone than ever.

He snuggled close to her, his head against her breast, and soon his regular breathing told her he was asleep.

*

Shanni stared at the doctor open-mouthed. 'I'm

150

with child, you say—but I can't be, surely?'

Dr Mortimer smiled and Shanni realized how stupid her question must seem. 'You're a healthy young girl, Shanni,' he said, 'and nature has taken her course. Aren't you pleased?'

Shanni did not know how she felt. She was confused, trying to count back to when she last saw the curse, and then she remembered: it had been shortly before she and Dafydd . . . but no, that was impossible, she must not even think the child could be his. 'I don't know what to say.' Shanni tried to gather her wits. 'I'm just so surprised, Doctor.'

'Why? You came to me feeling sickly and complaining of aching breasts. What else did you think it was?' He was laughing at her gently.

Shanni put her hand over her stomach, trying to imagine a child growing inside her womb. For a moment she was filled with excitement and then she started to count the days. She swallowed hard, trying to remember when she and Pedr had been together. They had a vigorous love life so in all probability the child was his. *Please let it be his,* she prayed silently.

The doctor misread her silence. 'It's perfectly natural, my dear. Women do it every day—give birth, I mean. You will be fine, so no worrying now.'

'You're right, of course, Doctor, and thank you. I'd better get home.'

'Anxious to break the good news to your husband, I imagine,' Dr Mortimer said. 'I'm sure Pedr will be delighted, and you will too, once you take it all in.'

Shanni left the doctor's house with mixed feelings. She walked into the park and sat on a tree

151

stump, trying to work out when the baby was conceived. The doctor had been vague about dates and times, and Shanni sought hope that the baby might be Pedr's child but she found none.

She clasped her hands together, trying to think things through in a sensible way. What if she had Dafydd's child? No one would know, would they? Dafydd was dark-haired, but so was Pedr. Both men were strong and well-built—perhaps even she would not know whose child she had borne. But did she want to be like Llinos Mainwaring, foisting an illegitimate child on her husband? Look at the trouble that had caused: Joe Mainwaring had gone to America, leaving his wife behind.

She sat for a long time, staring up into the sky, wondering what to do. She did not want to hurt Pedr—she loved him too much for that.

Could she live with a lie hanging over her head? And if not, what was the alternative? She closed her eyes, not wanting even to think of losing the child in her womb. But there seemed no other way out of the mess.

She made up her mind to go to see Mrs Keen, find out how to lose the baby. It was the only way and, really, it was not wicked, was it? Either she had the child and faced the consequences, or she could miscarry. It was a terrible choice but she had brought trouble upon herself when she chose to break her marriage vows.

She cooked Pedr a hearty meal of rabbit stew and fresh crusty bread—he was always hungry after a day at the pottery. When he came in, he grinned as he took her in his arms and hugged her close. 'Looking after me well, aren't you, *cariad*?' He planted a kiss on her lips. 'What are you after? A

152

new coat, or is it boots this time?'

'Hey, cheek! No, I had the day off from work so I thought I'd cook you something nice. I wasn't feeling very well and I decided the pottery office could do without me for a day or two. Perhaps you'll take a letter in to Mr Buchan explaining things for me.'

Pedr looked concerned. 'What's wrong, my little love? You're not really sick, are you?'

'Just a chill in the stomach, nothing to worry about. Now, come and eat your supper before it gets cold.' She sat at the table with him and stared in distaste at the stew. How could she even pretend to eat when she felt overwhelmed with guilt?

The idea of bearing Dafydd's baby made her want to vomit—yet how could she think of killing her child? Perhaps she could consider her options for a day or two. Tonight she would forget there was anything wrong and perhaps in the morning her mind would be clearer.

CHAPTER SIXTEEN

Llinos read the letter from Joe for the third time. He was not coming home—at least, not yet. He told her that their son was settling well into the life of the village and had made a great many friends. She felt angry as she crumpled the letter into a ball. There was no telling what her menfolk might be getting up to. She thought of the Indian squaw who had played such an important part in Joe's life. Had he found another just like her?

She stared out at the cold winter landscape: soon

153

it would be Christmas and she would spend it with only her younger son for company. She was a prisoner in her own house. Since the night of her row with Jayne, Llinos had been virtually a recluse.

She sank into a chair and put her head in her hands. Could she really blame Joe if he was enjoying the love of another woman? Abroad, life must be lonely for him and she was as much to blame as he was for the problems in their marriage.

Nevertheless, sitting here making herself miserable would do no good at all. It was time she paid some attention to the pottery. The old patterns were stale and a new line of decoration was needed if she wanted to keep up with the ever-increasing competition. It was almost with a sense of relief that she sat at her desk and took up her pen. At least in creating something beautiful she could put her anxieties out of her mind.

The patterns on her potteryware had ranged from exotic American Indian to the more usual willow pattern, depicting a stylized tree, a pagoda, and sometimes one or two figures. Now it was time for something fresh. Her pen flew across the page as she drew the mountains of Snowdonia, a bunch of daffodils, then finally, and most pleasing, two dragons facing each other, one red, one white.

She started a fresh page and composed the dragons in more detail, fining down the wings and emphasizing the talons before she became aware of the symbolism in her work. One dragon was bad, one good, both fighting for survival. Perhaps she was portraying her own inner conflicts. If so, she was the wicked dragon and had beaten the good one hands down.

An hour later she stretched her arms above her

154

head. She felt stifled—she needed some air. She rang for the maid to fetch her outdoor clothes: she would go for a walk.

The air was sharp and Llinos turned up her coat collar. She could hear the sounds of the pottery and see the shimmer of the kilns. The cheerful whistling of the apprentices brought tears to her eyes. It was all so familiar, so dear to her, and it seemed to be the one constant element of her life. She walked a little way from the house and down to where the river Tawe ran swiftly towards the sea. Her head felt full of cobwebs and she hoped the fresh air would clear her mind.

At first she saw the figure on the bank with little curiosity but as she drew nearer she could see that the woman was perilously close to the water's edge, about to walk into the river.

'Stop!' Llinos hurried forward, and saw the flash of red hair peeping from under the bonnet. 'Shanni, wait! Don't be foolish!' She caught the girl's arm and drew her away from the bank.

'What on earth are you thinking about?'

'Let me go!' Shanni's voice was flat, hopeless. 'I'm not fit to live.'

Llinos took a deep breath. 'If you think I saved you from the slums only for you to throw away your life like this you're sadly mistaken.' She dragged her onto the road. 'Whatever has happened, nothing is worthy dying for.'

Shanni began to cry, and Llinos hugged her. 'Please come home with me, Shanni.' She drew the unresisting girl towards the house and almost pushed her inside.

'Sit down by the fire in the drawing room, get the chill out of your bones. I'll ask the maid to bring us

155

a cup of chocolate.'

Shanni sat down on the edge of the chair, her hands in her lap. 'I didn't really want to die in the river,' she said, 'but I've done something dreadful.' She looked up, her eyes brimming with tears. 'I don't know what I'm going to do.'

'Well, you can talk to me for a start, see if I can help.'

Llinos rang the bell and the maid came into the drawing room. 'Bring some hot chocolate, there's a good girl, and be quick.' She waited until the maid had brought the tray, then sat opposite Shanni.

'So, why were you about to throw away your young life like that?'

'I don't know if I should tell you my troubles. It doesn't seem fair.'

Llinos had not seen the girl in such a bad way since the day she had taken her from the slums of Swansea and given her a home. She thought of Shanni as a girl of spirit, but now she was looking defeated.

'I'm having a baby.' Shanni dropped the words into the silence. 'And I don't think my Pedr is the father.' She glanced up at Llinos.

'I see.' Llinos hesitated. 'But we all make mistakes, Shanni, me included, and nothing is worth killing yourself over.'

'But you haven't heard the worst. I . . . I think the father is Dafydd Buchan.'

'Oh, no!' Llinos said. 'It can't be—Dafydd, surely he would never . . .' Her words trailed away.

'Well, he did.' Shanni's lips were trembling. 'It was only the once but it's then I must have fallen for a baby.'

Llinos tried to hide her shock: she must put

156

aside her own feelings for Dafydd. Common sense told her Shanni would not lie about such a thing. 'Can you be sure the baby is not Pedr's?'

'He was away at the time. I'm so ashamed, so frightened, I just don't know what to do.' She looked up at Llinos. 'Should I tell Pedr the truth, do you think?'

Llinos's hand shook as she poured the chocolate. She needed time to think. 'I don't know what you should do, Shanni, except that you certainly mustn't kill yourself. Think how devastated your husband would be.'

'But how can I live a lie?' Shanni asked. 'You told your husband the truth, didn't you? And it was the right thing to do because the child looked the spit of Dafydd. What if my baby looks like him too?'

'If you tell Pedr he'll want to kill Dafydd. It's only natural. Is that what you want?'

'Your husband didn't fight Dafydd, did he?'

'No, but Joe is a special sort of man.' Llinos took a deep breath, realizing how much her husband must have suffered for having another man's child under his feet. It was no wonder he had wanted to go to America and leave behind all the pain and humiliation.

'The chances are that the baby will look like you, red-haired and fair-skinned. Wouldn't it be kinder to keep your husband in the dark? As you said, it was only the one slip and you will never do it again, will you?'

'No, never.' Shanni was weeping again. 'It was after I'd . . . done it that I knew how much I loved Pedr. What I felt for Dafydd was always a dream, and when it became real it wasn't what I wanted.'

'I think it best if you keep all of this to yourself for now. Give yourself some time to think it all out carefully.' Llinos took a deep breath. 'Look, I'll be discreet—you know that. No one but you and I will ever know what has been said here today.'

'Thank you for listening to me,' Shanni said tearfully. 'I know that no one can help me but I'm so confused—I only know that I can't bear the thought of hurting Pedr.' She got up, her chocolate untouched. 'I'd better be going. Thank you for being so kind.'

'I'm sorry I couldn't do more for you than listen, but you will have to sort this out yourself, Shanni.' Llinos then felt she had been too abrupt. 'Shall I send for the coachman to take you home?'

'No, I'd rather be on my own. Thank you.'

Llinos watched Shanni walk down the drive towards the town, a pathetic figure, her shoulders bowed beneath the shawl she was hugging round her.

She returned to her drawing, but somehow it no longer seemed important. In a sudden burst of anger she pushed aside the papers. 'You swine, Dafydd Buchan—you treacherous swine!' Somehow, his dalliance with Shanni seemed a worse threat to Llinos than his marriage had ever been. She straightened her shoulders. She would go to see him, tell him to his face what she thought of him. It might not touch him, but it would make her feel better.

*   *   *

As Shanni walked, despair settled around her like a thick cloud. Llinos had been right: she must sort

158

out this problem alone, for if she told anyone the truth several lives would be ruined.

The wind and rain bit through her clothes. Why had she let herself come to this? She had risen from the slums, had seen at first hand what happened when a woman strayed, for her own mother had been publicly shamed for bearing a child by a married man.

She walked down to the beach and stared at the sea rushing towards the shore. The movement of the water seemed to calm her, and suddenly she knew what she must do.

She turned back into the winding streets of town, walking swiftly in case she changed her mind. She stopped at Fennel Court, which was worse even than she remembered, with its mean houses crouched together, each building housing many families. Her childhood house seemed to stare at her in disgust. The windows were grimy and the door, still rotten, hung off its hinges.

Mrs Keen lived in the end house. It was cleaner than the rest of the street and faded but cheerful curtains hung at the windows. Shanni knocked rapidly at the door. After an interminable wait, Mrs Keen opened it, more aged now but with the same bright stare that looked right through a person, as if reading hidden secrets.

'It's Shanni, Dora's daughter. Can I come in?'

The old woman led the way along the passage to the back kitchen where a cheerful fire sent flames leaping up the chimney. 'Sit down, girl.' Mrs Keen eased her bulk into a rocking chair. 'What you here for? In trouble, is it?'

'Yes, I'm in terrible trouble.' Shanni's voice cracked a little in fear. 'I should have learned my lesson when my mam was dragged out and put on the wooden horse, and shamed by the neighbours.'

'Aye, your mam was sorely punished for going to the bed of the wrong man. Surely you haven't been doing the same thing?'

Shanni bowed her head and swallowed. 'My husband was away and I—'

Mrs Keen put up her hand. 'I don't need to hear any more. I'm not doing my old trade, these days. Hasn't anyone told you?'

'Oh, please, help me! Tell me what I can do to slip the baby before it's too late!'

'You know what will happen to you, child?'

Shanni stared at the old woman fearfully.

'You will suffer, girl. Slipping a baby is not to be taken lightly. Have you thought long and hard about it?'

Shanni nodded. 'If I want to save my marriage I'll have to do it. Please, just tell me what I must take.'

'Wait by here then, girl.' Mrs Keen shuffled through the passage and Shanni wished now she was anywhere but in Fennel Court, waiting for a medicine that might kill her as well as the baby she was carrying. The thought was like a sharp pain.

Mrs Keen returned and handed her a brown packet. 'Here are some fern roots. I gathered them at midsummer.' Her eyes seemed to pierce Shanni's now. 'These are particular ferns, see? They're very rare, my girl, and very dangerous, so you must not let anyone else tamper with them.'

Shanni felt the rustling packet with a sense of hope. If they worked all her wickedness would be hidden away and no one need know what she had done. She would make it up to Pedr, if she had to spend the rest of her life doing it.

'You must bruise and boil the roots of the fern first, then add them to mead, or water and honey, and boil them up like a stew,' Mrs Keen said. 'When the potion cools add some of the leaves to the mixture and drink it at once. Use it sparingly, girl, or you will do more harm than good. Do you understand?'

'Thank you, Mrs Keen. I'm so grateful to you— you don't know what this means to me. What do I owe you?'

'Call it a gift for the sake of your dead mother, and I hope you've learned your lesson, girl, for if you haven't now, you will by the time your ordeal is over, believe me.' She opened the door. 'Go on, now, and don't tell anyone that Mrs Keen's been helping you, understand?'

Shanni left the house and walked along the court that had once been her home. Here, her mother had lain in great pain, and at the last had given birth to a dead child. Nothing could be worse than that, could it?

Briefly she considered throwing the packet away, but then she thought of Pedr, dear, trusting Pedr, and with a determined thrust she pushed it to the bottom of her bag.

CHAPTER SEVENTEEN

Jayne looked at Dafydd across the length of the dining-table and smiled a secret smile.

'So, you still haven't managed to buy shares in the railway, then?' She toyed with the idea of

161

telling him about her own investment but he scarcely looked up from his paper.

'I'll get some, don't worry,' he mumbled.

'Oh, I'm not worried.'

'Neither am I.' He looked at her then and put down his paper. 'I usually get what I want in the end. Now, don't concern yourself with business matters, Jayne.'

He was being patronizing, treating her like a brainless idiot. She threw her napkin on to the table. 'Don't talk down to me, Dafydd. I'm not a child.'

'Oh dear, have I offended my lady wife?' He stood up and planted a kiss on her head. 'I'd better be off if I'm to get any work done today. I hope you'll not be sulking when I get home.' He laughed, and Jayne could have slapped him.

'Oh, you are infuriating!' she said, but he was already gone, closing the door behind him.

She got up and left the dining room, wondering what to do with her day. Life was monotonous, and she had expected more from her marriage. She had hoped that in Dafydd she would find a soul-mate but he always treated her like a beautiful but silly child. It was a pity she had no close friends, someone of her own age in whom she could confide. She wished she had not quarrelled with Llinos, who had always been a friend, ready with a comforting word.

She could go and see Llinos, make her peace . . . Jayne made up her mind to try, and rang for the maid. As soon as the girl came to the door she said, 'Tell Norman to get the carriage ready—and fetch my good coat. It's cold outside and I don't want to get a chill.'

Later, as Jayne sat in the carriage watching the passing scenery she wondered how she would be received. She should begin by apologizing to Llinos and trying to repair their friendship. As it was, her only real friends were her papa and Father Martin, which did not say much for a woman of Jayne's standing. Llinos might be getting old but at least she was the daughter of a gentleman. She was also a good businesswoman, which Jayne admired.

Llinos was seated at her table in the drawing room, a sheaf of papers before her. Jayne stood inside the door, wondering what to say.

'Is everything all right, Jayne?' Llinos got to her feet quickly. 'It's not like you to arrive unannounced.'

'I just came to apologize for my awful behaviour to you.' The words tumbled from Jayne's lips. 'I'm sorry, Llinos, I've behaved like a child. May I sit down?'

'Of course,' Llinos gestured to one of the chairs, 'and don't apologize. I can understand how you feel.'

'But all that happened before Dafydd married me,' Jayne said quickly, 'and I'm truly sorry for what I did. I know you and Papa have always been such good friends and I was very wrong to try to shame you in front of his guests.'

'You're young, Jayne, and intolerance is the privilege of the young. Please, think no more of it.'

Jayne was surprised at how humble she felt in the face of Llinos's generosity. Llinos was a lady— and a fine one at that.

'Now we shall have some tea with a drop of brandy in it to keep out the chill,' Llinos said, and rang the bell for the maid. She continued, 'It's so

163

good to have the company of another woman. It's surprising how lonely it gets sometimes.'

'That's exactly how I've been feeling,' Jayne said. 'I haven't even one true friend of my own age.'

The maid brought in the tray and Llinos dismissed her. 'I'll pour, thank you.'

Jayne studied Llinos. Old she might be, but she was still a beautiful woman, and she didn't seem to care a jot that she had lost her position in society.

'Is everything all right with your father?' Llinos sounded anxious. 'I haven't seen him for quite some time.'

'He has a slight cold, but that's all.'

'Is it you, then? Are you well?' It was obvious that Llinos was not going to mention Dafydd.

'I'm very well, Llinos, and there is nothing wrong except perhaps . . .' Then words burst from her lips: 'Dafydd sees me only as a pretty child. He doesn't even make love to me very often. Can't he see I'm a passionate woman?' She hadn't meant to talk about Dafydd or say anything about their private lives together. 'I'm sorry, I shouldn't be disloyal.' She picked up her cup and looked into it as if she could take back her words.

'He is probably being considerate, that's all,' Llinos said slowly. 'I'm sure he loves you dearly.'

'I suppose you're right, Llinos.' Jayne sighed. 'But I do wish he'd let me show him I'm not brainless.'

'Tell him your feelings, then,' Llinos said gently. 'Men can be a little obtuse when it comes to their wives.'

'Even Joe?' Jayne asked.

'Even Joe, though he is special and I love him very much.' She looked at Jayne. 'I do love him,

164

you must believe me.'

'I know. I've seen you together. What on earth possessed you to take up with Dafydd?' She was saying all the wrong things but Jayne knew they had to come out: they had been buried inside her for too long.

'I don't really know the answer to that,' Llinos said. 'But I do know that I never stopped loving Joe through it all. And, Jayne,' she stared directly into Jayne's face, 'I would never ruin your marriage. I couldn't hurt you like that.'

Jayne felt comforted. She had underestimated Llinos, who was strong when she needed to be. She was not so sure, however, that Dafydd would resist the temptation to try to make love to Llinos if he had the opportunity.

'How's business?' she asked, moving the conversation to safer ground. 'I believe you have shares in the railway.'

Llinos nodded. 'I thought I'd buy before all the shares went. Of course, the Great Western Railway Company owns the majority of the shares.'

'I do know that,' Jayne said. 'I'm a holder myself, but that's a secret I haven't shared with my husband.' She found a perverse satisfaction in claiming Dafydd as hers. 'I'll tell him when the time is right.' She smiled. 'He frets because he's missed the boat. You and I were wise enough to see what was happening in Swansea.'

'Well, I'm impressed,' Llinos said. 'I always knew you had a good head on your shoulders but I didn't know you were interested in railway shares.'

Jayne was no longer concentrating on the conversation, but staring into space. Eventually she said, 'Can I ask you something?' She didn't wait for

165

a reply. 'I'm a little bit worried that I haven't caught for a baby yet. I've wanted one for some time but . . .'

'That's quite usual,' Llinos assured her. 'Nature will take its course, don't you worry.'

Jayne took a deep breath and changed the subject again. 'When is Joe coming home from abroad?'

'I don't know, Jayne, I wish I did.' She sipped her tea. 'His last letter told me he was well and that Lloyd was settling down in America, but I feel my husband and son are so far away from me that they might never come home.'

'They surely will!' Jayne said. 'Joe couldn't live without you, and as for Lloyd, well, he's always been a devoted son.' She leaned forward and touched Llinos's hand. 'Are we friends again?' She heard the wistful note in her voice but she was so lonely, so in need of a woman's company, that she did not care if her true feelings showed.

Llinos took her hand. 'Of course we're friends. I'm always here if you need me, you can count on that.'

By the time Jayne left the house it was growing dark and as she waved from the carriage she felt ashamed of herself. How could she have been so unkind to Llinos, who was so generous? Jealousy was such a waste of energy. What had happened between Llinos and Dafydd was over and done with long ago. And yet Dafydd was in love with Llinos, would always be in love with her, and there was nothing Jayne could do to change that.

*   *   *

166

Katie walked along the high street, not seeing the crowds of cockle-women and fish-sellers as they brushed past her. She was going to see Bull and get the truth out of him.

It was raining, a cold steady drizzle that soaked into her clothes. She passed the Mackworth Hotel and stopped beside the scene of desolation that would soon be the railway station at Swansea. She had seen it many times before but today, somehow, it looked even bleaker than usual.

Huts straggled along the side of the track and smoke from many fires filled the air with an acrid smell, pouring from chimneys that were little more than a piece of metal thrust into a hole in the roof. She stopped at the doorway of one where a woman was sitting on a stool, stirring a boiling pot. 'What do you want?' The woman was young but her eyes were shadowed, and the bulge beneath her skirt revealed the impending birth of her child.

'I'm looking for Bull Beynon. Can you show me where he lives, please?'

The woman nodded. 'Up along a few huts. Better than most, is Bull's place—you'll know it when you see it. What do you want him for?'

Katie was taken aback by the woman's open curiosity. 'Just some business, nothing important.' She began to pick her way through the mud. *Nothing important*, the words echoed in her mind; just her whole future.

When she came to Bull's hut she saw what the woman had meant about it being better than most of the dwellings on the trackside. It was built of good, solid timber, and from its size it had more than one room.

The door was closed and Katie hesitated,

wondering if she had the courage to face Bull and ask him for the truth. Well, she had come all this way in the rain and it would be foolish to give up now. She rapped loudly on the door, which was opened almost immediately.

'If you're selling pegs I don't want any, right?'

The woman was dark and beautiful, her hair was neatly brushed and she wore decent clothes.

'I've come to see Bull Beynon,' Katie said quickly. 'It's important that I have a word with him.'

The woman looked her over from head to foot. 'And what do you want with my man? Tell me that.'

'It's my business.' Katie was beginning to feel angry. 'Is he here or not?'

'No, he is not.' The woman paused, folding her arms across her full breasts. 'You're that Katie woman, aren't you?'

'That's right. Has Bull told you about me, then?'

'You'd better come in. I'm Rhiannon.' She stood aside and Katie stepped into a surprisingly comfortable room. Faded but clean curtains hung at the windows and the furniture, though sparse, was well polished. It was clear that Rhiannon kept her house as neat as was possible in the circumstances.

'I've heard about you, Katie Cullen, and I don't like what I've been told, not one little bit.'

'I'm not interested in what you think,' Katie said. 'I'm here to talk to Bull, not you.'

'Well, if you've come to claim Bull for yourself you're wasting your time, madam! Bull is my man. Everyone knows that.'

'He's been walking out with me,' Katie said firmly, 'and I won't believe he wants you instead of

168

me until he tells me himself.'

'Look, sit down.' Rhiannon's voice had softened. 'It's no use us two arguing the toss over him. He's a man and makes up his own mind about things, see? But I am his woman. I've lived with Bull for months now and I don't want to give him up.'

She sat opposite Katie, her arms on the table. 'He took me in when I was nothing more than a harlot, selling myself along the railways. I can't go back to that life, not after having a decent man take care of me. Please, Katie Cullen, don't take him from me, I'm begging you.'

Katie's mouth was dry and suddenly she was angry with Bull, so angry that she could not think straight. 'He's not been fair to you or me!' she said. 'He's kept the truth from me and I don't think I can forgive him for that.'

Rhiannon's face brightened. 'Then you don't want him like I do. I love every hair of that man's head. I tell you, I'll die if he throws me out. I can't go back to sleeping with men just to put a crust in my belly.'

Katie stared at Rhiannon for a long moment and knew she was telling the truth. She would be in terrible trouble without Bull to take care of her.

'See, Katie Cullen, you've got a job in a big house and a warm bed to go to at night. And you're younger than me. You can have any man you like, so don't take Bull.'

Katie could not ignore this plea from the heart. She got to her feet. 'Tell Bull I don't want to hear from him ever again.' She was near to tears and Rhiannon, generous now in victory, put her hand on her arm.

'Oh, I'll tell him, don't you worry,' she said

eagerly. 'You'll be all right. You'll meet a man more suited to you than Bull. He's a man of the road— he goes where the work is, see, and you wouldn't like that, would you, travelling round and living the way we do?'

Katie couldn't reply because her throat ached. She went out of the hut and felt the rain mingle with the tears running down her face. How could Bull deceive her so badly? How could he not tell her about Rhiannon?

'Find Bull's place, then, love?' The woman in the first hut was in the doorway. 'He'll be back soon if you want to wait for him by here.' She sniffed. 'I 'spects you had nothing but cheek from that Rhiannon. No good to man or beast, her. Scum, she is, living off men who should be home with their wives.'

'No, it's all right,' Katie mumbled, and hurried away, afraid of meeting Bull. How could she face him now without wanting to kill him?

By the time she got to the Morton-Edwards' house, she was soaked to the skin. The kitchen was warm, the fire roaring up the chimney.

'*Duw, duw!* Will you look at the girl! Like a drowned rat, you are, Katie love, and you been crying. What's wrong, then?' Mrs Grinter was fussing around her.

Katie kicked off her sodden boots. Her feet were freezing but it didn't seem to matter. Nothing mattered except that Bull had lied to her. But, no, he'd never lied, he just hadn't told her the truth.

'Come on, have a nice cup of tea and tell Cook all about it, there's a good girl.'

'It's Bull Beynon.' The words spilled from her numb lips. 'It's true, he's got a woman, I've seen

170

her for myself. She lives with him in a hut at the side of the railway track.'

Cook handed her a cup of tea. 'Plenty of sugar special in that, set you up a treat it will, good for shock, see?'

'He never said a word about living with a woman. He knew I wouldn't walk out with him if he told me the truth.'

'But, love, these navvies have women all the time, camp followers they are, no-goods who are there just to give a man a bit of comfort after a hard day's work. I told you, they mean no more to the men than a hot meal or a drink of beer on a pay-day. Don't you go fretting yourself over a little thing like that. He'll give her up once he marries you, you'll see.'

'He won't have the chance!' Katie said. 'I'll never speak to him again, let alone marry him.'

'Then you're a fool, girl,' Cook said severely. 'Any man wants a bit of comfort, like. It don't mean anything to them.'

'Well, it means a lot to me,' Katie said. She finished her tea and put down the cup. 'Thank you, Cook, but do you mind if I go up to bed? I'm so tired.'

'Go on you, girl, and think on what I've said. A man has needs, not like us, and if you're looking for one who never 'ad a woman then you'll look for a long time.'

Katie made her way up the back stairs, her wet skirts cold against her legs. Once in her room she stoked up the fire, glad that Mr Morton-Edwards was such a generous master. He'd treated her kindly ever since he'd run her down in the accident. That seemed a lifetime ago now.

One thing was certain, she would never trust any man again. 'Oh, Bull!' she whispered. 'How could you do this to me? I loved you so much.' But the only sound was of the rain dripping incessantly against the window, as if the whole of heaven was crying with her.

CHAPTER EIGHTEEN

Shanni stared into the green infusion of fern as if it were poison. And perhaps it was. How could she trust an old woman's knowledge of plants and the effect they would have on her unborn child?

No! It was not a child yet! She pushed away the thought. It was an unfortunate accident and must be put right, if she was to go on with her life. She picked up the cup and put it to her lips, closing her eyes tightly. The liquid was bitter, even though she had added honey to it as Mrs Keen had told her.

'Well, Mrs Keen, I hope you know what you're doing.' She tipped back her head and swallowed. It burned down her throat and into her stomach and Shanni panicked. What if it was lethal?

She put down the cup, staring into the dregs with distaste. As she heard Pedr's whistle she looked up sharply. He was coming up the path.

Quickly, Shanni hid the cup and set about laying the table for a meal, not that she could eat a thing but Pedr would be famished. She took up the loaf and began to cut thick rounds of bread. He liked his bread crusty and hot and tonight she wanted to please him.

'Hello, love, I'm home.' He came into the

kitchen and clasped her in his arms, planting a kiss on her upturned face. 'What's for supper?'

'Bacon and cheese and some lovely fresh bread. Let me go and I'll put out the food for you.'

'What about you?' Pedr shrugged off his coat. 'You're going to waste away to nothing if you don't start eating properly.'

'I've got a bit of an upset tummy and I think I'll make do with a cup of tea and a little bit of toast.'

Pedr sniffed. 'Funny smell in here, love. It's stronger even than the bacon. Not trying to poison me, are you?'

'No, silly! It's a remedy I got for my gippy tummy. Nothing to worry about.' It wasn't really a lie.

Pedr looked at her more closely. 'Do you think you ought to see the doctor, love? It may be you're going to have a youngling.'

His words shocked Shanni but she forced herself to smile at him, although she felt as if she was putting a dagger through his heart.

'No, it's not that, love. I've had my monthly curse.' She put his meal in front of him, fighting the nausea that the smell of bacon fat brought on. She made toast and sat opposite her husband picking at it with little enthusiasm. When would it start? She had little idea of what would happen to her. Mrs Keen had said something about bleeding but Shanni had not been sure what she meant.

'I'm worried about you, Shanni,' Pedr said gently. 'You look pretty bad to me.'

Shanni got up. 'Perhaps you're right, I should lie down for a bit. Will you bring me some tea up later on, love?'

'Aye, go on up you. I was going down the Castle

for a beer but I think I'll just stay in for tonight.'

'No, you go, love. I'm not that bad, I promise you.'

'We'll see.' Pedr put down his mug of tea and leaned back in his chair. 'Fine supper that, Shanni, you're a good cook and a wonderful wife. Have I ever told you that?'

'Once or twice! Now, go on out and leave me alone, for heaven's sake. I've only got stomach-ache and I don't know why you're making so much fuss about it. Go out with the men and give me a bit of peace, will you?'

'If you're sure, then, love. I'll just have a bit of a wash and then I'll be off, but I'll bring you some tea first.'

Shanni went upstairs to the small bedroom she shared with Pedr. The bed looked cosy and inviting. She slipped off her dress and, in her chemise, crawled under the covers.

It was good to lie down. The pain in her stomach seemed to ease as she settled herself more comfortably.

She didn't hear Pedr bring her tea for she was dreaming of babies, young ones lying in her arms, smiling at her, and when she woke in the darkness of the night there were tears on her cheeks.

*   *   *

Llinos sat at breakfast, thinking of the events of the past few days. Jayne had come to make her peace, which had been surprising enough, and, of course, she had found Shanni about to drown herself in the cold waters of the river Tawe.

'Damn you, Dafydd Buchan!' Llinos said softly.

'How many other lives are you going to wreck?' She poured another cup of tea. The house was quiet: Sion was busy upstairs with his tutor and the early morning silence seemed even to have quelled the clatter of the maids about their tasks.

She made up her mind, in spite of her promise to Shanni; it was her duty to see Dafydd and let him know of how Shanni was suffering. It might just teach him a lesson. He was no longer the young man eager to help the world but a selfish oaf who used women without a care for their future.

But she could hardly go to his house. She would have to send one of the servants to bring him here to the pottery. His visit would set tongues wagging again, but this was important. Jayne must be saved from the truth, if only for the sake of Llinos's friendship with her father.

It was early afternoon when Llinos heard the sound of hoofs. She knew Dafydd had arrived: she could hear him issuing orders to the stable-boy to rub down his horse. He must have ridden like the wind to get to her, yet the thought gave her little comfort.

He came into the drawing room like a breath of fresh air, his cheeks red from the wind, his hair standing out around his head like a halo. He looked so handsome but Llinos knew now how weak and treacherous he could be.

'What is it, Llinos? Are you ill?' He took her hands and drew her towards him, but she pushed him away.

'I am perfectly all right,' she said icily. 'Sit down, Dafydd, while I fetch you a strong drink. I think you're going to need it when you hear what I've got to say.'

'What is going on, Llinos?' Dafydd sounded impatient. 'I've been summoned here like an errant schoolboy and I want to know the reason why.'

'I'll come straight to the point. Shanni Morgan is pregnant.' She watched his face, trying to read his expression but he did not meet her eyes.

'What has that to do with me?'

'You know full well what it has to do with you! Don't lie to me on top of everything else.'

'All right. It happened once. She can't be having my child.'

'I found her about to drown herself in the river. I brought her home and made her tell me everything. Her husband was away when she fell for the baby. Oh, Dafydd, how many more lives are you going to ruin?'

He put his head in his hands. 'What a fool I was to be tempted by Shanni, but she's always wanted me, you know that, Llinos.'

'And if a woman wants you it justifies your outrageous behaviour, does it?' Llinos was aware she sounded like an indignant wife, but that was how she felt. 'And there's Jayne,' Llinos added. Dafydd looked up sharply. 'It's all right, she doesn't know anything. Your sordid secret is safe with me.'

'Why did Jayne come to see you the other day, then? Was she suspicious?'

In that moment Llinos realized she was free of him. Dafydd was a weak man, like all the rest, open to temptation and happy to indulge himself whatever the cost to others. The only man who was big enough to love her wholeheartedly in spite of her faults was Joe, but now he had gone away from her, perhaps for ever.

'She has no idea that you would betray her like

that, poor trusting girl. Her only complaint was that you didn't appreciate her. You treat her like a simpleton, Dafydd. I've seen you together, remember?'

'And that was *all* she came to see you about?' Relief was in his voice. 'Are you sure, Llinos?'

'I'm sure. But don't underestimate your wife, Dafydd. If you do, you will be doing her a grave injustice.'

'I love Jayne . . . in my own way,' he said lamely. He took up his glass as if to make a barrier between himself and Llinos. 'She's a fine girl and one day she'll bear me fine sons.' He looked at her sharply. 'I will always love Sion, have no fear of that.'

'You don't know how insensitive you are, do you, Dafydd? What about poor Shanni and Pedr? How are they going to sort out the mess you've made for them?'

'I was a fool, I admit it.'

'And that makes everything right, does it? For goodness' sake, go home, Dafydd! In future, try to let your head rule your urges. You've changed, you know. You were honourable once, when you wanted me to go away with you. Now you have a fling with a girl just for the fun of it! Isn't it time you grew up?'

'I was wrong to bed Shanni Morgan, but I don't see what I can do about it now. Is she going to tell her husband the truth?'

'How do I know? But instead of worrying about yourself I suggest you talk to Shanni, see if there is anything you can do to help her.'

'If Jayne finds out it will be the end of our marriage.' He put down his glass and moved to the door. 'Shanni hasn't come into work this morning. I'd better go up to her house.'

Llinos saw what he intended to do. He would not offer comfort to Shanni but beg or bribe her to keep quiet about what had happened. She took a deep breath. 'You disappoint me, Dafydd. All your principles have fallen by the wayside. At least now I am free of you for you are not the man I believed you to be.'

'And you are so perfect?' he said. 'I didn't force you to come to my bed, did I? What does that say about you, Llinos?'

He left as abruptly as he had arrived and Llinos watched him ride away. She felt relief that he no longer had the power to make her want him, but it was mixed with a lingering disappointment that the man she once loved had feet of clay.

*   *   *

Shanni had not slept again that night for the pains in her stomach had grown fierce, and by the time the dawn light was creeping through the window she thought she was going to die. She had kept quiet, pretending to be asleep as Pedr got ready for work. She usually made him breakfast but this morning he cooked it himself.

When she heard the door close behind him, she feared that she would die there alone—but she had brought the trouble upon herself and knew she must deal with it. After a while she tried to get out of bed but the pain drove her back, and she fell against the pillows sweating. After that she drifted in and out of a strange sleep in which nothing was real but the pain.

178

She was almost unconscious when the urge to bear down roused her. She turned over on her back and, crying, pushed with all her strength. She felt the blood gush from her and then came blessed relief from pain.

Cautiously she lifted the sheet and there lay a pathetically tiny scrap, so still, so beautiful. This was her baby and she had killed it. The blow to her was worse than Shanni had ever imagined. Until now, the thing inside her had been a mistake, something to be rid of as quickly as possible.

She realized that she must clear up before Pedr came home and tried to rise, but she was so weak and the blood was still flowing. She felt as if she was fading away, that all she wanted to do was sleep.

She became aware that someone was in the room. She opened her eyes and saw Dafydd bending over her. 'Shanni, what have you done?' His face was white.

'The baby is gone,' she said. 'It had to go—it was yours, not Pedr's. There was nothing else I could do.' Her voice was thin and threadlike, and Dafydd took her hand.

'You are ill, Shanni, you need help.'

She forced her eyes open. 'You would let me die to protect your good name, would you, Dafydd?' she whispered.

'Of course not, but by the time I find a doctor it might be too late. Is there a midwife round here?'

'Fetch Mrs Keen from Fennel Court,' Shanni said. 'She'll know what to do.' She felt the darkness close in on her again and gave herself up to it gratefully.

When she opened her eyes again it was to feel a

cold cloth around her belly. Mrs Keen was there, sleeves rolled up, her expression sober. 'I've cleaned everything away,' she said quietly, 'and I've just about stopped the bleeding.'

Shanni tried to focus her attention on Mrs Keen but she just wanted to drift away again into oblivion. She could hear Dafydd talking to the old woman, trying to explain that he was a concerned employer and had dropped by to see Mrs Morgan just by chance.

'Good chance for her, poor wee girl,' Mrs Keen said. 'She'd be dead by now if I hadn't been called. Freezing water stops the flow, see, sir? Without my help, she'd be a goner.'

Shanni heard the chink of coins changing hands and then heard Dafydd saying he'd best be leaving.

'Go on you, sir,' Mrs Keen sounded more cheerful now she had the money in her pocket. 'I'll stay till her old man gets home from work. She'll be all right now, sir. You just leave her to me.'

Shanni was so very tired, all she needed was to sleep. She felt her eyes grow heavy and then she drifted off into a sleep with no pain and no bad dreams. It seemed, for now at least, that her ordeal was over.

CHAPTER NINETEEN

Katie was tired: she had got through the last few days by working until she fell asleep. Eventually, Mr Morton-Edwards had told her she was looking peaky and needed to rest. She lay in bed now in her small room at the top of the house, trying to sort out her feelings. Her problems had to be faced and now was as good a time as any.

She allowed herself to think of Rhiannon, Bull's woman. She could still see her pale face, hear her begging Katie not to take Bull away from her.

Katie turned over restlessly. How could Bull have kept this from her? He had a woman, almost a wife, and had not even thought to mention it! That could only mean he didn't love her enough to give up his old way of life.

At last she slid out of bed and washed in the cold water from the jug on the washstand. The kitchenmaid would have been up an hour ago lighting fires and boiling water for the rest of the household to wash in comfort. She could see why Rhiannon thought she was living a life of ease.

When Katie went downstairs the kitchen was warm and welcoming and she stood by the fire holding out her hands to the blaze. 'Morning, Cook. A cup of tea in the pot, is there?'

'Aye, sit you down, Katie, and let me tell you the gossip. You went to bed early so I didn't have a chance to talk to you last night.'

'What gossip?' Katie was not really interested in Cook's stories but the old woman was kind enough and it did no harm to listen.

'That Shanni Morgan's had something terrible happen. She's a friend of yours, isn't she?'

'Well, yes, I suppose she is. What's wrong, then? Is she sick or something?'

'She's lost her little babba. A miscarriage, it was, and a bad one at that.' She leaned across the table. 'It's being said she got help from old Ma Keen to slip the poor innocent child so she's only got herself to blame if she's had to suffer.'

'That's awful!' Katie was shocked. 'I'm sure Shanni wouldn't want to get rid of a baby. She's married to a lovely man. Why would she do such a thing?'

'Well, keep this to yourself but from what I heard Mr Dafydd Buchan was mixed up in it. It was him what got old Mrs Keen to take care of her.'

'But surely Mr Buchan was just being kind? Shanni works for him.'

'That's as maybe but I got my doubts. That Mr Buchan's no angel. Didn't he give Mrs Mainwaring a child and her a married woman? A real rake is that Mr Buchan. I got no time for him myself.'

'Well, it's terrible news. I'd better try to see Shanni and find out how she is. Perhaps I can take her some pudding or something, Cook?'

'Aye, you can that, love, the master's told you to take some time off, hasn't he?' She stared closely at Katie. 'Nothing wrong with you, is there? You got no babba on the way, have you?'

'Of course not!' Katie said indignantly. 'I wouldn't let Bull or any other man take liberties with me.'

'I didn't think you would but I had to ask, mind. Right, I've got some cold meat pie in the larder and I'll do a nice egg tart—set the girl up a treat, that will.'

'Thank you, Cook. I'm sure Shanni will be very grateful.'

'Well, you slip off this morning, if you like,' Cook said, smiling. 'You can let us know the truth of it all when you come back.' She was a devil for gossip but Katie knew she had a good heart.

'Now, Katie, get some bacon and eggs down you, girl. You're thin as a sparrow and looking a bit sickly these last few days. It's that Bull Beynon, isn't it? You're grieving over the man. Look, forget about that woman he's living with. I've told you, she means nothing to him.'

'I'm all right, just a bit tired that's all.' Katie didn't want to talk about Bull or Rhiannon. The very thought of them together made her feel ill.

A little while later the pale sun of early spring was shining as Katie left the house. She was glad she was going out visiting because then she couldn't dwell on Bull.

When she reached Shanni's little house, the front door was closed and Katie knocked softly. 'Shanni, it's me, Katie Cullen. I've come to see how you are.'

Pedr appeared in the doorway, his usually ruddy face pale. 'Come in, Katie. My little wife could do with some cheering up, see.'

'Here we are, Pedr.' Katie handed him the basket Cook had prepared. 'There's some cold meat pie, some ham and a nice custard tart. Perhaps Shanni will be able to eat a little bit of it.'

Pedr's eyes misted with tears. 'Everyone is so good to us. Tell the cook thank you for me.'

'I will,' Katie said, and laid a hand on his arm. 'Try not to worry. Shanni's young and strong, she'll be all right.'

Shanni was lying in bed, propped against the pillows. She was pale and there were huge dark shadows under her eyes, but she smiled when she saw Katie. 'There's nice of you to call. Sit down, Katie, and tell me what's been happening outside in the big bad world. Gossiping about me, are they?'

'I think folks are sorry for you, Shanni. They've

heard you lost your little baby, that's all.'

Pedr came and stood by the bed. 'No one is gossiping, love,' he said. 'We didn't know there was a babba on the way, did we?' He looked at Katie. 'Shanni thought she had a bad stomach.'

'Go and make a cup of tea, love,' Shanni said. 'Me and Katie want to talk woman-talk.'

When Pedr had gone Katie asked, 'How are you really feeling?'

'I've got to talk to someone, Katie, or I'll go mad. I got rid of my baby. I'm so wicked, I don't deserve a man like Pedr.'

Katie was astounded. 'But why, Shanni? Didn't you want a baby?'

'Not now, not this way.'

Pedr came clomping up the stairs and Shanni put her finger to her lips.

'There, love, a nice cup of tea and a bit of custard tart. Try and eat a little bit, just to please me.'

'Go away, love.' Shanni flapped her hands at him.

When he'd gone she sighed heavily. 'I'm aching all over and my conscience is driving me crazy. I keep seeing it, a perfect little child lying there on the sheet, and I can't bear it.' Tears ran down her cheeks. 'It's my fault, Katie, it's all my fault.'

'No, love, don't think like that. It wasn't your fault, whatever you say, because these things happen to lots of women. The old wives say that if you lose a baby there was something wrong with it, so it might be all for the best.'

'But you don't understand, Katie. I did it on purpose. I took some stuff Mrs Keen gave me—I wanted to lose the baby.'

184

Katie took a deep breath. 'But why, Shanni?'

Shanni lowered her voice. 'The baby wasn't Pedr's.'

'Oh, you poor thing!' Katie took Shanni's hand and held it tightly. 'What happened? Were you attacked by one of the navvies?'

'No. I gave in to temptation. I'm such a fool but I thought I—' She took a deep breath. 'Oh, there's no excuse for what I've done and I'll never forgive myself.'

'You needn't say any more, Shanni. What's happened is your business and no one else need know about it.'

'Just let me talk, Katie.' Shanni fell back against the pillows, tears still streaming down her cheeks. 'I've got to tell someone and I know I can trust you.' She looked into her friend's eyes. 'I went with Dafydd Buchan when we were alone in the office one night. I'd always thought I loved him but I know that's no excuse.'

'I'm so sorry, Shanni, I really am, but don't go putting all the blame on yourself now. Dafydd Buchan is a grown man with a wife, and he should have known better than to take advantage of you.'

Shanni sighed heavily. 'Once we had . . . well, done it, I knew I didn't love him. I *never* loved him. The man I truly love is my wonderful Pedr. Oh, Katie, Pedr is such a good person and he loves me so much. How can I live a lie for the rest of my life?' She looked at Katie beseechingly. 'Should I tell him the truth, do you think?'

Katie knew that if she did, Pedr would want revenge. 'Shanni, Pedr would probably fight with Dafydd Buchan and then he would lose his job. And what about Mrs Buchan? How hurt she would be!'

'I've thought of all those things. I don't know what to do for the best.'

Katie squeezed her hand. Poor Shanni, she looked so ill and lost, Katie's own troubles seemed petty in the face of such pain. 'Look, don't do anything for now, just get better. Then think it all through carefully, that's the best.'

'But—'

'No buts. Put it out of your mind, and then, when you feel strong, you can decide what to do.'

'You're very wise for a young girl, Katie. What's made you so sensible when I'm such a fool? Perhaps it's because you haven't fallen in love yet.'

The door opened and Pedr came into the room. 'Any more tea for you, ladies?' He kissed his wife's head. 'And I won't have any more of this weeping, right? You're a strong young woman and we'll have plenty of babies when the time is right.'

'No tea for me, thanks, Pedr,' Katie said. She felt pity tug her heart as she watched Shanni touch her husband's cheek. They were so obviously in love that it was hard to imagine Shanni being unfaithful with another man. Katie must make sure she never did anything so foolish. It was just as well she had learned about Bull's woman before it was too late.

Pedr went out, closing the door behind him.

'He's so worried about you, Shanni. He must love you very much,' Katie said.

'I know,' Shanni said, 'and I'll spend the rest of my life making up to him for what I've done.'

It was with relief that Katie left the house a little later. She wished she had never called, had never been the one in whom Shanni had confided. Once she got back to the Morton-Edwards household

186

Cook would be waiting for the latest gossip and what could she say?

She walked towards town, leaving behind the potteries and the little huddle of houses. She turned into the Carmarthen road, trying to ignore the navvies working on the railway line. Then she caught sight of Bull: his big shoulders and tall frame made him stand out from the other men and Katie longed to run to him and throw herself into his arms. She turned away her face, hoping he wouldn't see her. But he did. Suddenly he was standing in front of her, barring her way.

'Katie, I must talk to you, please. Just give me a few minutes of your time, that's all I ask.'

She looked up at him. She had thought him so dear, so wonderful, and yet he was a cheat and a liar. 'What can you say, Bull? You have a woman and that's an end to it.'

'No. I took Rhiannon in because she was alone, defenceless. She needed protection from the other men.'

Katie stared at him. 'Are you telling me you live with her like brother and sister?'

He faced her squarely. 'I can't tell you that, Katie, but since I met you I haven't—'

'Stop! I don't want to hear it, Bull. You should have told me about Rhiannon.' She hesitated. 'Are you willing to send her packing, then, Bull? Would you do that for me?'

For a long moment he was silent. 'No,' he said at last. 'I wouldn't throw Rhiannon to the wolves. I owe her more than that.'

'Well, that's all there is to say. ' Her voice was cool, but part of her respected him for his loyalty.

'I'll be getting a house soon,' Bull said, 'and,

given time, I can make arrangements for Rhiannon to find work in a good home. I never meant to ask you to be my wife until I'd sorted out my affairs properly.'

'But you should have told me about Rhiannon. How do you think I felt when she begged me not to take you away from her? She loves you so much, Bull, and you've just used her in the same way as all the other men used her.'

'It wasn't like that. I was trying to help her. I gave Rhiannon a bit of security instead of watching her being passed from man to man. Was that so wrong?'

'I don't know, Bull,' Katie said wearily. 'All I do know is I can't share you, not with anyone. Goodbye, Bull. Please don't bother me again.'

Katie sounded strong, a woman in charge of her feelings, but once she had walked away from him the tears came and she knew that her world was coming to an end.

*   *   *

Rhiannon had watched the little scene between Bull and Katie, her heart in her mouth. She could see that they were arguing and she knew it was over her. Would Katie win him away from her? She tried to read Bull's expression. Was she being fair in trying to keep him for herself? She was denying him a good marriage and a family. Was that the way to show her love for him?

'Hell and damnation!' she said aloud. 'He's my man and I can't let him go.' She watched, with a sense of triumph, as Katie walked away, leaving Bull staring after her. It was clear that Katie had finished with him once and for all.

Slowly Rhiannon went back to the hut. She built up the fire and put a pot of water on to boil: she would make him a good meal, a nice chicken soup with chunks of potato, and some bread and cheese to come after. Rhiannon looked around her at the bare wooden walls of the hut, the crude window covered with paper-thin curtains. It was not much but it was the home she shared with the man she loved.

Later, when Bull came home, Rhiannon served his meal and sat beside him at the rough wooden table. 'Had a good day, Bull?' She dare not tell him she had seen Katie Cullen stop and talk to him. The last thing she wanted was to quarrel with him and hear the truth about his feelings.

'Average.'

'Heard any more about your promotion?' She was on risky ground but she had to know what was going on. 'When will you move into the new house?'

'I'm seeing the engineer tomorrow and I'll know more after I've spoken to him.' He pushed away his plate. 'I'm going for a drink with the men. I've got such a thirst on me I could drink the sea dry.' It was an excuse and they both knew it. Still, he would come home mellowed by the beer and perhaps he would make love to her, the way he used to before he met Katie Cullen. It was a vain hope but Rhiannon clung to it, knowing in her heart that she had already lost the battle.

CHAPTER TWENTY

'What on earth is wrong with you, Dafydd?' Jayne frowned as her husband walked across to the window for the umpteenth time that evening. 'You're so restless. Is business bothering you?'

He ran his hand through his hair, making it stand on end, and Jayne smiled: he was like a little boy wanting to confess a misdemeanour to his mother, but what could Dafydd possibly want to confess?

He returned to his seat and smiled absentmindedly. 'I'm just fretting over the damn railway shares,' he said. 'I missed getting my hands on some the other day.'

'How did that come about?'

'I got talking to Ben Knightly, the head of the bank. Seems the family of some old man wanted to offload the shares he held. If I'd got them I'd have a foot in the door at least.'

'Who did get them, then?' Jayne watched her husband's face. Had he known it had been her he would have confronted her by now.

'He wouldn't say, professional etiquette, but I do know it was his second-in-command who kept the shares for a favoured customer. Damn! I only wish Ben had come to me first.'

Jayne hid a smile. 'Well, Dafydd, you have enough money as it is without wanting to make more.'

She was wondering if this was the right time to tell him she had enough shares for both of them when he spoke again, impatiently, as though to a child. 'Don't be silly, Jayne! It's not just a case of money. There's a great deal more than money to consider but how can I expect you to know anything about business?'

Jayne swallowed an angry retort. If Dafydd chose to think of her as a foolish woman that was his loss. He strode to the door.

'Where are you going?' she asked, aware of the peevish note in her voice but unable to prevent it.

'To the club for an hour. I need the company of men of my own kind, ambitious men, who think it good to have an aim in life.'

'What makes you think I'm a fool?' She was standing now, her hands clenched at her side. 'If you only knew how much I resent your attitude to me!'

'Oh, I know, all right,' Dafydd said. 'You made your feelings clear to Llinos Mainwaring. How could you go crying to another woman about the way I treat you?'

'You've seen Llinos? When? Did you go to her home, then?'

'Yes.'

'Are you not satisfied with me? Do you have to cling to the skirts of an older woman? You're like a child looking for mothering.'

'Anything would be better than a wife who lies there like a piece of stone. I'm used to a full-blooded woman and all you are is a young, inexperienced girl.'

'So you would prefer it if I had been a trollop, lying with any man who took my fancy just as Llinos Mainwaring does?'

'Don't talk rubbish! Llinos is no whore, whatever you say. She loved me and was not afraid to show it

191

in bed. You, on the other hand, are a disappointment.'

'Oh, you think she's so good, so loyal. Well, I happen to know that Llinos and my father have been lovers for years.' It was a lie, but Jayne was past caring. She wanted to hurt Dafydd as he was hurting her.

'Don't make me laugh! Llinos and your father were never lovers. He's not enough of a man for her. He's vapid and colourless, just like his daughter.'

'Get out of my sight!' Jayne's voice was low. 'Go—before I forget that I'm a lady.'

She stood trembling in front of the fire long after the door had closed behind her husband. But he had never been a proper husband to her. He had never satisfied her in bed—and she wished now that she had told him so to his face.

At last she sat down and stared into the flames, watching the coals shift in the grate. It seemed that her world had shattered: she knew what Dafydd thought of her now and the truth hurt. She was cold and dead inside, her hopes and dreams vanished. But why was she surprised? She had sometimes suspected that her marriage was one of convenience. Yet she had clung to the hope that, one day, Dafydd would come to love her.

Perhaps even now if she had his children he would become a fond husband and father. Dafydd loved children—she could see the envy in his eyes whenever he saw his brother's family, so happy together even now when Ceri was so ill.

Tears welled in her eyes. Could she ever forget the way he'd talked to her, go to his bed knowing he thought her cold? Well, she would just have to make herself more welcoming to him because she had no intention of giving up on her marriage. She would make it work, whatever it cost her.

*   *   *

Mumbles Gentlemen's Club was housed in an ancient building facing the windswept waters of Mumbles Bay. As Dafydd entered the large, comfortable lounge he searched for a familiar face. The he caught sight of Jason Prentice from the bank with Ben Knightly. Eynon Morton-Edwards and Father Martin were with them, engrossed in conversation.

Dafydd watched them, a pang of anger running through him. No doubt they were discussing the state of the shares in the Great Western Railway. It was probably Eynon who had been favoured with a tip-off from the bank.

Dafydd walked across the room and stared down at his father-in-law. 'May I join you, gentlemen?' He forced a note of enthusiasm into his voice, and as Eynon indicated a chair he concealed a smile: Eynon would never slight his daughter's husband in public.

'Brandy for you, Buchan?' Eynon asked. He lifted his hand and at once a waiter was at his side. 'More drinks for us, and something for Mr Buchan.'

'Brandy, please.' Dafydd settled back in his chair. 'I do hope I'm not interrupting a business meeting. Talking about railway shares, were you?'

Eynon gave nothing away. 'Our business was concluded.' He looked at Dafydd over his glass and his eyes were blank.

'I hope you're feeling better, Eynon. Jayne told me you were ill.'

'It was just a chill. How is she?'

'My dear wife is well. She's planning to buy some fripperies, hats, things like that, so I thought I'd be better out of it.' He had no idea why he was making excuses to Eynon for leaving Jayne alone. Most men went out without their wives.

'I'm sure she has more on her mind than fripperies. Don't underestimate my daughter, Buchan,' Eynon said quietly, 'or one day she might just get the better of you.'

Dafydd frowned. What was the man talking about? 'In what way?' He smiled to soften the harshness of his question.

'Women are complex creatures.' Eynon did not answer directly. 'They have strange whims and fancies, it's true, but some, Jayne for one, have a brain as well as good looks.'

'Oh, I appreciate that,' Dafydd said. 'Jayne is an intelligent woman. That's why I married her.'

An uneasy silence fell, to be broken a few minutes later by Father Martin. 'Any sign of little ones on the way yet?' he asked jovially.

'Give us a chance, Father,' Dafydd said. 'We're just getting to know each other. There's plenty of time for children.'

'Sooner rather than later, mind,' Father Martin said. 'Children are a trial and they need a young mother to cope with them.'

'Not all mothers are young,' Eynon put in, with a touch of bitterness in his voice. 'There are one or two exceptions, as you well know, Buchan.'

Dafydd decided not to rise to the bait. 'Very true, very true.' He took his drink from the tray held before him by the waiter. 'Good health!' He swallowed it in one gulp. 'Bring more of the same,' he said, replacing his empty glass on the tray.

'Hey, steady on, man,' Father Martin said genially. 'I'm due to conduct a burial in the morning and I must stay sober for that or I might find myself in the grave with the deceased.'

Thereafter talk became general and Dafydd pretended to join in, but he knew his company was unwelcome. Father Martin threw him a look now and again in an attempt to include him, but that was more from a sense of charity than because he wanted to. Dafydd sat it out for just over an hour and then he rose to his feet. 'Well, gentlemen, I hope you will excuse me but I've pressing business to attend to.'

Eynon nodded and it was left to Father Martin to respond. 'God bless you, Buchan.'

Outside in the cold air Dafydd took a few deep breaths. Eynon Morton-Edwards treated him like a leper. He did not even observe the niceties of civilized society. Then a smile curved his lips: Eynon was cold because his son-in-law had seduced Llinos Mainwaring. He thought of Jayne and how she had thrown out that Llinos and Eynon were lovers. What a fool she was! Eynon would give all his wealth for Llinos to go to his bed, but she never would. He was warmed by the memory of her passion as she lay in his arms. What a woman she was, and what a pity he could never have made her his wife instead of shackling himself to the petulant Jayne.

The thought of going home was not attractive. Perhaps he should take a ride, clear his head a little. He walked to the back of the building where his horse was stabled and waited as the groom adjusted the girth and led the animal into the night air. Dafydd pressed a coin into his hands and he touched his forelock.

Without glancing back, Dafydd rode away from the town and followed the river as it wound its way through the manufactories where chimneys pointed to the leaden skies like a dark forest.

It was with little surprise that soon he found himself outside the pottery owned by Llinos Mainwaring. He dismounted and stood, rubbing his horse's flank, almost willing Llinos to appear. He saw the shimmering heat coming off the bottle kilns and breathed in the familiar smell of drying clay with a deep sense of loss.

Inside those walls were the two people he loved more than life itself: Llinos and Sion, the son born of a passionate union. At last he turned away. It was too late to go calling and, anyway, he knew he would not be welcome. He mounted his horse and rode as hard as he could to the loveless house he called home.

*   *   *

'Papa, how nice to see you looking so well.' Jayne kissed her father's cheek, and hugged him in an uncharacteristic show of affection.

'I'm delighted to see you too, my lovely daughter. Come and sit down. Let's have some tea together, shall we?'

Jayne took a seat and settled her skirts around her ankles. She looked at her father from under her lashes, wondering how she was going to broach the difficult questions she needed to ask. Last night

Dafydd had not returned home until the early hours of the morning and she suspected he had been with Llinos. When she thought of them together her stomach twisted into knots and she felt bile rise to her throat.

'To what do I owe the honour of a call from my little girl so early in the day?' Eynon asked.

'Nothing, really. I just need to get out for a bit, Papa. Where's the tea you promised me?'

Eynon rang the bell and the maid responded at once. 'Yes, sir?'

'Oh, Katie, fetch some tea, there's a good girl, and ask Cook for some of those scones she's been baking.'

Katie nodded, and Jayne noted briefly that the girl looked pale and wan. She ignored her but wished now she had kept Katie sweet: who knew what bits of gossip she might have picked up?

'The weather's brightening up now, thank goodness.' She looked out of the window, pretending to be interested in the garden. 'I see the daffodils are flourishing.'

When the tea arrived she wondered how to start the conversation, but Eynon settled back in his chair and steepled his fingers. 'Now, little darling, why are you really here? Is all well with you and Buchan?'

'Yes.' Her reply came too fast. 'Well, no. He came in very late last night and I was worried about him.'

'Yes, I can believe it.' Her father's tone was dry. 'But for most of the evening he was at the club.'

'At what time did he leave, Papa? He didn't come home to me until about three in the morning.'

Eynon sat up straighter. 'Good Lord!'

'Good Lord indeed!' Jayne fought for control. 'Who was he with until that time of the morning?'

'Now, don't jump to conclusions, Jayne. I know that he was piqued because he still has no shares in the Great Western Railway. Perhaps he went for a walk.'

'I have a distinct feeling that he went to see Llinos,' Jayne blurted out. 'Papa, he still loves her—I can see it plain as day. Why did I allow myself to believe he cared for me?' Her father took her hand and kissed it.

'Look, my lovely girl,' he said gently, 'most marriages are made without real love but it doesn't mean they don't work. Just wait until you have his children. Dafydd will be the finest husband and father you could ever find.'

Jayne frowned. 'Why are you taking his side?'

'I'm not, Jayne. It's just that I'm more used to the ways of the world than you are.' He sighed. 'As for him seeing Llinos, I doubt that very much. Young Sion has a spring fever and Llinos is an excellent mother. She would put her son before any other consideration, believe me.'

Jayne felt a glow of hope. 'Are you sure about that, Papa?'

'I'm sure, and even Dafydd would not be so foolish as to go visiting at that time of night.'

She brightened. He was right. Dafydd would not want the neighbours talking about his precious Llinos.

'What should I do, then, Papa?'

'Give it time, Jayne,' Eynon said. 'Be clever and forge the links so strongly between you and Buchan that he won't be able to break them. Have a family,

198

a brood of fine grandchildren for me to indulge.'
He smiled. 'It was because of you, my love, that I
was loyal to your mother when she was alive. Now,
cheer up. Once you give him a son Dafydd will be
tied to you for life.'

Jayne smiled at him. 'You're a wise old owl,
aren't you?'

'I've learned a few things about love and life,'
Eynon said. 'These lessons are not always easy to
digest, Jayne, but they're all about becoming an
adult.'

'Thank you, Papa.'

'What for?'

'Just for being a sensible old father.' She smiled.
'I'll be kind to Dafydd and not expect too much too
soon. He thinks of me as a child still, and that is
partly my fault for behaving like one.'

'So, now that's settled,' Eynon said jovially, 'let's
have another cup of tea.'

Later, when Jayne sat in her carriage travelling
towards her home, she thought over her father's
words carefully. Battling with Dafydd, throwing
accusations at him, would get her nowhere. She
must learn to curb her jealousy, to make herself a
model wife and mother. And tonight she would
make a start by luring Dafydd to her bed and
proving to him that she was an adult, passionate
woman.

CHAPTER TWENTY-ONE

Bull had changed. Looking at him now over the
scrubbed table in the little hut Rhiannon could see

from the slope of his broad shoulders and the lack of spark in his eyes that he was unhappy. She knew that her chat with Katie was to blame, but she couldn't tell him the truth and risk losing him.

'You haven't eaten much of your rabbit stew, Bull,' she said gently. 'You've been working hard all day and you need good food in your belly.'

'I'm not hungry, Rhiannon.' He avoided her eyes. 'I think I'll just go down to the Castle and have a drink with the boys.'

'But, Bull, it's getting late for walking into town, and you know what they can be like when they've been paid. Please, Bull, I don't want you involved in any fighting.'

Bull was already on his feet, swinging his coat over his shoulders. 'Don't worry about me, girl, I'm used to dealing with the men. I wouldn't have lasted long as foreman if I'd let them walk all over me, would I?'

Rhiannon glanced at the battered clock on the shelf over the fire. It was just on nine. 'You're going to meet her, aren't you?' The words tumbled from her lips before she had time to think. 'She comes out of choir practice about now, doesn't she? Come on, Bull, don't lie to me.'

She saw his features harden. 'Be careful, Rhiannon.' His voice was terse. 'You are not my keeper and I don't answer to any man, so why should I answer to you?'

Rhiannon was past caring about what she said and the anger she'd suppressed for the last few months rose up inside her. 'Be careful, is it? Do you mean you'll hit me if I don't shut my mouth, Bull?' She faced him, hands on her hips, cheeks red. 'Go on, then, hit me! Be like all the other men in my life and take your anger out on me!'

He sighed. 'Rhiannon, I have never hit you and I have no intention of doing so, but you can't order me about. Just get that into your head.'

Rhiannon hardly heard him. 'You don't care about me any more. You haven't lain with me for months. Ever since you met that Katie Cullen you've been a million miles from me. It wouldn't work, Bull. Katie needs a proper home, a respectable man. She wouldn't look at you.'

'Stop there now, Rhiannon.' There was warning in his voice, but Rhiannon ignored it.

'She came here.' She knew she was playing with fire, but the words spilled from her lips. 'Gave me a message, she did. I was to tell you to keep away from her. She doesn't want you, Bull. That sort of woman wants a gentleman for a husband.'

'And what did you say to her?' He moved away from the door. 'What did you say?'

'I didn't want to hurt you, Bull, but take it from me that girl is not the one for you. She's little more than a spoiled child.'

Bull was white to the lips and Rhiannon's anger faded. She had gone too far.

'Rhiannon, I think it's about time you found yourself another man.' His words fell like slivers of ice into her consciousness.

'No, Bull! I'm sorry, I really am, I don't know what came over me. I shouldn't have told you about Katie coming here.'

'Look,' he paused, 'you know I'm going to be promoted to manager, don't you?' He tried to speak calmly. 'I'll have a proper home soon.' He took her hand. 'I don't want to hurt you but I might as well tell you straight that you have no place in

201

my life any more.'

'Don't say that, Bull, please don't say that! I love you so much that it's like a pain inside my heart. I need you, Bull, I can't go back to the life I lived before, you know I can't.'

'That's up to you, Rhiannon,' he said. 'You can stay in this hut for as long as you need and perhaps, later, I could find you a position in one of the big houses.'

'I don't want to skivvy for the rich women of the town. Scrubbing floors and curtseying to the gentry is not my idea of living.'

'Well, as I said, that's up to you. I can't be held responsible for the way you choose to run your life.'

'But, Bull, haven't I been good to you? I've washed your clothes and cooked your food and lived at the side of the track for a long time and never complained. I love you, Bull, more than Katie could ever love you.'

'Tell me, Rhiannon,' Bull said quietly, 'what did Katie really want when she came to see me?'

'Oh, go and ask her!' Rhiannon turned away, her face in her hands. Bull knew then that she had been keeping something from him.

'I intend to.' He opened the door and the chilly evening air rushed into the hut. Rhiannon hurried across the room in time to see him striding away in the direction of the town. 'Bull, will you be back tonight?' she called, but her words were carried away on the wind.

*   *   *

Jayne was worried. She thought that by now she

should have conceived Dafydd's child. She was beginning to wonder if there was anything wrong with her. She had spoken to her doctor, but old George Sullivan had only told her to be patient and let nature take its course. But nature was not taking its course: it seemed to need a helping hand.

She could always go to see Mrs Keen, the midwife. She had brought many babies into the world, and it was said she had helped some to slip out, too. Any disfigured or damaged child was quietly smothered at birth. At least, that's what Jayne had heard.

Apart from being the local midwife, Mrs Keen was something of a sage. She would give medicine to those who needed it. But how discreet was she? Jayne wouldn't like everyone gossiping about her. No, she could not lay herself open to gossip of that sort. But early the next day, Jayne found herself riding her pony away from the western part of the town and towards Fennel Court where Mrs Keen lived.

If the old woman was impressed by Jayne's good clothes and air of good breeding she did not show it. Jayne glanced around the tiny house and noted that while it was sparsely furnished it was spotlessly clean. That cheered her a little.

'Sit down, ma'am,' Mrs Keen said politely, 'and tell me what ails you. Perhaps I'll be able to help.'

'I'm not sick,' Jayne said diffidently. 'It's just that I've been married for a while now and I would dearly like to have a baby.' There. The words were out.

Mrs Keen nodded. 'Well, I have to ask if your husband is vigorous in the bedchamber, ma'am. I'm sorry to be so personal but it is important.'

'He's like most husbands.' Jayne heard a touch of bitterness in her voice. 'He comes to me when he's ready and not before.'

'As you say, that's what most husbands are like. So there's no problems, then?'

'Not real problems, only the everyday ones that confront a married woman.' Jayne had no intention of going into detail.

'Very well,' Mrs Keen said. 'I can give you something to take that will make you relax while your husband . . . Well, you know, and then you might just catch for a baby.' She was about to speak again when someone knocked at the door. She got to her feet. 'Excuse me, I won't be a minute.'

Jayne shrank back into her seat as the old woman opened the door. She didn't want to be seen.

'Can I come in, Mrs Keen?' The voice was familiar and Jayne sat up to listen intently.

'I got company now, Shanni,' Mrs Keen said, 'but are you feeling better? You still look a little pale. Why don't you come back later and I can give you something for your blood. Slipping a baby always takes it out of you.'

Jayne muffled an exclamation of shock. Shanni Morgan had been expecting a baby and Mrs Keen had helped her to lose it? But why? Shanni was a respectable married woman and there was no reason on earth why she should not have children. Unless . . . unless the child had not been her husband's.

'I'm feeling awful poorly, Mrs Keen,' Shanni said, and Jayne noticed that she had slipped back into the language of Fennel Court.

'Well, that will teach you not to go with the

gentry,' Mrs Keen said. 'They don't care where they sow their seeds as long as they get their satisfaction.'

So Shanni had slept with a gentleman, but what man of breeding would sleep with the likes of her? A dreadful thought came to her. The one man Shanni saw day in and day out was Dafydd.

Jayne got up from her chair so abruptly that it tipped over and crashed to the hard flags. She pulled the door wide open, her fury mounting. 'Shanni Morgan, you've been with my husband! Admit it, you slut!' She slapped the girl hard across the face. 'Go on, tell me the truth! It was Dafydd's baby you were carrying, wasn't it?'

Mrs Keen ushered them back into the room and closed the door. 'Calm down, ladies, don't let the whole of Fennel Court know your business!'

'I don't care who knows the truth!' Shanni was as angry as Jayne. 'And I admit it! I bedded your husband.' Her face was white except for the red marks left by Jayne's hand. 'If you're not woman enough for him, then you're the one to blame for it, not me.'

Jayne felt faint with shock: even as she had flung out her accusation she had hoped Shanni would deny it.

'When did this happen?' she asked dully. 'Tell me, Shanni, I have to know.'

'It was only once.' The words came out like a sigh. 'I was at the office late and Dafydd came in.' She looked up defiantly. 'I think he was bored with all the domesticity you heaped on him.'

Jayne was too upset for anger now. 'And he slept with you and you caught for a baby?'

'Yes.' Shanni's reply was brief and to the point.

'How do you know it was his child? Couldn't it have been your husband's?' She was trying to come to terms with the knowledge that Dafydd had been unfaithful, but it was all like a bad dream.

'My husband was away,' Shanni said, her hostility fading. 'That's why I was at the office so late. I was lonely for him.'

'So lonely that you took another woman's husband?' Jayne said bitterly.

'I always thought I was in love with Dafydd. I realize now it was only a dream. It was the idea of him I loved, not the man.'

'And your husband knows about this, does he?' Jayne asked. 'Or would you like me to be the one to tell him?'

Mrs Keen had remained silent but she came forward now and shook her head. 'Don't do that, ma'am. Don't make the boy as unhappy as you are. He doesn't deserve it.'

'And I don't deserve it either!' Jayne said sharply. 'I came here to ask for help because I wanted a baby, and I find this slut getting rid of my husband's child.' Suddenly she was weary. 'I'd better go home and think about all this.' She brushed the creases from her skirt absentmindedly. 'It's pointless trying for a baby now that my life is in ruins.'

'Jayne,' Shanni said quietly, 'I'm so sorry. I shouldn't have blurted all that out the way I did. I'm sorry for what I did, and I'm even more sorry that you had to know.' She pushed back her red hair. 'If you want to tell Pedr the truth I can't stop you, and perhaps I would even be relieved to have it all out in the open.'

Out in the open? That was the last thing Jayne

206

wanted. She could imagine the sniggers, the hands over the mouths as people gossiped about her and laughed.

'I suggest that what's been said in this room remains a secret between us three,' she said at last. 'I'm not being noble and thinking of your husband, I'm protecting myself.'

She left the house and untethered her pony, swung up into the saddle and guided it out of the mean streets and onto the main road into town.

When she reached home Dafydd was there. He barely looked at her as she swept into the drawing room. He was pouring himself a glass of fine wine.

'Had a nice morning, Jayne?' he asked. 'Been buying yet more fripperies?'

'No,' she said, in a low voice. 'I've just been talking to your mistress.'

He looked up at her sharply then. 'What do you mean?'

'You know what I mean.'

'If you're harping on about Llinos again let me assure you—'

Jayne cut him off mid-sentence. 'I'm talking about your latest conquest, Shanni Morgan.'

'You're talking rubbish! Go and bathe, Jayne. You smell of horse.' He turned his back on her. Infuriated, Jayne swung him round and slapped his face as hard as she could. 'Don't you dare turn your back on me! I'm not the one who's done wrong. Look at you—just look at you! You'll lie with any whore. I should have listened to my father when he warned me against you.'

'Don't I wish you'd listened to him too?' Dafydd drank the wine in one gulp and poured more. 'How dare you come here and accuse me? Where's your proof?'

'Shanni Morgan admitted everything.'

'So you'd believe the girl you call a slut rather than me, is that it?'

'I was down at Fennel Court,' Jayne said wearily. 'I was asking the midwife to give me something to help me conceive your child. Isn't that amusing?' she said bitterly. 'Shanni came to the door. She didn't know I was there and I overheard her talking to the old woman.' She looked up at Dafydd then. 'Has it sunk in yet? She was having your baby, Dafydd!' Jayne's voice was filled with anguish. 'She's got rid of it, while I'm longing for a child.'

Dafydd was shaken. 'How would she know the child was mine?' He spoke guardedly. 'She's married to Pedr Morgan, you know.'

'Yes, but he was away when you took his wife. The poor man doesn't know he's a cuckold.'

'Is this the truth, Jayne?'

'Would you know the truth if it smacked you in the face?' She got to her feet. 'I don't want you to ever come to my bed again, Dafydd, do you understand?'

'You are my wife and you will do as I say,' he replied. 'I need heirs and you are going to give them to me.'

'No,' Jayne said, 'I am not. And now I am going upstairs to bathe and get rid of the stink of horse. We don't want the smell to offend my so-particular husband, do we?'

Lunch was served as usual in the dining room and Jayne sat opposite Dafydd, scarcely able to look at him. She would keep the pretence of a marriage if only to save herself embarrassment and ridicule. If people knew the truth she would be branded as the woman who could not keep her man and she couldn't bear that.

He tried to talk to her but she responded only when the servants were clearing away. Once alone with him she fell silent, determined to ignore him.

'Jayne, we have to live together. Please don't keep this up—it's simply too tiresome for words.'

She gave him a steely look. 'Oh, listen to the poor hard-done-by husband! I suppose making love to that slut was a diversion for you, a relief from my "tiresome" company. And you even made her with child—that I can't forgive.'

'How can *you* be so sure it was my child Shanni was expecting?'

'I told you, I was there when she said so.' She stared directly at him. 'How *could* you, Dafydd, with a woman of the lower orders?'

'Oh, that's important to you, isn't it, Jayne? I stooped below your exalted image of yourself and slept with an honest working-woman. When did you ever do a day's work, Jayne? You're a spoiled, ignorant girl, with less intelligence than the average hound.'

'You can be as insulting as you like.' Jayne threw down her napkin and stood up. 'But I have more intelligence than you give me credit for.'

'Really? Well, I've yet to see evidence of it.'

'Listen to this, then, Dafydd Buchan! I've acquired a great many shares in the Great Western Railway Company and that's more than you could achieve, isn't it?'

'You're lying.'

'Am I? Go and talk to Jason Prentice at the bank, if you don't believe me.' She stared at him, hating him. 'I've been one step ahead of you all along the way, can't you see that? Your big mistake was to underestimate me. You're nothing but a bigoted fool.'

He moved swiftly and caught her arm. 'How dare you go behind my back and get shares in the railway? Have you forgotten I'm your husband?'

She shook off his hand. 'Don't manhandle me, Dafydd. I'm not some back-street whore.'

'It was your duty to include me in any deals you made, but I suppose your powerful father helped you, did he?'

'Can't you understand that I have a mind of my own, Dafydd? You might have married a girl but now I'm a woman.'

'And, as I told you, you are still my wife. Kindly remember that.'

'That's rich, coming from you! Perhaps *you* are the one who should remember their marriage vows, not me.'

'Men take mistresses all the time. You've told me you're a woman so now behave like one.'

'But poor little Shanni wasn't even given the "honour" of being your mistress, was she? She was just a plaything when you were bored.'

'Oh, for goodness' sake, forget that—this business of the railway is far more important. We could have doubled the amount of shares we owned if you had let me in on the deal.'

'You're the one being dense now, Dafydd,' Jayne said. 'I bought all the shares that were up for sale. You are to blame, not I, if you were left out of it.'

'You vixen!' For a moment he looked as though he would strike her, then he turned away.

'Before you leave the room let me make something clear to you. I'll never let you near me again now you've been with that—that harlot!'

'We'll see about that.'

He looked as if he was about to start arguing again, but Jayne spoke up quickly. 'I'm going to lie down, and if you even think of coming to my room I'll tell the whole world what you've been up to with Shanni Morgan, starting with Llinos Mainwaring. Now, wouldn't she be thrilled to hear such news?'

'So you'd wash your dirty linen in public? That's not like you, Jayne.'

'Well, as I said, I've changed, and the price of my discretion is that you keep away from me. I don't want you to touch me ever again. Do you understand?'

'Go to hell!' His face was red with anger.

Jayne brushed past him and hurried up the stairs. Once in her room she fell onto the bed. She had won some sort of victory but it was an empty one. Her marriage was over before it had had a chance to begin. She turned her face into the pillow and cried as if her heart would break.

CHAPTER TWENTY-TWO

'Katie, girl, why don't you stop moping about the place? I thought you were going out today to see Shanni.'

Katie looked up at Mrs Grinter and made an effort to smile. 'You're right. It's my day off and I shouldn't be sitting here wasting my life.' She got up from her chair.

'Aye, it's your day off *again*!' Cook grinned. 'You

211

have more days off than anyone I know. Still, it's a lovely spring day, the sun is shining and a young girl like you should be glad to be alive. Just forget that Bull Beynon and enjoy being young and healthy. Me, now, I have the bone-ache in every part of my body.'

'Oh, Cook, can I get you anything?'

'No, it's all right, love. I got my own remedy.' She winked and took a bottle of brandy from under the table. 'Couple of these and I won't be aching so much. Now, go on with you. See your friend Shanni and get out from under my feet, girl!'

'I'll get my coat and then I'll be off.' Katie picked up the basket Cook had loaded with good things for the invalid.

'Give Shanni my best, mind.' Cook eyed the basket. 'Tell her I baked her a *Teision lap* cake special.'

As Katie left the house she heard the birds singing and felt the soft breeze against her face, and knew that Cook had been right. It was time she put Bull Beynon out of her mind. She hadn't seen him for several days now and it seemed that he had made his choice between Rhiannon and her.

As she reached the top of the hill Katie paused, noticing how pretty Shanni's house looked in the sunlight. The windows were shining and the flowers were blooming in the little garden.

When she knocked and pushed open the door she was pleased to see Shanni sitting at the table peeling potatoes. 'You're looking much better today, Shanni. You've got more colour in your cheeks.' She put the basket on the table. 'Some goodies from Cook. She's a funny old woman but she's got a heart of gold.'

212

'That's very kind of her. Tell her thank you from me. Though I expect she's gossiping about me like everyone else in Swansea.'

'People gossip for a few days then go on to talk about someone else,' Katie said, and sat down. 'Are you really better, Shanni?'

'My body is, but I don't think my conscience will ever get over what I've done.'

'Give it time.' Katie felt the words were inadequate but she could find no others.

'Anyway, what else is going on in Swansea, Katie? They say the railway station is almost finished. I suppose there'll be a great deal of pomp and ceremony when it opens.'

There was a sudden rap at the door and Shanni frowned. 'Who's that, then? It's not rent day yet. Come in, whoever you are, don't stand there on the step making a nuisance of yourself.' There was no reply and Shanni got up with a sigh. She opened the door. 'Hello, Bull, what brings you here?'

'I would like to see Katie. I saw her coming up here and I followed her. I want to tell her I've got a house at last. If that's all right, Shanni.'

'You'd best come in, then,' Shanni said reluctantly.

Katie swallowed hard as Bull came into the room. 'I wanted to see you, Katie, to explain—'

'Well, that's too bad because I don't want to see you. How dare you come here? Just go away.'

'Please listen while I explain how things are. Rhiannon has told me what she said to you but she bent the truth to suit herself.'

'So it's not true that the poor girl would go back to selling herself for money? Not true that you chose her over me? Oh, Bull, just go. I don't want to see you ever again. Is that plain enough?'

Shanni took Bull's arm. 'Better go. This isn't the time or the place to sort your affairs out, Bull.' She closed the door behind him with a click. 'Well, that told him a thing or two. Are you happy now?' There was a hint of reproach in Shanni's voice.

'Yes, of course I'm happy,' Katie said defiantly. So why did she feel that her world had turned upside-down?

* * *

The town was thronged with people, cockle-women called out raucously advertising their wares, and dray-horses clip-clopped heavily on the cobbles, fetlocks fringed with hair that lifted in the breeze.

Llinos breathed in the scents and sounds of the town she loved. Swansea was where she had been born and where she would die. She thought of Joe far away in America with her first-born son Lloyd, and wished briefly that she was with them under the sunny skies of the plains. But then, looking around her, she knew she would never leave Swansea. She was growing too old to travel. She couldn't bear to make the long, arduous journey by sea and then by bone-rattling cart to the village where Joe had been born.

'Good morning, Llinos.' The voice came from behind her and she turned to see Jayne alighting from her carriage. The relationship between them was still a little strained: although Llinos had accepted Jayne's attempt to make amends she was still wary, suspecting that Jayne's overtures had not been entirely sincere.

'Hello, Jayne. You're looking well.' Llinos was

214

being polite for Jayne looked anything but: her cheeks had no colour and her eyes lacked sparkle.

'You're very kind.' Jayne kissed her cheek. 'Llinos, come and join me in the tea-rooms for a little while. I need a friend to talk to. If you can spare the time, that is.'

'Of course I can,' Llinos said quickly. 'How is your father?'

'What I want to talk about has nothing to do with him.' She led the way into the Mackworth Hotel and swept into the tea-rooms as though she owned the place. She was growing up, Llinos thought, and that was only to be expected now that she was a married woman.

Llinos settled herself into the seat held by the waiter and waited patiently for Jayne to speak. She looked so tired: even her skin looked dull. 'What's wrong, Jayne?' Llinos frowned. 'In spite of everything I'm very fond of you, you know.'

'Llinos, since I married Dafydd have you ever . . . well, has he made advances to you?'

Llinos's eyebrows were raised in surprise. 'Of course not! I wouldn't allow it. Once Dafydd married you, made his vows before God, he was lost to me for ever and we both knew it.'

Jayne waited until the tea had been served before she spoke again. 'He has been with Shanni Morgan.'

Llinos was shocked to the core—how on earth did Jayne know that? 'He did *what*?' She was playing for time, not knowing what to say.

'He was intimate with her and she was with child by him. How could he do that, Llinos, and with a girl of the lower orders?' Her voice was filled with anguish.

215

'Where did you hear this? You know how people love to gossip for the sake of it, and what they say is not always true.'

'It is true.' Jayne's head was bent, her voice low. 'I heard it from Shanni's own lips.'

'Why would she tell you that? It doesn't seem like Shanni to make trouble. I don't think—'

'I was at Mrs Keen's house and I overheard them talking. Mrs Keen helped her to get rid of the baby.' Jayne paused, and swallowed hard. 'She said it was all Shanni's fault for lying with a gentleman.'

'Well,' Llinos spread her hands wide, 'Dafydd isn't the only gentleman in the area.' She hated lying to Jayne, but how could she admit that she already knew the truth?

'I confronted her.' Jayne was shaking her head as if even now she could not believe what she was saying.

'She admitted it?'

'Yes, Llinos. In fact, she threw it up in my face, taunted me with it.'

Llinos swallowed hard. Dafydd was a changed man: the lover she had known would never have stooped so low. Would he? He had seduced her without thinking about Joe's feelings, and had fathered a son on her as if that was of little consequence. She wondered if she had ever really known him at all.

'Well . . . did you talk to Dafydd about it?'

'Of course I did. I told him our marriage was over, except in name. I won't let him near me again. I'll never forgive him, never.'

'Did he deny it?'

'He tried to, like the coward he is. And I thought I loved him—it just shows how wrong you can be.'

216

She sipped her tea, her eyes downcast.

Llinos felt an overwhelming pity for the girl. She wanted to comfort her but knew that Jayne would hate a public show of affection.

Jayne lifted her head and looked directly at Llinos with tears in her eyes. 'I only had one way to get back at him. I told him I had substantial shares in the Great Western Railway. He was so surprised it was insulting.'

'Jayne, I don't know what to say.' Llinos felt so angry with Dafydd—how could he have been so foolish as to seduce Shanni? 'What on earth possessed Shanni to risk her marriage for a sordid encounter with him?'

Jayne shrugged. 'All I know is that they betrayed me.' She looked up at Llinos almost apologetically. 'I know I hated you for having had Dafydd before me but at least he was free and single then.' She dabbed her eyes. 'I'll never trust another man.'

Llinos knew exactly how the girl felt. She poured more tea to give herself time to think. She searched for words of comfort, but there were none: Jayne was practically a newly-wed and already her husband had been unfaithful. She decided to change the subject. 'So you've got more shares in the railway, then? That was astute of you, Jayne. They're going to be like gold dust before long.'

'I know, and I'm going to set my mind on being a good businesswoman. If I can't be a happy wife then success must be my aim.'

'But, Jayne, your father will leave you his estate one day. You'll have more money than you can ever spend.'

'That's not the point, Llinos.'

'Then what is? Showing Dafydd that you can

manage very well without him is not going to mend your marriage.'

'Listen to me properly, Llinos. I don't want to mend it. The marriage is over and done with. I'll live with him, for the sake of appearances, but my love was wasted on him.'

'Don't do this to yourself, Jayne. Surely you want children one day. They will be your reason for living—you'll know that when you hold a baby in your arms.'

Jayne drained her cup and set it down in the saucer. 'I don't think I want to talk any more, Llinos,' she said quietly. 'Nothing will change what's happened, however much we go over it.' She glanced at Llinos from under her lashes. 'My husband already has a son—maybe more than one, for all I know.'

Llinos felt her colour rise. 'As you pointed out, Jayne, that was before you and Dafydd were married.'

'But you were a married woman, and anyone less honest than you would have passed off the child as her husband's.' She rose to her feet. 'For all I know there could be many little by-blows running around Swansea.'

'There's no need to be cruel, Jayne. Sion is not just a by-blow, and I don't think Dafydd sees him like that either. For what it's worth, I think this thing with Shanni was a silly mistake. He won't do it again.'

'Llinos, you're bound to defend him—you probably still love him.'

'No, Jayne, I don't.'

'Well, that's good for you, and now I have to go.'

Rhiannon looked around the hut, pleased that it was as clean and cheerful as she could make it. She had sewn bright new curtains to replace the faded ones and had covered the bed with the same fabric, which made the hut look more like a home. From the blackened pot over the fire came an appetizing aroma, and a loaf of fresh bread was already cut in slices, awaiting Bull's return. If he did return.

Since he had told her to find a new man and a new home, Rhiannon had kept her jealousy to herself. She had not mentioned Katie Cullen again, and neither had Bull. Rhiannon hoped it was all over, a moment of madness, because what would a strictly brought-up girl like Katie want with a man who worked the railway?

A figure loomed in the open doorway and Rhiannon looked up expectantly. She was disappointed. 'Oh, it's you, Seth, what do you want?'

He came into the room, smiling broadly. 'I hear it's over between you and Bull.' He slid his arm around her waist. 'Well, I'll be happy to take you on, girl. No need for you to go scraping about for a man.'

'What are you on about, Seth? You're talking in riddles.'

'No, I'm not. You and Bull are finished. He's courting Katie Cullen—it's being talked about all around the camp. So come on, I'll take you in and you won't have to go whoring like you was before.'

Rhiannon pushed him away angrily. 'You're wrong there, Seth. I'm not leaving Bull for anyone. I'm his woman and he'll break the neck of any man that says different.'

'But haven't you heard, girl? He's getting his house today. Some nice little place in Waterloo Street.'

The colour drained from Rhiannon's face. 'Who told you this?' she asked slowly, as if afraid of the answer.

'Bull told us all yesterday, same time as he said he'd still be watching us to see we did our work properly like he did when he was foreman.'

'When's he getting this house?'

Seth had his arm around her again. 'Today, like I said.'

'I don't believe you. I can't see Bull leaving me without a word of explanation. Look, all his things are still here, his boots, his moleskin trousers and . . .' She stopped as it dawned on her that the clothes Bull had left behind were working clothes, and if he was manager he would no longer need them. 'I can't believe it,' she said. 'Seth, go and leave me to think, will you?'

'All right, love, but remember I made an offer for you first.' He grinned. 'Your worth has gone up since you was Bull Beynon's woman, and any man in the camp would give you a bed, but as I said, I was the first to ask so remember that.'

He left the hut, and Rhiannon collapsed onto the floor. 'Oh, God in heaven, it can't be true! Bull wouldn't leave me like this.' The tears flowed down her cheeks. 'Bull, my love, my darling, don't leave me!'

After a while, she got up and, with an effort, lifted the cooking pot from the fire. Then she washed her face in the water brought freshly from the Baptist Well spring, and combed her hair into

220

some sort of order.

She would go to Waterloo Street and find out if Seth was telling the truth. It was just possible he'd been trying it on with her—after a bit of free loving from a woman he knew only too well.

Rhiannon winced as she thought back to the days when she had plied her trade as a wanton. Then she had accepted any of the navvies who would pay for her services. It was not something she liked to remember, and whatever Bull decided, she would not go back to the old life. She would rather starve.

A gentle breeze was blowing along the track, and from somewhere out of sight Rhiannon could hear the distant sound of a pickaxe against unyielding rock. Perhaps this was the end of her life as a navvy's woman. One thing was certain: she could never live at the side of the railway line and see Bull at work all day if he was living with Katie Cullen.

It did not take Rhiannon long to walk along the high street and through the town towards Waterloo Street, which looked a friendly, ordinary place. The doors of most of the houses were open and smoke issued from the chimney-stacks. It was quiet for hardly a soul was about, and it had an air of respectability that made Rhiannon realize how hopeless it was for her to expect to live there with Bull Beynon.

Greatly daring she knocked at one of the open doors. She heard shuffling footsteps and an old woman came into view.

'What d'yer want? Not selling pegs or cockles, are you, girl? I don't want to buy anything, I can't afford it. I'm just an old woman, as you can see.'

'I'm not selling anything.' Rhiannon forced a smile. 'I just wanted to know if someone has moved into Waterloo Street today or even yesterday.'

The old woman wrapped her shawl more closely around her thin shoulders. 'I 'spects you are talking about Mr Beynon. He's some kind of manager or other, is that it?'

'Which one is his house, can you tell me?' Rhiannon asked eagerly.

'He's moving into number five, just along the end of the road there. He's not about now, though. I saw him go out some time back. Gone down the Castle, I suppose, that's where all the railwaymen meet.'

Rhiannon moved away, aware that the old woman was watching her. She strolled past number five but there was no light in the window and no smoke rising from the chimney. He had not moved in yet.

Would he persuade Katie to live with him, now that he had a fine house? But Katie was the type to wait for a wedding ring on her finger.

'Chin up, girl,' Rhiannon said aloud. It was pointless to feel sorry for herself: whatever Bull decided there was nothing she could do about it.

She turned for home. Perhaps he was there . . . and perhaps he would keep her as his mistress when he moved into the house in Waterloo Street. Rhiannon would be content with whatever part of Bull he decided to give her.

Her steps quickened. Perhaps, after all, the future was not as bleak as she had imagined.

CHAPTER TWENTY-THREE

The spring sunshine was bringing out bright blossom on the trees. The air blowing in from the sea was balmy, and Katie walked along the beach with her boots in her hands, bare feet digging into the sand, wishing Bull was with her.

She sat down on a flat rock and stared out at the deceptively calm waves of Swansea Bay. Across the water she could see the hills of Devon in bright relief, a sure sign of rain. Within an hour the weather would be stormy, like her feelings. She remembered how Rhiannon had begged her not to take Bull away from her, and how, her heart broken, Katie had walked away. She looked out across the sands, stretching for five miles around the curve of the bay, half expecting Bull to come riding along on a white charger to sweep her off her feet. But the beach was deserted except for the plaintive cry of seagulls on the still air.

Katie wiped her eyes on her petticoat and went back towards the road. She leaned against the wall to pull on her boots, the sand gritty between her toes.

'So there you are, Katie Cullen. You've got him now, haven't you?'

The voice startled her. 'Rhiannon! What are you doing here, and what do you mean I've got him?'

'What I'm doing here is my business, but Bull's left me. Don't pretend you don't know,' Rhiannon said bluntly. 'He's taken all his stuff up to the house the engineer found for him.' She began to cry. 'I asked you to leave him alone, didn't I? Bull

223

was the only man who ever treated me decent, like. How am I going to manage on my own, tell me that, Katie Cullen?'

'The same way as I manage without him.' Katie was surprised at the hardness in her voice. 'I don't depend on any man to keep me.'

'Oh, mind, now, miss.' Rhiannon brushed away her tears. 'It's all so easy for you, isn't it? Where would I get a job in a good household? Tell me that.'

'The same way most girls do. Go up to one of the big houses and ask. Nothing's given to you on a plate in this life and it's time you knew that.'

'Oh, it's all right for the likes of you,' Rhiannon said, 'with your good clothes, your washed face and neatly combed hair. What do you know about living on your wits?'

'You haven't used *your* wits very well, though, have you?' Katie said. 'I wouldn't sell my body for food in my belly and clothes on my back, not when there's plenty of honest work for the taking.'

'So if I go up to Eynon Morton-Edwards and ask him to give me a position he'd take me on, would he?' Fresh tears rolled down Rhiannon's face. 'Within a week I'd be in his bed. He'll be no different from any of the men I've been with, except he has money.'

'Mr Morton-Edwards is a good man!' Katie protested. 'He would never take advantage of any girl. He's always been a perfect gentleman to me.'

'Well, he wouldn't want a girl like you, would he?' Rhiannon said spitefully. 'You're a Miss Goody Two Shoes. Any man would want me, with my looks and experience.' She sighed heavily. 'Who am I trying to fool? I don't get no respect from men, see, Katie. The only man to show me any feeling at all was my lovely Bull. And now he's gone, left me, and it's all your fault. What am I going to do?'

'Find work,' Katie said more kindly. 'If you don't want to go into service see what else is about. Go to the shops in Swansea and get a post as an assistant.' Suddenly she was exasperated. 'I don't know why I'm bothering with you. Do what you like, I don't care. Perhaps you can't do anything properly except sleep with men.'

'I could do the work you do any day of the week,' Rhiannon said angrily, 'but can't you see how the other servants would gossip about me, calling me a harlot, blaming everything that goes wrong in the house on me?'

'What if they did?' Katie challenged. 'Don't you think the men you go with will call you even worse names and their wives accuse you of ruining their marriages?'

'I don't know what to think. I just can't imagine my life without Bull in it.'

'You'll have to face up to it, Rhiannon,' Katie said. 'You must have known that Bull would leave you one day.'

'He didn't plan to, not until you came on the scene,' Rhiannon said bitterly. 'I've worked for that man until my fingers were raw, washing his clothes, cooking his food and warming his bed, and what thanks do I get?'

The idea of Rhiannon in bed with Bull was so painful that Katie turned and walked away. 'Just do whatever you like,' she said, in a parting shot. 'It's nothing to do with me, and I couldn't care less what happens to you.'

She continued uphill towards the Big House, aware that Rhiannon was behind her. She stopped and turned. Her voice hard with anger as she said, 'What do you think you're doing, following me like some stray cat?'

'I'm going to take your advice. I'm going to see if I can get a job like yours.'

'Huh!' Katie hurried on.

'You could at least wait for me or are you going to warn the other servants that I'm coming and put in a bad word for me?'

Katie turned round. 'For goodness' sake, stop feeling so sorry for yourself. I've lost Bull too. Do you think I'd have him now after what he's done? You say I've ruined your life, well, you've ruined mine too.'

Rhiannon caught her up, panting a little from the exertion. 'I know, I'm sorry.' She sounded almost humble. 'But Bull was mine, see, my man, and I loved him with all my heart. You hardly knew him. All you saw was the Bull who could charm the birds off the trees. You never saw the real man.'

There was probably a great deal of truth in what Rhiannon said but Katie was not going to admit it.

'And *you* never saw *us* together,' she said. 'We went out to supper with friends, he would meet me from choir practice, we were a respectable couple. You're the one he had to hide away in a rough shanty-town.'

'Oh, I know I'm not respectable, you don't have to rub it in. I'm just a trollop. But if you help me I can do better, I can try to be a good servant like you said.'

'It's asking a lot of me,' Katie put her basket on the ground and, her hands on her hips, faced

226

Rhiannon, 'and you've got the cheek of the devil, I'll give you that.' She was silent. 'I'll do my best for you, though I don't know why I'm bothering.' She pointed to the house on the rise above them. 'See, we're almost home now.'

'Home,' Rhiannon said wonderingly. 'I don't think I've had a proper home since I was a child.'

Suddenly Katie felt sorry for her. 'Well, as it happens, Cook's looking for a new kitchenmaid. I could put in a word for you.'

'You wouldn't have to help me if you'd left Bull alone.'

As Katie led the way into the cosy kitchen Cook looked up. 'Oh, there you are, Katie. And who's this you've brought with you?'

'Rhiannon wants to work for Mr Morton-Edwards. Do you think he'll see her?'

Cook continued to roll out the pastry but her eyes narrowed as she studied Rhiannon. 'I know you, girl. I've seen you down the market. You're one of them shanty-town girls, aren't you?'

'Come on, now, Cook, give her a chance,' Katie said gently.

Cook shook flour off her hands. 'If the master takes her on there's nothing I can do about it, but I'll not make friends with a loose woman—so you just keep out of my way.'

'Look,' Rhiannon said, 'this is my chance to make a better life for myself. Even the Good Book says to forgive, doesn't it?'

'Aye, I suppose it does. But don't you bring your loose ways up here.' Cook looked at Katie. 'I'll see what the master says about all this.'

Katie sighed with relief and pushed the kettle onto the hob. As she waited for it to boil, she

227

watched Cook slip the round of dough over a plate and neatly cut away the overhanging edges.

'What's your name, girl?' Cook looked up briefly from her work.

'Rhiannon . . . Rhiannon Beynon,' she said. 'At least, that's what the other women called me.' She smiled for the first time since she had entered the kitchen. 'Along with other names not suitable to repeat in decent company.'

A glimmer of a smile crossed Cook's lips. 'Right, then, Rhiannon, hand me some lemon curd while I beat some egg whites for the meringue.'

Once the pie was safely in the oven Cook sat down opposite Rhiannon. 'You was with Bull Beynon, then?' she asked, stirring a generous amount of sugar into her tea. She looked at Katie. 'And what do you make of all this, her wanting a job here an' all?'

Rhiannon spoke up quickly. 'You've said you'll help me, haven't you, Katie?'

Katie hoped vainly that Cook would change the subject.

'Our Katie don't seem too sure of that. What happened with Bull, then? Didn't he want you to live with him in his new place?' Cook smiled wickedly and answered her own question. 'But, then, it wouldn't pay him to have a trollop in tow, not now he's got a better job and a respectable house to live in.'

'I know I'm a trollop, Cook,' Rhiannon said firmly. 'I don't need my nose rubbed in it.'

'Oh, nothing personal, mind,' Cook said. She got to her feet. 'I'll go to see the master now. I've got to ask him how many will be here for supper anyway.'

Rhiannon fell silent and Katie looked anywhere but in her direction. How *would* she feel having Bull's woman working with her, day in day out? It wouldn't be easy.

A few minutes later Mrs Grinter returned. 'Mr Morton-Edwards says he'll leave it to me to decide whether we keep you or not,' she said, 'so let's get to work, Rhiannon, and see how you shape up. You can help with the washing up for now. Later we need potatoes peeled and floors will want scrubbing. There's enough to do in this kitchen, goodness knows, and we need another pair of hands. You look like a big strong girl, so let's see how we get on.'

Katie glanced at Rhiannon, who looked daunted. 'You'll get used to it, don't worry.' In spite of all that had passed between them, she hoped Rhiannon would make a go of the job. Anything must be better than the life she'd led before.

Katie was polishing the curving banisters when the drawing-room door opened and Mr Morton-Edwards came into the hall. 'Ah, Katie, get Father Martin's coat, will you, please? Has Cook reached a decision about the new girl?'

Katie looked at her feet. She was still shy in the presence of her master. 'Yes, sir. Cook's given her work to do in the kitchen.' She glanced up briefly. 'I think Rhiannon will fit in, sir.'

'I'm glad to hear it.' He turned to Father Martin and shook his hand. 'Goodbye, old friend. If you're sure you can't stay to eat with me, I'll see you tomorrow.'

Katie handed the vicar his coat and opened the front door for him. On the step he stopped and looked down at her. 'I know all about Rhiannon,'

229

he said. 'I minister to all the railwayfolk, including the women.' He frowned. 'I know she was living with Bull Beynon, and as you were walking out with him that puts you in a difficult position. It shows a great spirit of Christian charity that you are willing to work with her. You are, aren't you?'

'Yes, sir,' Katie said.

'You don't really mean that, do you, Katie?' The look of sympathy on his face almost made Katie cry. 'Look, my dear, Bull wanted to make you his wife. Doesn't that mean anything to you? You're a respectable young woman and you must find it difficult to understand the loose-living ways of the navvies, but we mustn't judge lest we be judged.'

'Yes, sir.' Katie wished he would leave her alone: he was only driving the hurt deeper.

'I can see you're not happy about all this, Katie,' Father Martin said, 'but Bull only took in Rhiannon because she was being badly used by the other men. He gave her a home when no one else would have her but that doesn't mean he loved her.'

'He should have been honest with me from the start then, Father,' Katie said. 'It's the deceit I can't abide.'

'That's a little unrealistic, Katie, surely?' Father Martin seemed determined to talk the matter through. 'Bull took that way of life for granted and he could hardly ask you to understand that he was living with another woman, could he?'

'Why not? He should have tried. Anyway, sir, it's over between me and Bull.'

'Are you sure, Katie? Will you throw away a chance of love for the sake of your pride?' When Katie didn't answer he went on, 'Most men will

230

have enjoyed a dalliance with one lady or another before they settle down. That's how things are in the world, my dear. Why not give him another chance? I'm sure he deserves it.'

Mr Morton-Edwards came to her rescue. 'Go about your business, Martin,' he said smiling. 'You're gossiping like an old woman there.'

Katie had only just closed the door behind Father Martin when the bell rang loudly in the quiet of the hall. Mr Morton-Edwards glanced towards her. 'Please, Katie, answer that for me, and tell my visitor I'll see him in the library, would you?'

Katie opened the door as he disappeared from sight. The evening light made her blink and it was a moment before she realized Bull was standing on the step. 'Oh, it's you.' She swallowed. 'The master says you're to go through to the library.' She pointed. 'It's the fourth door across the hall.' Although she tried not to look at him her eyes were drawn to him. He was unfamiliar in his new clothes, with his hair neatly trimmed and a hat in his hand. 'Katie,' he said softly, 'I love you. Please give me another chance.'

'I have work to do.'

He caught her arm. 'Please, Katie, won't you give me a chance to explain things to you?'

His nearness was driving her mad and she wanted to hit him for the pain he'd caused her. 'We've been through all this,' she said quietly. 'You were living with Rhiannon, she was like a wife to you, and you kept that from me.'

'Because I knew you would be shocked and hurt. I wanted you to get to know me and thought then you might understand my reasons for taking her

231

in.'

'But you and she were . . . Well, she wasn't just a housekeeper to you, was she?'

'No, she wasn't—but I'm an ordinary man, Katie, I need a little love and comfort after a day on the line, working my body almost to breaking point. I'm no plaster saint and I can't apologize for what I did before I met you.'

He had a point. 'Bull, just give me a little time, and then perhaps we can try again.'

Bull's face lit up. 'Do you mean that, Katie?'

'Yes, I suppose I do.'

The door from below stairs opened and Rhiannon rushed out. 'Oh, Bull, I knew it was your voice I heard. Have you come to fetch me? Is that why you're here?' She clung to him tightly.

Bull looked from Rhiannon to Katie, his colour rising. 'What are you doing here, Rhiannon?'

'Katie helped me get a job in service—so you see I've changed now, Bull, I'm respectable.'

'I'm sorry, Rhiannon.' Bull disengaged himself from her embrace. 'I meant what I said. You have no place in my life now, I'm sorry.'

Rhiannon fell back, then turned on Katie. 'See what you've done? You've set him against me. I'll never forgive you for this, Katie Cullen.' She retreated towards the kitchen.

Before Katie could speak she heard the master call, 'Katie, if that is my visitor send him in at once.'

'I'll speak to you later, Katie,' Bull said, as he went towards the library. 'We can talk properly then.'

As the door closed behind the two men Katie sat on the stairs, still clutching the duster, and asked herself why life was so complicated. Her heart was telling her to listen to Bull, to forgive him, but her head was telling her she could not trust him.

She wanted to cry but instead she rubbed her cloth into the tin of beeswax and began, very carefully, to polish the banister.

CHAPTER TWENTY-FOUR

Llinos looked at the letter again. At last Joe was coming home to her. Lloyd was staying with 'his people': he had chosen a bride from the tribe of Mandan Indians and he was remaining with her on the plains of America. Llinos sank into a chair. Now that the damage was done and their son had been coerced into living like a savage, Joe was coming back to her.

'You fool, Joe!' Llinos said to herself. She'd had plans for Lloyd, plans that had involved him marrying well, living a gentleman's life in Swansea, giving her grandchildren. 'Joe, how could you do this to me?'

Eventually, she folded the letter and put it into a drawer. It was pointless to write a reply because Joe would be half-way across the Atlantic by the time it arrived in America. As for Lloyd, he no longer seemed to care about her: there was not even a personal note from him in Joe's letter. It seemed that her elder son had shaken the dust of Swansea from his feet for good.

Llinos smoothed down her hair. She was meeting Eynon in town and she didn't want him to see that she was upset. Eynon, her dear friend, he was always honest with her, would never betray her. Llinos sighed. She guessed that her meeting with him this afternoon had something to do with Jayne: Eynon always consulted her when he was uneasy about his daughter.

It was a fine warm day and as her carriage drew up outside the Mackworth Hotel tea-rooms Llinos told herself she would enjoy her afternoon with Eynon. She would forget her woes and laugh with him as she used to.

He was there before her, waiting in the plush lounge with a glass of brandy at his side and a cigar in his hand. He rose to greet her with a smile of pleasure. 'Llinos, how good to see you.' He took her gloved hands and kissed her wrists. 'As beautiful as ever.'

His hair was perhaps a paler shade of gold now, touched with white, and his face bore the marks of time, but his eyes were as bright as they always had been.

'Will you have wine, Llinos, or tea perhaps?'

'Tea, please. Let's take it in the conservatory— this sunshine is too good to miss.'

The waiter led the way, carrying Eynon's glass on a silver tray as if it were a priceless treasure. The respect he was accorded by the people of Swansea meant that Eynon was treated with great courtesy wherever he went.

The sun-splashed conservatory was a pleasure to behold, with plants and inviting soft sofas. Llinos felt almost content. Here with Eynon there was no need for polite conversation: they were at ease with each other, a mark of their lasting friendship.

'Any news of Joe?' Eynon had seated himself opposite her, and as their eyes met, Llinos's resolve not to talk about her problems evaporated.

'Funny you should ask,' she said dryly. 'I had a letter this morning.'

'Not good news, then.'

'It seems that my son has found an American Indian wife and intends to settle there with her.'

Eynon took her hand. 'I can see you're upset, Llinos, but Lloyd is a man and must make his own way in the world.'

Llinos smiled briefly. 'You sound like Joe.'

'Perhaps I've learned to be more philosophical about things now that I'm an old man.'

'Stuff and nonsense, you'll never be an old man! If I admit you're old I'll have to be old myself and I can't allow that, can I?'

The waiter brought the tray of tea and set it on the table: the fine bone china was almost translucent in the sunlight. 'Why can't life always be so pleasant, Eynon?'

'Because the people around us complicate it,' Eynon replied. 'You and I should abandon our families and run away together, live on some sunny island off the Spanish coast.'

'That sounds wonderful.'

'But it's an impossible dream, isn't it, Llinos? You have your family and I have mine, and they go on needing us. At least Sion is too young to be a trouble yet.'

'He's a joy.' She drank some tea, and looked at Eynon over the rim of her cup. 'But you want to talk to me about Jayne, don't you?'

'You're a witch, girl! How do you always know what I'm thinking?'

'Feminine intuition.'

'Well, I *am* worried about Jayne, it's true, but that's not the only reason I want to see you, Llinos.

235

I just love being with you.'

Llinos hid a sigh. 'What's wrong with Jayne?'

'The poor child is unhappy, and I don't know what to do about it.'

'Has she talked to you?' Llinos was determined not to give anything away. If Jayne chose to discuss her marriage with her father that was her business, but Eynon would hear nothing about it from Llinos's lips.

'No, but she and Buchan hardly speak to each other. The atmosphere between them is so strained it's almost impossible to have a decent conversation with them.'

'Have you any idea why?' Llinos tried to hide her discomfort.

'I think something is seriously wrong but I don't know what it is. Do you, Llinos?'

'Would Jayne tell me about her marital problems?' She was not being honest with him but it was not her place to tell him the truth about his son-in-law.

'Jayne has bought a substantial amount of railway shares and Dafydd is angry about it,' Eynon said. 'I think that's what started the downward slide.'

'Why should Dafydd worry about the shares?' Llinos said. 'After all, they both have more money than they will ever need.'

Eynon smiled wryly. 'It's not about the money, though, is it, Llinos? It's about power, about Jayne doing what Buchan could not in buying into the Great Western Railway.' He smiled proudly. 'She was one step ahead of him there.'

'Jayne is an astute young lady.' Llinos poured more tea and tried to be calm. If Eynon knew what

236

had really gone wrong in his daughter's marriage he would take a horse-whip to Dafydd as sure as night followed day. 'Dafydd is a man and Jayne will always outwit him.'

'You're very sure of female superiority. And they say man has the better mind.'

Llinos smiled. 'Ah, but it was a man who said that.'

Eynon lifted his hands in defeat. 'I give in. I can't win an argument with you or with my daughter.'

'And that proves my point. But if you want my advice, just keep away from Jayne's marriage.'

'Can I do that, though, Llinos?'

'You *have* to, or you'll be in the wrong whatever you do or say. Just lend a sympathetic ear and say as little as possible. Haven't you learned yet that a parent's place is to be in the wrong? Jayne will sort out her own problems—she's a capable young woman.'

'I suppose you're right. Now, let's forget Jayne and talk about other things,' he made a wry face, 'because whenever I think of Buchan I have the strongest urge to kill him.'

Llinos had not realized Eynon's feelings went so deep. She steered the conversation into safer channels and they talked about their childhood, and Llinos's latest dragon patterns.

'This is pleasant, Eynon,' Llinos said. 'Remembering the past is so peaceful.'

'We're good for each other, Llinos,' Eynon said. 'You and I are like a pair of gloves—meant to be together.'

'Go on with you!' Llinos said. 'You're a sentimental old fool.'

'I thought you told me I wasn't old.' When

Eynon laughed his whole face lit up and Llinos saw, as she often had, what an attractive man he was. It was a pity she had not fallen in love with him. How uncomplicated her life might have been if she had.

Eynon touched her hand. 'You're still a beautiful woman, Llinos—fine eyes, hardly a touch of grey in your hair and a figure most young girls would envy.'

'Flatterer! But I confess I was thinking much the same of you. I think you grow more handsome as the years go on.'

'You see? A matched pair as I said.'

The door to the conservatory swung open and Llinos saw Dafydd Buchan walking towards her. By the look on his face he was not happy. He came across the room with measured steps and Llinos knew that something was very wrong.

Without asking, he sat down and faced Eynon. 'I've spent all morning looking for you,' he said abruptly. 'You have to talk sense into your daughter. She's a stubborn, foolish woman.'

Eynon bristled. 'How dare you come in here and interrupt us without so much as a by-your-leave?'

Dafydd ignored him. 'Many a husband would take a stick to her for the way she's behaving,' he grated.

'I would not advise you to do anything of the sort.' Eynon's voice was filled with loathing. 'If you lay a hand on my daughter I will thrash you myself.'

'You don't understand,' Dafydd persisted, still not looking at Llinos. 'She refuses to do her marital duty by me.'

As his words sank in Eynon smiled. 'Is that all? I thought she had at least taken a lover or two. Good heavens, man, haven't you learned the art of seduction yet?'

Llinos tried to defuse the situation. 'Dafydd, please lower your voice,' she said, 'or do you want the whole of Swansea discussing your grievances?'

He looked at her then, his eyes cold. 'This has nothing to do with you. It must be sorted out man to man.'

Llinos was appalled. She had never thought Dafydd considered women inferior to men but now he was telling her to keep her place. She picked up her bag and gloves. 'Perhaps I should leave you two *gentlemen* to get on with it, then.'

'No!' Eynon said. 'Please, Llinos, stay. I won't have this—this blackguard drive you away. I'll take you home when I'm ready.'

He turned to look at Dafydd. 'So my daughter does not wish to share your bed.'

'That is so. How am I to get children if my wife will not obey me? Tell me that.'

'I'm afraid I've no advice to offer on that score.' Eynon grinned. 'I was never in such a position.'

'I'm not lacking in manhood, as Llinos will confirm.' He did not look at her but Llinos was outraged. Humiliated and angry, she wished she was anywhere but in the sunny conservatory of the Mackworth Hotel being insulted.

'I must go.' She got up, almost tripping in her haste.

Just then Jayne came into the conservatory, serene, in control of herself. As always, she looked elegant, hair shining and curled, her clothes freshly pressed. She crossed the floor and stood beside her husband.

'So, Father, are you going to tell me to do my duty and be a good wife?' She sounded amused rather than angry. 'If so, you will be wasting your breath.'

'Sit down, Jayne, and you too, Llinos. People are staring,' Eynon said. 'Come, let's talk this over like civilized people.' He was still angry, but for the sake of appearances he was doing his best.

Reluctantly Llinos took her seat again. She knew Jayne's iron will, and the girl looked very sure of herself.

'Jayne,' Eynon said, 'I'm not going to lecture you. You are grown-up, a married woman, and you must sort out your own affairs in private.'

'Huh!' Jayne's eyes were on her father. 'It's not me having the "affairs" but my precious husband.'

Llinos took a deep breath. The worst was going to happen: Jayne was about to tell her father everything.

'Jayne, shall we talk privately?' she asked gently, but Jayne was in no mood to listen.

'I've had enough of secrecy,' she said, 'enough of covering up for my loving husband.'

'Covering up?' Eynon frowned, 'What do you mean, Jayne? What's happened?'

Jayne smiled thinly. 'My dear husband has been unfaithful to me, Father. He's bedded with Shanni Morgan, a common little slut if ever I saw one.'

The conservatory was filled with people but silence had fallen on the room as everyone stared at Jayne Buchan.

'Jayne, don't do this to your father,' Llinos said quickly. 'Let's go home and talk this over, like sensible adults.'

'I'm not going home with *him* ever again.' She stared at her husband. 'If he wants harlots he can have them, but he's not coming to me afterwards. I won't have it.'

'Jayne!' Dafydd's voice was hard. 'Keep your voice down. You sound like a fishwife.'

'I thought fishwives were your preference, these days.' Her voice was heavy with sarcasm. 'And, to be honest, I'd rather be without your favours—they were never up to much anyway.' She smiled at Llinos. 'A quick fumble and it was over. I'm surprised you bothered with him after a man like Joe.'

'Enough of this!' Llinos's voice rang out in the silence. 'I won't be involved in such a disgraceful scene. How dare you bring my name into this disgusting tirade?' Her colour high, she swept out of the room and made her way through the lounge to the glass doors and into the street, her cheeks burning. Her reputation was low enough already in the town but now it must have sunk even further.

She lifted her head to allow the breeze to play on her face. One thing was certain: she wanted nothing more to do with Jayne or with Dafydd. Yet as she walked along the street, for the first time in her life Llinos felt old and ugly.

CHAPTER TWENTY-FIVE

Shanni stared in horror at her husband. Pedr was red-faced as he stood in the kitchen, his hands clenched. He had left home in a good mood to drink at the Castle with the navvies, and had come home in a furious temper.

'Tell me, then, my dear wife,' his voice was harsh, 'if you let Dafydd Buchan under your skirts how many others have been there?'

Shanni swallowed hard. 'Where on earth did you get that idea from, Pedr?'

'Don't bother to lie to me, Shanni.' He sat down and put his head in his hands. 'There was a row down at the Mackworth Hotel and your name came into it. You were even having his child! How could you, Shanni? How could you do that to me?'

Shanni wished the ground would open and swallow her. 'I'm so sorry, Pedr,' she said desperately. 'I didn't mean it to happen, honestly, and it was only the once.'

'Oh, is that supposed to make me feel better? You lie down for my employer without a thought for me and you tell me now it was only the once. Why? Didn't you satisfy him, then? Or was it done when he was bored and you were handy for him?'

Shanni began to cry. 'I don't know why I did it— I don't care for him, I love you, Pedr.'

'You love me! You love me so much that the minute I'm away you're bedding another man. You call that love, do you? I don't know how I'm going to live with this.'

'Please, Pedr, don't cry.' Shanni saw his tears with horror. 'I didn't mean to hurt you, I really didn't.' She knelt on the floor beside his chair. 'Pedr, I want to make it up to you. Will you just let me try again?'

'I don't know if I can ever forgive you, Shanni. I don't know what to do.' The tears were streaming down his cheeks. 'I want to kill you, Shanni. I want to put my hands around your throat and strangle the life out of you. And yet I love you, God help me!'

'I deserve it all,' Shanni sobbed. 'I've made the worst mistake of my life because it's you I love,

Pedr. If you give me another chance I promise with all my heart I won't ever stray again.'

'How can I trust you, Shanni? How can I work for the bastard who took my wife?'

'We'll go away,' Shanni said. 'Move to another part of the country, work at a different pottery.' She put her arms around his neck and hugged him close. 'I love you so much, Pedr, I really do. I'd give my life for you—please believe me.'

She pressed her cheek to his and their tears mingled. 'I'm sorry, so sorry, Pedr. What a fool I've been. I wouldn't blame you if you never wanted to see me again.'

He held her close then, his arms warm around her. 'You're my woman, Shanni, and I can't live without you.'

'What have I done to you, my love?' she said brokenly.

Pedr took a deep, shuddering breath. 'We'll sort it out. I'll find work somewhere else as you say, move right away from Swansea, go where no one has ever heard of that bastard Dafydd Buchan.'

Shanni closed her eyes and breathed in the familiar scent of her husband. She knew she would go to the ends of the earth with him, if he asked her to. She kissed his cheek, his forehead and then his lips, and they clung together like children lost in a storm. 'I hate Dafydd Buchan but I hate myself so much more,' she said, her voice full of tears.

'Hush now, we'll say no more about it. Let us try to pick up the pieces and see if we can get on with our life, Shanni.'

'We will, Pedr. I'll be the best wife in the world, I promise you.' She got to her feet and wiped away the tears with the back of her hand. 'Now, my love, shall I make us a nice cup of tea?'

Pedr nodded, unable to speak, and as Shanni pushed the kettle onto the fire she made a silent vow that, whatever it cost her, she would make it up to Pedr.

*   *   *

Katie was arranging flowers when Mr Morton-Edwards came into the house. His face was unusually flushed and his mouth set in a thin line. His daughter was with him and she looked pale and upset but in control of herself. Katie bobbed a curtsey and took their coats.

They went into the drawing room and closed the door. 'I don't think I can even make a pretence of living with him, Father.' She made no attempt to lower her voice. 'I have no respect left for my husband. He's a weak, stupid man.'

'Jayne, I'm furious with Buchan for the way he caused a scene but most married men have their mistresses.'

'Well, then, their wives are at fault for allowing it!' Jayne said angrily. 'I will not be intimate with a man who has taken another woman.'

Katie felt sorry for Mrs Buchan: it seemed they were in the same boat. Not that she and Bull were married.

'But, Jayne, think of the scandal if you were to leave your husband. What part would you take in society then? You would be shunned by all the wives, who would see you as a threat.'

'I would hate to be left out of everything, but how can I bear to be in the same house as Dafydd?'

'Don't you love him at all, Jayne?' Mr Morton-

244

Edwards asked quietly. 'You were so hell-bent on marriage that I believed he was everything in life to you.'

'Well, he is—he was.' There was a tremor in Jayne's voice. 'But my pride will not allow me to—'

'To hell with pride!' her father said sternly. 'Go home to your husband before you lose him altogether.'

'But, Papa, how can I allow him into my bed after what he's done?'

'It was only once, you say?'

'As far as I know.' Jayne sighed. 'But if he's been unfaithful once what's to say he won't be again?'

'There are no guarantees in life, Jayne, and it's time you learned that. Make the best of the happy times and put up with the bad. That's what most wives do—husbands, too, come to that.'

There was a sudden thundering on the front door and Katie almost knocked over the flowers. She opened the door and drew back as Mr Buchan stormed into the house.

He walked straight past her and into the drawing room. All Katie could hear then was subdued voices, so whatever passed between the married couple she did not know, but a few minutes later Mr Buchan emerged and his wife was with him.

Jayne's pale hair was ruffled, her cheeks were red and tears stood in her eyes. 'My coat, Katie.'

Katie helped her into it, then stood back as Mr Buchan led his wife away. She saw the droop of Jayne's shoulders and knew how she was feeling.

'Ah, Katie.' Mr Morton-Edwards was standing in the doorway of the drawing room, making an effort to behave as though nothing was wrong. 'Ask Cook to serve supper early tonight. I'll be going out.'

'Yes, sir.' Katie bobbed a curtsey and left for the kitchen.

Mrs Grinter patted the seat beside her. She'd sat down for a few minutes' rest. 'Tell me what's been going on above stairs.'

'Mr and Mrs Buchan had a falling out,' she said, reluctant to gossip yet not wishing to snub Cook. 'She came home with her father but Mr Buchan appeared and he's taken her home with him.'

'Well, I knew that much!' Cook frowned. 'What was they saying, though? Is he confessing he's done wrong or what?'

Katie hesitated. 'Well, the row was about Shanni Morgan.' She took a deep breath. What was the point in being discreet when her so-called betters were behaving like children? 'Mrs Buchan knows he put Shanni in the way for a baby.'

'*Duw, duw!* No wonder she's mad at him. I don't blame her one little bit.' She clucked her tongue in disapproval. 'Some of these gentry are no better than they should be.'

Katie was tired and dispirited. Why were men such fools for a pretty face, even Bull Beynon, a man she had thought she could trust? 'Is there any man true to his vows, Cook?' she said softly. She saw Rhiannon smile at her naïvety and felt a little foolish.

'Bless you, no, child. Show a man a trim ankle and he falls for it every time. If you saw what I've seen over the years you'd have no respect for men at all. That's why I'm on my own, see? What about you, Rhiannon? What do you think about men? Are you getting over that Bull Beynon now?'

Rhiannon sighed. 'I suppose I've got to.' She looked at Katie. 'I was wrong to warn you off Bull.

246

He's not mine any more, he's made that plain enough even for me. One of us might as well be happy.'

'I don't know I can trust him again,' Katie said reluctantly.

'I suppose he took it for granted that you knew, you silly girl.' Rhiannon shook her head. 'What do you think men and women from the track do? Play at house like children or what?'

Cook leaned her fat elbows on the table and saved Katie from having to reply. 'What's my orders for supper then? I 'spects you've got something to tell me, haven't you?'

'You're to serve supper early, the master is going out,' Katie answered.

'I'd better get to work, then. The soup's done and the roast's in the oven but I've yet to make the custard for the pudding. Get me some eggs from the cold larder, will you, Katie? And you, Rhiannon, get me a nice big mixing-bowl.' She clapped her hands. 'Time to go back to work, girls.'

*   *   *

It was Sunday, the church bells were ringing clearly on the soft breeze and Bull was gazing at the unfamiliar street outside his window. On the trackside the men would be leaving for the public bars, the women sitting outside on the grass verges and the smell of roasting meat would pervade the air. He felt very alone.

Now that the line had been laid into Swansea, he'd begun his duties as manager and he revelled in the extra responsibility but he felt he had lost the camaraderie of the navvies.

247

The churches and chapels were emptying now and respectably dressed worshippers were on their way home. Bull saw a family coming along the road, a father, mother and three young children, all clutching prayer-books. Somehow it was a comforting sight.

He was about to turn away from the window when he saw her, and his heart pounded in his chest like a drum. Katie was still a little way off but he would have known her anywhere. He held his breath. Was she coming to see him? He could scarcely believe it when she hesitated at his gate then pushed it open and came along the path to his house.

He opened the door before she could knock and stood back for her to enter. She smelled of fresh grass and flowers, and there was a bloom on her cheeks as she looked up at him. 'I thought I'd come calling, Bull, is it all right?'

He resisted the temptation to pull her into his arms and kiss her full lips. 'Of course it's all right. You can knock on my door at any time.'

He led her into the parlour and watched as she seated herself, carefully arranging her skirts around her small feet. 'Does this mean you're willing to try again, Katie? It's so long since we've talked properly I thought you'd changed your mind about us.'

'I had to have time to think things through,' Katie said. 'And I'm seeing things a little differently now, but I must ask, have you really finished with Rhiannon for good?'

'We haven't seen each other since she started work up at the Big House,' Bull said. 'She'll tell you if you ask her—Rhiannon was never a liar.'

'She's told me that you and her are finished.' Katie's smile was tremulous. 'She said one of us might as well be happy.'

'That's generous of her.'

'It's not only Rhiannon who's made me see things differently,' Katie said. 'There was a bad row up at the house between Mr and Mrs Buchan, and I realized that no man is perfect.' She smiled more confidently. 'No woman either.'

'So we're walking out again, then?'

'I suppose so.'

'I won't take liberties with you, Katie. I won't push you into anything you don't want.'

'I know.'

'Can you trust me now, Katie? I promise on my oath never to do anything to hurt you again.'

'It looks like men think nothing of taking a mistress. Are you sure you won't be like that, Bull? You won't go running back to Rhiannon if we have a disagreement or something?'

'Let me just prove it to you, Katie. I didn't take any other woman the whole time I was with Rhiannon, and I admit I was wrong not to tell you about her straight off.'

'I realized you needed a woman to care for you, to cook and wash your clothes and see to your comforts, but it never crossed my mind she'd share your bed.' She looked down at her hands. 'And when I saw Rhiannon, when I saw she was real flesh and blood and so beautiful, I was angry and jealous.'

At her words Bull felt a thrill of pride: Katie was admitting that she had been jealous of Rhiannon, which showed she cared about him. 'I promise I'll never make you feel like that ever again.'

Katie looked so demure, so untouched and somehow vulnerable sitting there with her skirts spread around her that Bull had to resist the temptation to grab her and shower her with kisses. 'Shall we go for a walk?' he asked tentatively. 'It's a lovely day.'

'I'd like that.' Katie rose to her feet with alacrity, and Bull knew she had been uncomfortable at being alone with him in his house.

He felt ten feet tall as he walked down the broad, tree-lined street with Katie on his arm. She was so sweet, so tiny, and with her hair in shining curls beneath her hat, she was all he could ever want in life. She was a rare treasure, and he was so lucky to have her.

'I'll make you happy always, Katie,' he said, and though he considered himself a strong man, he was surprised to find tears of happiness in his eyes.

CHAPTER TWENTY-SIX

Llinos watched, her heart thudding, as she saw her husband alight from a hansom cab outside the pottery buildings. He was thinner, his shoulders were stooped, and he looked like a sick old man. Then, as he came closer, she could see that his skin was golden, highlighted by the sun on the American plains. He still looked so handsome that her heart ached for what they had once been together: faithful lovers, devoted husband and wife.

But that was before Joe's squaw had come on the scene—Joe had been half in love with Sho Ka, though he never would admit it. Llinos knew she was not blameless either, for she had been besotted with Dafydd Buchan, but she had never loved him as she loved Joe. Perhaps even now it was not too late to make a fresh start.

'Joe! It's good to see you home again.' She hugged him, and when she smelt his familiar scent she felt like a girl again. His lips lingered on hers for a long time, and then, arm in arm, they walked through the hall and into the drawing room.

'Llinos, my beautiful girl, my little firebird, if only you knew how much I've longed to hold you like this.' He kissed her properly now that they were alone, his lips hot. Joe was a passionate man, so how had he lived without her for all these long months?

She held him away from her. 'You didn't console yourself with a young squaw, did you?' She hated the suspicion that rose inside her like a snake, but somehow she felt the words had to be said.

'I'm an old man now, Llinos.' Joe had chosen to ignore her sharpness. 'I have energy only for my wife.' He kissed her again and she pressed herself to him, feeling the old magic his touch roused in her.

'Joe, my darling, how did we let our love slip away from us?' She rested her head on his shoulder. 'We were meant for each other, why did we spoil it?'

'Let's forget the past, Llinos,' Joe said softly. 'We're here together now so let's enjoy each other. Come, sit down and let me tell you the news of our son.'

'Is Lloyd happy?' Llinos tried to keep the bitterness out of her voice. Joe should have brought him home so that he could tell her face to face that he was happy. 'And is he well?'

'He sends his love,' Joe said. 'I've brought you letters from him, and a drawing of Lloyd with his bride by one of the old braves. Lloyd is accepted as one of the tribe, and though I know it upsets you, you must believe he's happy.'

'That's all I want for him, but I can't help feeling I've lost him.'

'No, you'll never lose him. He's your firstborn son.'

His words were like a rebuke, even though he had not meant them that way. 'How is Sion?' The question was forced from him, and Llinos knew that the past still hurt him.

'He is well, Joe. I enrolled him in a good school a month ago, and he writes to me every week.'

Joe held her hand and kissed it but Llinos knew what he was thinking. 'With him out of the way, you won't be reminded of my infidelity, will you, Joe?'

'I wasn't going to speak of it but now you've brought the subject up I'd like to know if you've seen anything of Buchan while I've been away. I know he's the boy's father, but I can't abide the thought of him being in my house.'

Llinos pushed aside the old feelings of guilt. 'Sion has known only one father and that's you, Joe.'

'You haven't answered my question.'

'I've seen little of Dafydd Buchan. He's a married man,' she frowned, 'though it seems he has trouble remembering that. He's been involved in a scandal and Jayne is bitterly hurt by it.'

'What sort of scandal?'

'The usual sort. He got Shanni Morgan with

252

child. In a moment of madness the poor girl lost so much.' Before Joe could speak Llinos held up her hands. 'I know, that is exactly what I did, and I can see now how foolish I was. But please believe me when I say I can look at him now and feel nothing for him.'

Joe smiled then. 'You've never lied to me, Llinos, my love, and I know you wouldn't start now.'

'So can we make this a new beginning for us, Joe?'

'I think we can, my little firebird.' He took her hand and kissed it. 'I might be getting on in years but you still have the power to move me, Llinos.' He turned her hand over and nuzzled the softness of her palm. 'And looking at you now, how beautiful you are, I know I've always loved you more than anyone else in the world.'

He drew her close and Llinos vowed she would never do anything to hurt him again.

*   *   *

Katie sat on the grass verge that ran along the edge of the bay and stared out at the ships in full sail. 'Aren't they beautiful?' She glanced shyly at Bull. 'With the sails bending to the wind they look like nuns bowing to their devotions before the altar.'

Bull touched her hand lightly, and Katie allowed him to curl his fingers in hers. 'It's wonderful being here with you, Bull, with the sun shining and the birds singing.' Katie sighed. 'I wish today could last for ever.'

'Once we're married, we'll be together always, Katie.' His voice was gruff and she knew he was as moved as she by the beauty of their surroundings. 'I have to ask you something, Katie,' Bull's fingers tightened around hers, 'and please don't be angry, but how is Rhiannon settling into the job?'

She felt as if a cold hand had touched her heart. 'She seems to be well enough.' She was aware of her icy tone, and so was Bull.

'Katie, I love you so much, but I am still concerned about Rhiannon's welfare.'

'I know, and I do understand, but it hurts me to hear you talk about her.'

Bull smiled. 'And that makes me realize how much you care for me.'

'And now I must be getting back to the Big House or I'll be in trouble.' She scrambled to her feet. 'Cook's waiting for the vegetables for tonight's dinner. Mrs Buchan is coming over and her husband with her.' She made a face, and glanced away from Bull to hide her blush. 'I can't forget the row they had the other day. It was awful.' She paused. 'Though I suppose it's no concern of mine what they do.' She smoothed the creases from her skirt. 'I can understand Mrs Buchan being hurt, though,' she said. 'Her husband was unfaithful and they haven't been married all that long.'

'Don't let it upset you, Katie. The gentry look after their own and tonight everyone will act as though nothing is wrong, you'll see.'

He stood up, brushed the sand from his clothes and held out his hand to her. 'Come on, then. Let me walk you home. Every minute I spend with you is precious to me, Katie.'

They stood close together for a moment, and Bull looked down at her, his eyes alight with love. 'Can I kiss you, Katie?'

254

'You can kiss my cheek,' she said playfully, but Bull took her seriously.

He stood for a moment, not looking at her, and then, just when Katie was thinking she had offended him, he smiled. 'You little tease.' He took her in his arms and kissed her gently at first but then with growing passion. Katie felt breathless and wanted the moment to go on and on, but at last she pushed him away. 'I must watch my manners and remember what a nice, respectable girl you are, Katie,' he said, with a twinkle in his eye.

'Now who's teasing?' Katie giggled.

They fell into step, Bull measuring his tread to hers. 'You're such a tiny thing,' he said softly, 'so fragile, so different from Rhiannon I'm afraid I'll crush you.'

'I'm a woman, Bull,' Katie said, 'and the only way you'll hurt me is if you keep on talking about Rhiannon.' Her voice was sharper than she intended and Bull looked at her quickly. He was smiling.

'It's not funny!' Katie said, though an answering smile tugged at the corners of her mouth. 'Stop laughing at me, Bull.'

'I'm smiling because you're jealous,' Bull said, 'and I'm flattered.'

She looked up at him, so strong, so wonderful . . . then stood on tiptoe and, to the surprise of them both, she planted a kiss on his lips. They were both silent, laughter gone as they gazed at each other.

'Oh, Katie!' Bull groaned. 'I love you so very much.' He would have kissed her again but she lifted her skirts and ran across the grass to the Big House. At the gates, she stopped to look at Bull, who was still watching her. She waved, resisting the urge to run back and kiss him again. If this was love it made her breathless.

As she entered the house and made her way to the kitchen the smell of roasting meat and freshly baked bread made her feel hungry.

'So you've decided to come back home, then, have you, Katie?' Mrs Grinter said. 'I suppose you think those vegetables are going to peel themselves while you dally around doing goodness knows what.'

'Sorry, Cook, I saw Bull and we stopped for a minute to have a chat.'

'I'd guessed that much from the light in your eye and the colour in your cheeks. I hope you're acting like a good Catholic girl should.'

'I don't know what you mean.' Katie was aware that Rhiannon was watching her.

'You didn't allow him any liberties, did you?'

'Well, no, I suppose not.'

'What do you mean by that?' Cook put a pie in the oven and closed the door before she looked up at Katie.

'Well, I did allow him a kiss.'

Rhiannon gave a little laugh. 'Bull Beynon isn't one to be satisfied with that for long, I can tell you.'

'Well, that's as may be,' Cook said, 'but I dare say a body can't come to much harm out there in broad daylight. Come on, then, give Rhiannon the vegetables and then you should be getting upstairs to see what the master wants. Mrs Buchan's coming tonight and the master's always in a funny mood when she brings her husband into the house and I don't blame him.'

'They stick together, though, the gentry,'

256

Rhiannon said. 'It's all right for a so-called gentleman to take a woman, and it's the woman who gets the blame every time. Men are such weak creatures.'

'Mind, now, miss!' Cook said. 'Who are you to pass judgement on your betters?'

'Only speaking my mind, Cook,' Rhiannon said defiantly.

'A word of warning, girl, just watch who you speak your mind to. I'm telling you that for your own good.'

It was with relief that Katie left the kitchen and climbed the short flight of steps to the hallway. Rhiannon's cold stare was unnerving, and it was clear to her that they could never be friends.

She stood in the sunlit hall looking at the patterns the stained-glass windows cast on the polished floor and smiled. Bull was hers now, and she would make sure he stayed hers.

*   *   *

Jayne climbed into the carriage and sat as far away from Dafydd as she could.

'Do we have to visit your father yet again?' he said sullenly. 'You're like a child running home to Daddy at every whip stitch.'

'Did you have to choose Shanni Morgan?' The words burst out of her.

Dafydd looked at her coldly. 'I don't see that who I bed is any of your concern any more. If my wife refuses me no one can blame me for wanting other women. And I'll wager that every man in Swansea would agree with me, even your beloved father.'

257

'That's unfair!' Jayne said. 'You slept with that—that whore when we were leading a normal married life. You can't start blaming me for what you did.'

'You were never responsive to me, Jayne. Have you asked yourself why I sought the company of another woman?'

'Oh, so it's my fault now, is it?'

'I suppose it is.'

'Well, your love-making left a lot to be desired. How would you like it if I found another man?'

'You won't do that, Jayne, you're far too interested in your own reputation to risk losing it.'

He was right, and Jayne knew that she would not risk the scorn of her peers for any man.

'Then I can well do without the quick fumble to which you subjected me.'

'You only say that because you feel insulted that I turned to another woman.'

'And you have an over-inflated idea of your prowess. Believe me, Dafydd, I don't want you in my bed and I never did. Our love-life was a disappointment to me from the beginning.'

'And your performance, in comparison with other women's, failed miserably.'

The carriage jerked to a halt and Jayne tried to calm the anger that filled her, but in that moment she hated Dafydd. 'By the way,' she said, as she alighted, 'I've managed to get hold of some more shares in the railway.' She smiled. 'It seems I'm better at business than you are, my dear husband.'

Dafydd frowned as he followed her into her father's house. 'Now,' she said, pausing, 'we will behave as though nothing is wrong, shall we?' She was talking to Dafydd as if he was a child, but to her surprise he nodded.

'If this evening is to be endured I'll play any part you like, even that of a devoted husband.'

Jayne looked at him and saw a handsome man, but a flawed one. She did not love him, probably had never loved him. Well, she had made her vow of chastity and would keep it.

Katie was in the hall ready to take the coats and she bobbed a curtsey, but Jayne scarcely noticed her. With her head held high, she made her way across the hall and into the drawing room, where her father was waiting. 'Jayne, my dear child, you're looking remarkably well.' Eynon kissed her.

'I am well indeed, Father.' She brushed aside the fringe of hair that fell over his forehead. 'You need your hair cut. Why don't you get a good woman to look after you?'

Before her father could reply the door opened and Llinos Mainwaring entered the room on the arm of her husband. Jayne winced at the irony as she watched her father kiss Llinos's cheek and shake hands with Joe. The talk was general, though Jayne noticed that Dafydd spoke scarcely a word. She wondered if he was aware that his presence was unwelcome. Somehow, she doubted it.

Later, at supper, Jayne found herself beside Llinos. When the meal was over and the women withdrew she would have an opportunity to tell Llinos what a fool she had been ever to let Dafydd into her life. It was with false cheerfulness that she sat through the meal and talked and laughed. But her mind was racing and anger took away her appetite. Dafydd didn't notice: he was playing his part of happy husband to perfection. What a hypocrite he was. Looking at him now, she could see beneath his good looks and assured charm to

259

the weak, foolish man she knew him to be.

CHAPTER TWENTY-SEVEN

Eynon was sitting in the sunlit window of the library with a book on his knee but he was not reading: he was thinking about Dafydd Buchan. The advice he'd given Jayne was sound: unless she turned a blind eye to her husband's moral lapses she would make a show of herself throughout Swansea. But he would not let the insult to his family pass without punishing Buchan.

He would have liked to damage the man financially but that seemed impossible: his business ventures were sound as a rock. Perhaps a good beating would make him regret hurting the daughter of Eynon Morton-Edwards.

The front-door bell rang. That would be Martin—he was due to arrive at any minute. Lucky man, all he required in life was to serve God, and put as much food into his belly as he could. Martin always had a soothing effect on him.

But it was not Martin. It was Jayne.

'How lovely to see you, Jayne.' He hugged her. She was visiting him so often these days it was clear that she needed her father's support.

She disentangled herself from his arms. 'It's bad news, Papa. Poor Ceri Buchan died at three o'clock this morning.'

'I'm so sorry to hear that,' Eynon said. 'He was always a gentleman and he will be sorely missed.'

'Especially by his wife and children.' Jayne took a seat and fanned her hot cheeks with her hand.

'I'm going to ask you a great favour. Will you come to the funeral?' She held up her hand. 'I know how you feel about Dafydd, but this would be out of respect for Ceri and his family.'

'Of course I'll come,' Eynon said, 'so long as I don't have to play the fond father-in-law to his brother.' The bell rang again. 'It will be Martin, this time,' he added. 'He's fifteen minutes late.' He was relieved he wouldn't have to talk any more about Dafydd Buchan. 'Martin, come and say hello to my beautiful daughter.'

'You get more lovely each time I see you,' Father Martin said, and kissed Jayne's hand. He eased his great bulk into a chair and folded his hands across his belly. 'I have to say, Jayne, how sorry I am about Ceri Buchan. I didn't know him well, but he was a fine man.'

'A pity his brother wasn't cast from the same mould,' Eynon muttered. 'Anyway, Martin, a glass of wine?'

A smile spread across the vicar's angelic face. 'That sounds very good.'

'I've just been asking Papa to come to the funeral with me.' Jayne looked to Father Martin for approval and he nodded.

'And I expect he has agreed. No one has anything against poor Ceri Buchan.' Then Father Martin leaned forward. 'And, Eynon, it looks like your Jayne has made a shrewd move in buying all those railway shares. They're going up at an amazing rate. Anyone who sells now will make a lot of money.'

'But the shares will go on climbing for a long time yet,' Jayne put in. 'I won't sell mine. Indeed, I might pick up some more when I talk to my friend at the bank.'

Eynon laughed. 'Will you listen to my daughter, Martin? A woman with such a business sense, have you ever seen the like?'

'Not since Llinos Mainwaring saved the pottery from ruin,' Father Martin said. 'It seems you surround yourself with intelligent women, my friend.'

Eynon nodded, pleased. 'Well, Jayne,' he said, 'are you going to let your husband know that more shares are available? I understand he's desperate to lay his hands on some.'

'No fear!'

Jayne had spoken so fiercely that Eynon laughed. 'That's the spirit, girl! You're your father's daughter, all right, don't you agree, Martin?'

The clergyman held up his hand. 'Don't drag me into this. I'm a man of the cloth and I'm supposed to forgive all sins.' His tone was stern but there was a twinkle in his eye. 'And man might sin, but as long as he repents all must be forgiven him.'

'Balderdash!' Eynon said. 'Buchan has upset my daughter and I'll never forgive him.'

'Well, then,' Father Martin said, 'let's compromise and say you mean the man no harm. Be charitable, Eynon, for no man is without sin, not even me.'

'Oh, Uncle Martin,' Jayne put her arms around his neck, 'you haven't committed a sin in your life.'

'But I have.' He patted his belly. 'I commit the sin of gluttony every day of my life.'

'Well,' Jayne got to her feet, 'I'm not answering that! Anyway, I think I have urgent business at the bank.'

Eynon took Jayne in his arms. 'Now, look after

262

yourself, my dear, and let me know about the funeral when you have the details.'

When Jayne had gone he sank back into his chair. 'I can't help it, Martin, but Buchan makes me so angry.'

'Why?' the vicar asked gently. 'Is it because of your daughter or our sweet Llinos?'

'A bit of both, I suppose,' Eynon conceded. 'Buchan has shamed my family publicly and he treats Jayne like a fool.'

'And Llinos?'

'You know what I feel about her. And how can I trust Buchan to look after Jayne when he brought Llinos nothing but shame?'

'I know how you feel, old friend,' Father Martin nodded sagely, 'but these things have a habit of resolving themselves. "As ye sow so shall ye reap".'

'Buchan has been getting away with things for far too long,' Eynon said. 'I never liked the man and I never will.'

'Leave it to Jayne. She will see that Buchan suffers for what he's done. Women have a way of meting out vengeance as a surgeon wields a knife.' When he smiled he looked more cherubic than ever. 'That's why you see so many men patronising the local beer shops. And that reminds me, where is that drink you promised me?'

'What do you say if we forget the wine and have something stronger?'

'Excellent!'

Eynon poured him a generous quantity of brandy. 'Now,' he said, 'let's talk about anything but family matters, shall we?'

*　　　*　　　*

263

Jayne took the first opportunity to go to the bank for a meeting with Jason Prentice.

'Good morning, my dear Mrs Buchan. Please take a seat.' He held the chair for her and Jayne smiled warmly up at him.

'I appreciate all you've done for me, Mr Prentice.'

'This time I could only manage to get a few shares. I wish it could have been more but other bankers have their sources too.' He leaned forward confidentially. 'I heard on the grapevine that Mrs Llinos Mainwaring got there before us. However, I think these –' he took a sheaf of papers from his drawer '—will give you a strong voice in any negotiations into which the other shareholders might enter.'

'I'm so grateful.' Jayne allowed her gloved hand to cover his.

'I have to look after my best customers,' he mumbled. 'And you, Mrs Buchan, are one of my dearest—I mean *very* best customers.'

'Well,' Jayne removed her hand and stood up, 'I'll not forget your kindness, Mr Prentice, and some time, I feel sure, I might be able to reward you for your astuteness and loyalty.'

She left the bank, feeling as though she was walking on air. The acquisition of the shares had been a good business move, another weapon in her armoury against her husband. Dafydd would learn that he couldn't play fast and loose with Jayne Morton-Edwards. One day he would discover that she was made of sterner stuff than he had ever imagined.

She wondered how in just a few months all her

joy in marriage had vanished. It hadn't taken her long to learn that her husband was not the great man she thought him.

*   *   *

Dafydd stood beside his brother's grave and listened while Father Martin intoned the words that would send Ceri to his last resting place. He could hear women weeping and, indeed, tears blurred his own eyes. Ceri had fought a courageous battle against his sickness until it had overwhelmed him.

He was relieved when the service ended and the mourners began to leave the cemetery. Jayne was walking ahead of him, her arm around one of Ceri's children. His mouth tightened. They would never have children of their own, not while she kept him out of her bedroom, but short of forcing himself on her there was nothing he could do.

Father Martin fell into step beside him. 'Once again may I offer my condolences, Mr Buchan?'

'Thank you, Father,' Dafydd said.

They walked in silence for a moment. Then the clergyman stopped and looked at him. 'Still, you have your lovely wife to comfort you. Jayne is a clever woman, and it's easy to underestimate her.'

Dafydd looked at him sharply.

Martin smiled beatifically. 'I'm impressed with Jayne's business sense—it's unusual in a well-brought-up young lady. She's acquired even more shares in the Great Western Railway while I . . .' he shrugged '. . . would not be able to buy even one.'

Dafydd digested the fact that, once again, Jayne had outwitted him. She knew he wanted some of the shares and it was her wifely duty to tell him if there were some on offer. He endured the traditional after-funeral tea with scant patience— he couldn't wait to let Jayne know how angry he was. He glanced at her and saw that her cheeks were blooming. If he did not know better he would say she had a lover.

At last it was time to leave his brother's house. He patted his sister-in-law's shoulder and kissed her cheek. 'Try to rest for a while,' he said. 'You look all in.'

'Thank you for your support, Dafydd,' she said gently. 'You've been a pillar of strength.'

He climbed into the carriage and seated himself beside Jayne. 'Thank heaven that's over,' he said feelingly. 'I never could stand funerals.'

'I'm sorry,' Jayne said. 'I know you're going to miss Ceri badly.' She sounded truly sad. 'He was a lovely man but, then, the Lord seems always to take the good ones first.'

He glanced at her to see if she was being sarcastic but there was real sympathy in her eyes. He touched her hand, but she snatched it away. 'For heaven's sake, Jayne! I *am* your husband.'

'I can't forget that I'm tied to you, can I, Dafydd? I despise you and all you stand for.'

'I have noticed,' he said. 'Is that why you grab all the shares in the Great Western Railway like a greedy child?'

She shook her head. 'Do you know something, Dafydd? I actually feel sorry for you at this moment.'

'Well, you needn't waste your pity on me. I can easily do without your wifely duties but trying to best me in business is insulting to say the least.'

266

Jayne relaxed against the upholstery and actually smiled. 'That's what you can't forgive, isn't it? That I succeeded where you failed.'

'It was not business acumen that brought you those shares but your ability to make sheep's eyes at that fellow at the bank. And your father's influence didn't go amiss either.'

Jayne's laugh grated on his nerves. 'What's funny about that?' he demanded, feeling that the argument was slipping away from him.

'I'm laughing because I used my feminine attributes *as well as* my brain to get what I wanted, and you don't like it.'

She looked so lovely with her pale hair lifted from her face and her large eyes bright with triumph that for the first time he felt a real desire to make love to her.

'Look,' she said, more gently, 'I might be able to get my hands on one or two of the shares for you if you like.'

He was silent, not wanting to be beholden to his wife.

'Just think,' Jayne said, 'the Great Western will get stronger, other lines will be built. The railways are our future, don't you agree?'

'You might just have a point,' he said slowly. He was suspicious of her motives in making the offer now but he could afford to buy the shares and take a loss on them. 'I might take you up on that, Jayne,' he said at last, then leaned back in the carriage and closed his eyes. Perhaps it was time he began to woo his wife in the way a loving husband should. Clearly there was more to her than met the eye . . . but however much he might admire her, even desire her, she would never have his love.

CHAPTER TWENTY-EIGHT

Shanni finished packing her bag and snapped the catch shut with an air of determination. Soon, she and Pedr would shake the dust of Swansea off their feet for good. Standing there, in the little bedroom of the home they had made together her courage failed her. Leaving everything she knew was not going to be easy.

Pedr came into the room hauling a box of their possessions; papers fluttered off the top onto the floor and Shanni picked them up. 'What are these, Pedr?'

'Can't you see what they are?' His tone was sharp. 'Or have you lost your senses yet again?'

Shanni ignored the barb. 'Of course I can see what they are—they're patterns from the pottery—but why are you taking them?'

'Potting is the only job I know and I'll need to find work in England. With these,' he took them from her, 'I'll have something to bargain with.'

'But why should an English pottery owner care about Llanelli patterns?' Shanni frowned. 'The painters up there are skilled and they have their own.'

Pedr put down the box and closed the lid. 'Many potteries use the same designs and I think the Persian Rose pattern would suit any painter, even those living in Staffordshire.'

'But that's stealing!'

Pedr looked at her. 'Wasn't Buchan stealing from me when he took you?'

'Look, Pedr, I don't know why I let . . .' Her

words trailed away. 'Please, Pedr, try to forgive me. I know it's hard to forget what I've done but I'll never let you down again.' A few minutes passed before she spoke again. 'Are you ready, Pedr? We're getting the mail in half an hour.'

'I'll just tie this box securely then I'll be as ready as I'll ever be.' Shanni saw him looking around his home, and his regret at leaving it was plain to see in his eyes. Shanni realized now that not only had she shattered Pedr's trust in her but that she was driving him away from all he held dear. 'Do we have to do this, Pedr?' she asked, in a small voice. 'Can't we stay here and try to put the past behind us?'

'With everyone pointing the finger and calling me a cuckold? You're not thinking straight, Shanni.'

'But not many people know about it, do they?'

'Well, now,' Pedr began to make his way downstairs, 'let's see, there's Buchan himself, and his wife and his father-in-law. Then there's Mrs Mainwaring and her husband. Oh, and, of course, Mrs Keen and her customers. I couldn't face the pitying stares, Shanni, I just couldn't.'

In the small kitchen, he put down the box and gazed at the cold dead fireplace, the neat furnishings. Shanni took him in her arms, her head against his chest.

'Oh, Pedr, what a fool I've been. What a silly, evil woman I am.' Pedr was standing stiffly, his arms at his sides, and Shanni began to sob. 'I love you, Pedr, I would give anything to turn back the clock, you know that.'

He sighed and rested his chin against her hair. 'No one can do that.'

269

She looked up at him. 'I know, but we must stop tearing each other apart or our marriage will be over.'

'You're right, I know you are, but it's the very devil thinking of you letting that man touch you—never mind make love to you.'

She cupped his face in her hands. 'I'll make it up to you, Pedr, you'll see. Now, let's pull ourselves together and go and get the mail. Our new life is just about to begin.'

*　　　*　　　*

'Not long now before the station opens at Swansea.' Bull glanced at Cookson, who was bending over a sheaf of plans. 'I can't wait to see the Great Western train pull in alongside the platform.'

Cookson looked up, shading his eyes from the bright sun shining through the office window. 'You'll get to meet the great man himself, Bull.' Cookson's face was full of pride. 'Mr Isambard Kingdom Brunel will be the first to step off the train at Swansea. How I admire that man.' He dipped into his pocket and drew out a silver flask. 'Here, have a nip of this.'

'Thank you, sir.' Bull swallowed some. 'Damn!' he spluttered. 'That's hotter than the fires of hell.'

Cookson shrugged. 'I don't notice it myself—used to it, I suppose. Right, let's get over to the high street and see how the work is progressing, shall we?'

The two men left the building and stood in the street while Cookson checked his papers. 'Let's take the carriage, shall we? We'll travel in style this

270

morning.'

The groom touched his hat and handed the reins to Bull. 'Here we are, sir. The beasts are gentle enough. They shouldn't give you any trouble.'

Bull clucked his tongue and lifted the reins, and the horses jerked the carriage into motion. As he sat far above the heads of the shoppers he felt as if he owned the world. He looked around him and everything seemed different, but it was not the town that had changed, it was Bull.

He was looked upon as a gentleman now. He wore well-cut clothes and a shiny hat, but for him the real satisfaction came from his work. He was asked for his opinion on important matters, such as which gauge would serve the railway best. Mr Brunel wanted all the tracks to be broad gauge but that plan had attracted opposition.

The drive across town took less than half an hour, and when the two men alighted they stood shoulder to shoulder, gazing at the scene before them.

'We've made good progress,' Cookson said. 'A congratulatory drink is in order, I think.'

Bull shook his head: he did not need the stimulus of drink. The sight of the navvies working side by side with the masons and carpenters was excitement enough. This was all he could ask of life. He had a worthwhile job and a beautiful wife-to-be, what more could he want?

Soon he was pointing out difficulties, solving problems, fulfilling all his ambitions. That morning, Bull Beynon was a happy man.

*   *   *

Rhiannon was exasperated with Cook. 'Can't you forget that I was a camp follower for one day?' she challenged.

'Well, can you? That's more to the point, my girl.' Mrs Grinter was in one of her moods again. 'You're so used to lying on your back all day that it's hard to get a day's work out of you.'

'That's not fair!' Rhiannon said. 'I do more than my share here, and in any case I did a lot more than lie on my back.' She knew it was foolish of her to rile Cook—the other woman had the power to make life a misery for those working under her if she chose.

'I had to look after Bull, mind,' Rhiannon said, more quietly. 'He needed clean clothes and good food to put in his belly, and who do you think did that for him?'

'As well as warming his bed.' Cook was not to be mollified. 'Decent women do that every day of their lives and a job of work as well. You lived like the gentry, my girl, and now you don't like to work hard for a living.'

'Gentry?' Rhiannon said sharply. 'What gentry ever lived in a hut with tiny rooms, cheap curtains and a door that was coming off its hinges?' She warmed to her subject. 'And when you stepped outside you were sometimes knee-deep in mud.'

'Well, that's what you'll go back to if you don't shape up, girl.' Cook sniffed. 'Perhaps that's all you're good for—'cos you're not good at anything else.'

Rhiannon was silent. Perhaps the woman was right. Surely her old life was better than the constant grind of fetching coal for all the fires in the house and carrying heavy jugs of water up three flights of stairs? But, then, she would never find another man like Bull: he had treated her with respect, protected her from the other men. She had been so happy with him.

'Don't just stand there, girl. Go to town and get me some yeast—do something useful for a change.'

'I thought Katie usually did the errands, Cook,' she said. 'I don't know why you send her, though, she always spends half the day roaming around Swansea.'

'Katie's busy upstairs,' Cook said, 'and, in any case, if I say you must go then I expect you to obey me.'

'All right, Cook, I'll go and willingly.' Come to think of it, an hour or two out of the house would do her good.

Later, as she walked downhill towards Swansea, Rhiannon's anger drained away. It was a clear, sunny day and a warm breeze was blowing in from the sea. This was the weather the camp women liked, when the sun shone and they could sit outside to cook the food for their men and spend the time in idle gossip. Rhiannon missed the camaraderie of the other women. But she ached for Bull at night when she lay in her narrow bed; in the dark hours she longed for the times she had spent curled up against her man, content and warm, happy with her lot. Now, because of Katie Cullen, she had lost everything.

There was an air of festivity about the town. Along some of the streets flags were being strung between the houses, and windows had been cleaned until they sparkled like diamonds in the sun.

Perhaps she could go to see the new station,

273

which was going to open shortly—she might even catch a glimpse of Bull. Her heartbeat quickened. If he saw her again he might realize what he was missing. Bull was finding no comfort in Katie's arms: she was a maiden and would remain so until the wedding ring was placed on her finger.

Rhiannon walked along the high street and here the road teemed with people. Horse-drawn carriages vied for position and street peddlers shouted their wares. And then she saw him. For a moment she was breathless with love for him. He stood head and shoulders above the rest of the crowd and the sight of his dear face brought tears to her eyes. 'Bull.' She hurried forward and stumbled against him in her haste. He caught her arm to steady her. 'Bull, how are you keeping?' She tried to sound casual but every instinct was telling her to throw herself on his mercy and beg him to take her back.

Suddenly she realized the engineer was standing alongside him and she drew back, but Mr Cookson was smiling at her approvingly. 'This is your lovely lady, then, Bull, is it?'

'This is Rhiannon,' Bull said, 'but we are not together any longer. Rhiannon works as a maidservant these days.' He smiled as he held her away from him. 'How are you doing up at the Big House, Rhiannon? Is Mr Morton-Edwards a kind master?'

'Yes, very kind.' Rhiannon swallowed hard. 'But it's not the life for me, Bull. I feel cooped up, smothered by the other women there, all of them thinking they're better than me.'

'You'll get used to it, Rhiannon,' Bull said. 'I'm sure it's nice for you to have clean sheets to lie on and good food to put in your belly.' He glanced at the engineer. 'Hadn't we better get along, sir?' He distanced himself from Rhiannon, and she felt bitterly hurt.

'Just a minute, Bull,' Cookson said, 'I could do with a housekeeper—that's if you are interested.' He smiled at Rhiannon. 'You will be the only *young* lady in a bachelor's residence. My cook is old as the hills and will be glad of a pair of hands to help her out. Mind,' he continued, 'I can't offer you the luxury that you find in Mr Morton-Edwards' household but you should be comfortable enough all the same.'

'That's very kind of you, sir.' Rhiannon glanced at Bull, wondering how he felt about the engineer's offer. There was no doubt that Mr Cookson and he were becoming good friends so if she took up a position with him she would see Bull more often. 'If you really mean it, sir, I would like to work for you very much.'

'Well, then, that's settled. Now, you must give notice at the Big House and then Bull will show you where I live, won't you, Bull?'

'Yes, sir.' Bull did not sound too pleased but there was nothing he could say without offending his boss.

'I know where you live, Bull,' Rhiannon said. 'When I've worked out my notice I'll come to your place, shall I?'

'I suppose that will be all right,' Bull said reluctantly, 'though perhaps you could let me know about your plans through Katie.'

'I'll just come to your house. Thank you, Mr Cookson, for your generous offer. I'll be very happy working for you, I'm sure.' She glanced round. 'I suppose I'd better get on, I've shopping to do.'

Before Bull could protest Rhiannon melted into the crowds. She was jubilant—she would have the chance to see Bull again, to be with him at his new house.

Perhaps when he saw her employed at the engineer's home he would realize she was respectable now. It was with a happy smile and a light heart that Rhiannon did her shopping and set off for home. Just wait until she told Miss High and Mighty Katie Cullen that she was seeing Bull again. That would take the smile off her face.

*   *   *

'You don't mind me taking on the girl, do you?' Cookson grinned at Bull, who shook his head.

'Not a bit, sir. I'd like to see Rhiannon happy. She's a good girl.'

'And a good bedfellow too, by the look of her. Made for loving is that girl and I've been without a woman for too long.'

Bull was not sure that Rhiannon understood the terms of her employment but, he reasoned, she was better off with a man like Cookson than being passed around the navvies. It was clear that the job at the Big House was getting her down and soon, for one reason or another, she would be out of work. The only life she knew was keeping men happy. He felt a flash of guilt at the way he had left her: she was a loyal woman and she had loved him dearly. He had been more than a meal ticket to her, far more.

'You'll be good to her, sir?' he said. 'That goes

276

without saying, I suppose.'

'I'll take care of her, don't you worry, Bull. That's the trouble with you—you've too much of a conscience. Get rid of it. It will hamper your progress up the ladder.'

'I'll try, sir,' Bull said, but the enjoyment had gone out of the day and Bull felt sure that nothing good would come of this morning's meeting with Rhiannon.

CHAPTER TWENTY-NINE

As he stood outside in the sunshine, watching his coachman methodically grooming one of the horses, Eynon was in a furious mood. Yesterday Jayne had come to him in tears. 'Papa,' she'd said, 'gossip has it that Dafydd has taken a mistress, some common woman called Serena. He's flaunting her in public. It seems he no longer cares what anyone thinks of him. How could he insult me like that?'

The man had not only insulted his daughter, he had besmirched the fine name of Morton-Edwards and Eynon decided he had to be punished.

'Jacob,' he said to the coachman, 'do you know any men who are handy with their fists?'

Jacob looked up at him in surprise. 'Aye, sir, I do that.'

'Will you sort something out for me, then?'

'That goes without saying, sir.'

'It's Buchan. I want the man horse-whipped for what he's done to my girl.'

Jacob nodded. 'I understand, sir. If I was a

younger man I'd see to it myself.'

Eynon handed him a bag of money. 'I don't want to know anything that would connect me with the beating, is that clear?'

'Clear as daylight, sir.'

Eynon made his way back to the front of the house and paused, looking up at the blue bowl of the sky. 'You are going to get what you deserve at last, Buchan!'

He could not pretend, even to himself, that Buchan's latest infidelity was at the top of his list of grievances against the man. Rather, it was the last straw. Buchan treated women as if they were of no account. The man was a scoundrel: he had no sense of honour and must be punished.

Eynon sighed in satisfaction. Later he was to meet Llinos in town, they would sit in one of the coffee-houses and talk and laugh together as they always had. His love for her had grown ever stronger as the years progressed. Even her fall from grace had not destroyed it. He had been angry with her, but his devotion had not faltered. Now that Joe was home he had less opportunity to see Llinos but they met at least once a week, and with that Eynon had to be content. If some other man had to possess Llinos, there was no one better than Joe Mainwaring.

The front-door bell jangled insistently and presently Jayne came into the sitting room, skirts billowing, cheeks flushed.

'Dear heaven, it's so hot today! How are you bearing up, Papa?' She hugged him.

'I'm all the better for seeing you, my darling. Come along, sit down, and I'll send for some cold cordial.' He rang the bell and Katie bobbed into

278

the room, her face wary when she saw Jayne. Eynon concealed a smile. If only Katie knew the real Jayne: in her heart she was as gentle as a lamb. 'Fetch us some cordial, there's a good girl,' he said, 'and if Cook's made some of those fine Welsh cakes, bring those too.'

Katie dipped her head and vanished, and Eynon hugged his daughter again. He felt so glad that he was going to teach Buchan a lesson, but he would not mention it to Jayne, not now, perhaps never.

'Have you heard the news?' Jayne did not wait for a reply. 'That hussy Shanni Morgan has left Swansea, and just as well too.'

Eynon frowned. Shanni was another of Buchan's victims. 'Poor girl,' he said. 'She had such promise once.'

'I don't know how you can feel sorry for her,' Jayne said sharply. 'She lay with my husband, and goodness knows how many other marriages she has ruined. It seems her mother was just the same, a loose woman.'

'Jayne, my love, learn a little tolerance. I understand your anger, but Shanni was duped by a clever man.'

'So was I,' Jayne said, with uncharacteristic humility. 'But my eyes are open now, Papa, and I won't ever let a man get the better of me again.'

'That's my girl!' Eynon smiled at her. She looked so beautiful, so innocent, that his heart almost failed him. 'If ever you want to come home you're more than welcome, you know that, don't you?'

'Yes, Papa, I do and—' Jayne was interrupted by a knock.

Katie came in with a tray on her arm. 'Cook says the Welsh cakes are freshly made, sir, and rich with fruit, just as you like them.'

'Thank you, Katie, and thank Cook for me,' Eynon said.

'You spoil your servants, Papa. I don't know why Katie or Cook needs thanking—they get their money and their keep, don't they?' She touched his hand. 'But your kindness is part of the reason I love you so much.'

'Servants are human beings like us,' Eynon said, 'and have feelings, believe it or not.'

'I know that. There's no need to stoop to sarcasm.' She looked at him reprovingly. 'Now let's talk business. The station is set to open in a few weeks' time, then? I'm really excited about it, aren't you?'

'I suppose so, though I don't know what effect the iron monster will have on our countryside.'

'Papa!' Jayne scolded. 'You sound like one of the peasants who think the devil will come out of the train, along with the steam from the funnels.'

'I'm not that bad.' Eynon eased himself into a more comfortable position in his chair. 'Now tell me, how are the share prices doing today?'

He scarcely listened to her reply, though, because he was thinking about Buchan and how the man was going to get just what he deserved.

*   *   *

Katie was in the kitchen with Cook and Rhiannon. The other servants were still busy at their chores, and the rattle of crockery could be heard from the scullery. One glance at Rhiannon told her that the girl was bursting to tell her something. Somehow, Katie felt it would not be very pleasing to hear.

280

Cook broke the silence. 'All right, Rhiannon, tell us what's on your mind.'

'Well,' Rhiannon glanced at Katie, 'I saw Bull when I was in town.' Katie's heart missed a beat.

'Go on,' Cook said impatiently, 'what about it?'

'He's asked me to go and live with him in his fine house, that's what.'

'It's not true! He would have told me that himself,' Katie stated.

'Well, has he asked you to move in there with him, Miss Prissy Prissy?'

'No, of course not!' Katie felt the colour rush into her cheeks. 'He would never suggest anything improper like that.'

'Not to you, perhaps,' Rhiannon said smugly, 'but, then, you're the type who waits for the ring and the church and all that. It don't always pay, see?'

'I don't believe Bull would ask you to live with him,' Katie said firmly. 'If he felt that way why did he leave you alone in the hut at the side of the railway track?'

Rhiannon looked coy. 'I think he's missing the love and comfort I always gave him,' she said. 'Men get used to having a woman to warm the bed for them.'

'No need for vulgarity!' Cook spoke sternly. She stared at Rhiannon, her eyes narrowed. 'I don't believe you either, my girl. He wouldn't want you when he's got a smart girl like Katie, now, would he?'

'Well, you'll all see. I'm going to give my notice in and you'll have to believe me, won't you?'

'I won't be waiting until then,' Katie said. 'I'll be going down to town first thing to see Bull. I'll soon

281

prove that you are a liar.'

'Go you,' Rhiannon said. 'He'll only tell you what I've told you, that I'm going to move in with him.'

'I think you're just making this up to hurt Katie,' Cook said. 'Who'd want you after all the men you've been with?' She held up her hand as Rhiannon went to speak again. 'Just keep your mouth shut, girl. You're getting too big for your boots, you are. I never liked you or approved of your loose ways and the sooner you go the better I'll be pleased.'

'Right, then.' Rhiannon got up. 'I'll go now. You'll see then if I'm a liar or not.'

'You wouldn't dare leave without giving the master your notice, 'cos if you did you'd never get any decent job again.'

'Get it into your head, Cook—you too, Katie—I don't need another job. I've got Bull to keep me now. I'm going to live in a fine house and sleep in a good bed and be with the man I love.' With that she rushed from the room.

Cook looked at Katie and shook her head. 'I'll believe it when I see it,' she said. 'The girl is play-acting. She'd no more leave at this time of night than fly to the moon.'

Katie was not so sure. Rhiannon had seemed too certain of herself—and if she left the house where would she sleep if she was lying about Bull?

After a while Rhiannon came back into the room carrying her bag. 'Well, I think you'll believe me now.' She stared at Katie triumphantly. 'I'm going to Bull and you can't do a thing about it.'

She let herself out of the back door and Cook sat open-mouthed, staring at the door, as if waiting for

Rhiannon to reappear.

'Well, I'll be blowed!' she said. 'She's actually gone.' She fanned her hot face. 'I don't know where that girl's going to end up—murdered in some back alley, like as not.'

Katie felt numb. 'Do you think she's really going back to Bull?'

'Don't know, I'm sure,' Cook said. 'But if I was you I wouldn't let things rest there.'

'I won't.' Katie felt a surge of anger. 'I'll be going to Bull's house first thing in the morning and I'll clear this up once and for all. If he thinks he can play me for a fool he's got another think coming!'

'That's the way, girl.' Cook nodded. 'When you see your man I'm sure everything will be sorted out once and for all.'

*   *   *

Rhiannon stared around her at the dark hillsides and strained to see the track leading down to the town. Her bag seemed to be growing heavier by the minute and she cursed herself for being a fool. She should have waited until morning, and even then she could not be sure of a welcome. It was true that Mr Cookson had asked her to work for him but he would not expect her so soon and certainly not at this time of night.

She sighed with relief when she saw the lamp-lit windows of the houses growing nearer: in the darkness she had felt as if she was alone in the world. She tried to gather her thoughts. The only thing she could do was go to Bull's house—surely he would not begrudge her a night's lodging.

Unsure of the way in the dark Rhiannon took

several wrong turnings and found herself in unfamiliar territory. She was afraid to stop and ask directions in case someone thought she was plying her old trade.

At last she found the house and knocked at the door almost timidly.

After a long time it was opened. 'Rhiannon!' Bull sounded none too pleased to see her. 'What on earth are you doing here at this time of night?'

'Can I come in, Bull?' she asked. 'I've walked such a long way and this bag is so heavy.'

He hesitated, and she thought he was going to turn her away, but then he stepped back to allow her into the hallway. He was frowning, and Rhiannon could see that he did not want her there.

'All right. Put down your bag at the bottom of the stairs and tell me what's going on.'

Rhiannon took off her coat and followed Bull into an elegant sitting room. A good fire burned in the grate and a glass of some golden liquor stood on the table. It was all very cosy, all ready for Katie to move in as Mrs Bull Beynon. The thought brought a bitter taste to Rhiannon's mouth.

'Why are you here?' Bull sounded angry. 'I am no longer responsible for you, Rhiannon. Please get that into your head.'

'I know.' She held up her hand. 'It's just that life up at the Big House is awful with the other servants picking on me.'

He stared at her for a long moment. 'You're usually very good at holding your own, Rhiannon, so don't put on the helpless act now because I don't believe it.'

'I'm sorry, Bull, I don't mean to put you out but please let me stay tonight. Tomorrow I'll go to Mr

Cookson and get my job there and you'll be rid of me.'

'How is it going to look, Rhiannon, you sleeping at my house and no one else here? I don't want to start off my life as manager with any scandal hanging over me.'

'I'll get up early and go before it gets light, but I can't walk alone in the darkness, Bull, it frightens me.'

'I know.' His voice was kinder. 'All right, then, just for a few hours.'

'Thank you, Bull, I knew you wouldn't turn me away. You're too good a man for that.'

'You can take the back bedroom—and remember, no funny business. What we had together is over, finished. I'm going to marry Katie. I love her and I won't do anything to hurt her.'

'I understand, Bull. Just show me the room and I'll be out of your sight.'

'It's up the stairs at the back of the landing. You can't miss it.' His tone was sharp. 'And, Rhiannon, if you ever do this again I'll turn you out into the night.'

'I understand, Bull.' Rhiannon went upstairs and into the back bedroom, leaving the door ajar. The room was not lit and no fire burned in the grate, but the bed looked comfortable and inviting and, suddenly, Rhiannon realized how tired she was.

She undressed and crawled under the blankets. It was a warm night but she was shivering.

The next day Rhiannon was up early and she had lit the fire and put the bacon on to fry before Bull got out of bed. He came down to the kitchen and, without a word, went through into the yard. She heard him wash at the pump, and when he

285

returned to the kitchen, his hair was damp and his skin shone. She ached with love for him, a hopeless love that would never be returned.

They ate breakfast in silence, and when Bull pushed away his plate and got to his feet, he stood waiting for her to move. Reluctantly Rhiannon rose too, staring at him as if memorizing his every feature.

'Go over to Mr Cookson's house right away,' Bull said. 'He lives just round the corner in the large white house surrounded by railings. Say you're out of work and ask is it possible for you to start at his house right away.'

'All right, Bull,' Rhiannon said, 'but will you do me one last favour?'

'What is it?' Bull sounded suspicious.

'Will you bring my bag round to me later. It's so heavy—my arms are still aching from carrying it.'

Bull sighed. 'Rhiannon, I hope you know that if you don't start working for Cookson you're on your own? I don't want you coming back here.'

'What about my things?'

'I'll leave the bag in the front garden and you can pick it up any time you like. I'm going to get my jacket now so I'll see you out.'

He was determined to see her on her way and Rhiannon almost broke down in tears. He would not change his mind: he was too much in love with Katie Cullen even to think of anyone else.

He led the way into the hall and opened the front door. She glanced up at him in his clean shirt with the collar open revealing his neck. On an impulse she stood on tiptoe and kissed him. 'Goodbye, Bull,' she said softly, 'and I mean it this time. I'll not bother you again.'

She stepped out into the street and forced a smile. 'Good luck to you and Katie,' she said, and added under her breath, 'you're going to need it.'

She strode along the street, with her head high. She turned once to wave at Bull and he waved back. Neither of them noticed the small figure of Katie Cullen standing on the opposite side of the road, her hand pressed to her lips and tears rolling unchecked down her cheeks.

CHAPTER THIRTY

Llinos paused outside the door of the conservatory. She could hear Joe and Sion speaking softly. Sion was home for the holidays: he looked well and happy and she wondered what he and Joe found to talk about so seriously.

'I know you're not my real father,' Sion's voice wobbled a little, 'but I love you very much, Papa, and I think you love me too.'

'I do love you, Sion, and you *are* my son, as far as I'm concerned. Who told you I wasn't your real father?'

'No one told me, Papa, but I hear people talking. In any case, I can see the likeness between Mr Buchan and me. I'm not a stupid boy.'

Llinos resisted the urge to rush forward and comfort her child.

Then Joe spoke again. 'You're certainly not stupid, you're an intelligent boy, and I'm proud of you. So is your mother. We both love you very much.'

'Yes, Papa, but I've wondered if you love Lloyd

better than me. He's your real son, isn't he?'

'I am his father by nature, but I'm your father by choice, and one way is just as valuable as the other.'

Sion nodded thoughtfully. 'I understand.' Joe drew the boy into the circle of his arm.

'I want to ask you something, Sion. If . . . when I have to go away, you'll look after your mama for me, won't you?'

'Course I will. I'm a man now.'

'But you're not too old to get a kiss from your papa, are you, Sion?' The boy hugged him, a smile illuminating his face. He looked so much like Dafydd in that moment and yet, strangely, it was as if something of Joe had rubbed off on him too.

Forcing back her tears Llinos went into the sunlit conservatory. 'Good morning to you, gentlemen. I hope you both ate a hearty breakfast.' She sat beside Joe on the scroll-backed sofa. 'You were both up with the birds this morning, weren't you? And what's this about you going away, Joe?'

'Men's business. Nothing to interest you.'

Llinos kissed his cheek. 'All right, I won't pry—and, Joe, I'm so lucky to have a man like you.' She saw Sion looking up at her as if for reassurance. 'And such a wonderful son, too.'

'Enough of all this sentiment,' Joe said gruffly. 'I know you're on holiday from school, Sion, but you still have to do some work on your books, so off with you and get some studying done.'

When her son had gone Llinos leaned against Joe, her cheek against his collar. She could smell the fresh scent of grass and flowers and sunshine about her husband, and love for him flowed over her like a tide. 'You're so good to me, Joe,' she whispered. 'I love you so much that sometimes I think my heart will burst.'

He took her hand and smoothed her palm with his thumb. 'These are our golden days, Llinos, and we must make the most of them.' He stroked her cheek. 'We might not have many of them. We must promise not to look back on our mistakes but to go forward, enjoying the time we have left with each other.'

She nodded, knowing she would cherish this moment for as long as she lived. And yet somehow his words brought a chill to her heart.

'What do you mean, Joe, we might not have many days left?'

He smiled. 'Well, we're not getting any younger, are we?'

'That's true but I don't need reminding of it, thank you.' Joe was right, though, they must count their blessings now. So what if her elder son was living in America? He was a man and he must make his own choices in life. She hoped for his sake that he would be happy.

'It's strange cutting the ties, Joe,' she said. 'Letting go of our children seems to be the hardest thing to face.'

'He will be happy,' Joe said, reading her thoughts. 'Lloyd is intelligent and sensitive, rather like his mother.'

'I've not always been sensitive, though, have I?'

'We've both made mistakes, indulged our own selfish needs, but that's all behind us.'

'You're right,' Llinos said. 'And I must tidy myself up, I've promised to meet Eynon in town. Would you like to come with me?'

He shook his head. 'We don't have to be together every moment to prove we love each other, do we?'

Llinos went into the hallway, then glanced back at her husband. Something about him was different: he looked the same but there was an aura about him that she couldn't fathom, a sort of sadness that hung around him like a cloak. He was very pale too and there were lines around his eyes that she'd never seen before.

'You are all right, aren't you, Joe?'

'Go on out and stop worrying about me!'

'I'll be off then.' Llinos ran back to kiss Joe's cheek. 'I won't be long.' She stepped out into the fresh morning air, yet somehow she was reluctant to leave her husband alone. Still, she would be back before long, and then they could sit and talk for the rest of the day, and at night they would make love.

*

Joe sat in the conservatory for a long time, gazing out at the garden, admiring the way the sun brought the bed of roses into focus. Usually the dust from the potteries settled everywhere but today everything looked fresh-washed and clean.

It was quiet, with only the occasional chirping of birds to break the silence. Joe closed his eyes, determined to enjoy his respite from the world of reality. Eventually he moved back into the comparative dimness of the house. With Llinos out visiting, he must begin to put his affairs in order.

*   *   *

'You're looking well.' Eynon pulled out a chair for her to sit at the small table. 'What would you like to drink—strawberry cordial, perhaps?'

'That would be lovely, Eynon. The heat makes

me thirsty.'

He leaned forward and took her hand. 'Are you content with your life, Llinos?'

'You know I am,' she said.

'And Joe?'

'Joe and I made a new start this morning. We've pledged to put our sordid past behind us and enjoy what Joe calls our golden years.'

'Good idea.' He fell silent, wondering if he would ever possess the flame that was Llinos Mainwaring.

'You seem very quiet, Eynon.' She smiled fondly at him, and Eynon forced a smile in response.

'Just admiring the scenery.' He looked directly at her. 'Have I told you lately that you're still the most beautiful woman I've ever met?'

'Well,' she said, 'not in the last few minutes.'

'What is it, Llinos? I can see you are worrying about something.'

'I don't know, I might be imagining it but Joe doesn't seem quite himself. It's nothing I can put my finger on but there's an air of resignation about him that makes me uneasy. How do you think he looks?'

Eynon smiled. 'Like a man who has everything he wants in life. Stop worrying about shadows, Llinos. Haven't you learnt by now to take every day as a blessing?'

'You're right. Now, how's Jayne?' Llinos asked, changing the subject. 'She was looking very well last time I saw her.'

'She's well enough, got her father's flair for business, I'm proud to say.'

'So her business affairs are flourishing?'

'Yes indeed,' Eynon said. 'That girl has brains

291

and beauty and she deserves a better man than Buchan.'

'It's my turn to tell you not to worry,' Llinos said. 'Jayne's turning into a fine, independent woman and she'll make her mark on the world, I'm sure. Has she secured any more shares in the Great Western Railway?'

Eynon shook his head. 'No, but then Jayne already has enough to make her quite powerful. She will oppose any plans Buchan may have for a takeover and so will the other more powerful shareholders. I'll keep Buchan out if I die in the attempt.'

'No talking of death, please.' Llinos smiled fondly at him. 'It's far too morbid a subject for a day like this.'

Eynon reached over and touched her hand. 'Quite right. Come along now, drink your cordial— it's time we took the air. Shall we walk along the promenade for a while?'

'That sounds nice,' Llinos said, obediently draining her glass.

'Right then, the promenade it is,' Eynon said. 'And I can show everyone that I've got the most beautiful woman in the world on my arm.'

Outside in the sunshine, Eynon breathed in the fragrant smell of the sea and sighed. Right now he was the happiest man in all the world.

*   *   *

Llinos and Joe sat in the dining room side by side at the long table, but she noticed he was scarcely eating any of the roast beef and vegetables.

'It was nice seeing Eynon this morning,' she said.

'He seemed in high spirits, praising Jayne to the skies as always.'

'Eynon is a good man.' Joe put down his fork. 'Llinos, I don't want to eat. I want to have an early night.'

'I'll come with you. I'm not hungry either.' She looked at Joe worriedly: he was paler than usual and his hands were trembling.

'Joe, are you sick?' she asked, suddenly frightened. 'Something's wrong. Come on, Joe, talk to me.' She got up from the table and put her arms around his shoulders, resting her cheek against his hair. 'I know you're not well. Have you seen a doctor?'

'Come upstairs, my love.' He pushed back his chair and took her in his arms. 'I want to be with you, to seal our love the way we've always sealed it.'

She followed him up to their bedroom, and watched him as he undressed and climbed into bed, realizing suddenly how thin he had become. She joined him, and they made love. Afterwards, he kissed her gently, with none of the urgency of the young but with infinite depth of feeling.

Llinos held him close. 'Joe, please tell me the truth. You're very sick, aren't you?'

He held her in his arms. 'I have been seeing dreams as I did when I was young. Remember how I knew you before we'd even met? Now the Great Spirit is telling me I'll have to start on my long journey soon. The only thing I'm sad about is that I have to leave you alone, my little firebird.' He spoke softly and Llinos felt her heart begin to pound.

'What do you mean?' Llinos stammered.

'The parting is coming sooner than I thought,

293

but don't mourn for too long. Just remember the happiness we've shared together.'

'No, Joe! What are you saying? I can't live without you!'

Joe propped himself up against the bed head. 'You will live a long time without me, my love, but I'll always be watching over you.'

'Please, Joe, don't talk like that,' she said desperately. 'We must get a doctor, the best in the world.'

'No doctor can help me, my love.' Joe kissed her cheek. 'I did hope we'd have longer together but it's not to be.'

'What about Lloyd? We must fetch him home.' Llinos was grasping at straws. 'You can't die without saying goodbye.'

'Our son and I have said our goodbyes.' He took her hand. 'But it's going to break my heart to say goodbye to you, my darling wife.'

'No, Joe, please, you don't have to die! Perhaps your dreams are wrong?'

'Hush now. Life has taken its toll on me and now I'm ready to leave it.'

'I can't believe you're ready to leave *me*,' Llinos protested. 'I know your kin in America have their own beliefs and their own way of leaving this world, but you mustn't think you have to follow them.'

'I know that, my love,' he said, 'and because of my upbringing I know there's no use in fighting destiny.' He drew her closer and she felt his warmth. 'Come, let's go to sleep together, my lovely firebird—and, Llinos, try to accept the inevitable as I do.'

She lay against the pillows, alone with her terrified thoughts. Joe couldn't die: he was just worrying too much. In the morning she would send for the doctor, then everything would be all right.

The next few days were torture for Llinos. She brought in doctor after doctor but none of them could find anything wrong with Joe. And yet he was fading away before her eyes.

She couldn't sleep. Every night she lay curled close to him, feeling the safeness of him, knowing she couldn't face life without him. It was the night before the Sabbath at about three in the morning when Llinos heard her husband sigh. She had kept the candles lit and now she drew one closer to her and looked down at Joe.

His eyes were open and he smiled, looking as young and handsome as the first time she'd set eyes on him.

'I have to go now, my lovely.'

'No, Joe, please, don't leave me.'

'My heart will stop beating but my soul will go on loving you, believe me, little firebird. Now, just hold me close.'

She held him, his head against her breast, and she willed him with all her strength to live. And then, quite suddenly, he was still. She looked down at him. His face was in repose as if he had gone to sleep, but she knew that his spirit had left his body. Her Joe was dead.

*   *   *

The funeral took place on a day filled with sunshine. Bright, cloudless skies made a mockery of the black-clad figures of the mourners. The hearse, drawn by two black horses, carried inside it the only man Llinos had truly loved.

She clung to the hand of her young son as Father Martin conducted the burial service. Standing by her were her only close friends, Eynon and his daughter Jayne. Few of the Swansea inhabitants had thought it necessary to turn out for the funeral of a foreigner. They had shunned Joe in life and intended to pay no respects to him now that he was dead.

Llinos thought she had cried all her tears but now, with Joe's coffin being put into the ground, more came.

'Ashes to ashes,' Father Martin intoned, 'dust to dust.'

Llinos bowed her head and prayed for comfort, but there was none. Her life might go on but it would be barren without her Joe.

Then the service was over and Llinos felt Eynon's hand on her arm as he drew her away from the grave. Sion's grasp on her hand tightened and Llinos made an effort to wipe away her tears.

'Don't cry, Mama,' Sion said softly. 'Papa is gone to the Great Spirit but he will always be there to look after us.'

'I know, darling.' Llinos lifted her head and walked proudly through the gates of the cemetery. Now she must learn to live without her beloved Joe.

CHAPTER THIRTY-ONE

Katie watched as the funeral procession passed by her, feeling sorry for the mourners. There were not many, just the widow and her son, and Mr Morton-

Edwards with Jayne.

Katie felt a deep sympathy with Mrs Mainwaring; she was covered in black, even her face hidden by a veil, but she could tell by the stoop of her shoulders how unhappy she was. Mr Mainwaring had seemed a strong, healthy man, but life could play strange tricks on people. Perhaps, Katie thought, she should take warning from all this. She shouldn't let life pass her by. She should see Bull, ask him why Rhiannon had been in his house that morning. There might be a reasonable explanation.

She went into the churchyard and watched as the kindly Father Martin performed the ceremony. His words were just audible to her as she stood in the shelter of the trees. She felt the solemnity of the occasion and tears came to her eyes. She wanted to run away through the winding streets of Swansea and fling herself into Bull's arms. Surely all that mattered was that they loved each other.

He had done his best to see her—he had even called up at the Big House several times but she had refused to speak to him. Had she been too hasty?

She watched as Mrs Mainwaring walked by, holding her son's hand. Mr Morton-Edwards nodded to her as he went past, but he did not stop to talk. He caught up with Mrs Mainwaring, put a hand under her elbow and guided her back towards the carriage.

Katie waited until everyone had gone, then went up to the grave and bowed her head. She did not know much about Mr Mainwaring, except that he had been a kindly gentleman, good and gentle to all he met. She turned and left the churchyard, walked slowly back along the road. The summer sun was going down and the shadows falling against the ground were violet, shading away into a deep purple.

Katie stood at the crossroads and wondered if she should go back to the Big House or try to see Bull. She found herself walking towards his home, and though her heart was thumping in her chest she knew she must try to put things right between them. She stood for a long time outside his house. The evening was drawing in and lamps were being lit in windows. But the windows of Bull's house remained dark.

All at once a jealous rage filled her: was he even now with Rhiannon in that hut they had once shared at the side of the track? Was he holding her and kissing her and telling her he loved her?

She tried to think calmly. Tomorrow was the opening of the line into Swansea, and Bull was probably with Mr Cookson the engineer making final plans. She might as well go home.

The walk to the Big House took almost an hour, and by the time she arrived at the back door the sun was setting.

'*Duw, duw!* Where have you been all day, Katie Cullen?' Cook was taking a meat pie out of the oven, pans were boiling on the range and the kitchen was stiflingly hot.

'It's my day off, remember?' Katie said. 'I went for a walk and I came across the funeral of the American Indian gentleman. I stopped to pay my respects.'

'Oh?' Cook placed the pie on the hob. 'Was he buried in a decent church, then? I thought he was a heathen.'

298

'I don't know about that but he was a kind man,' Katie said. 'He must have been, to take care of the little boy the way he did.'

'Aye,' Cook said. 'You're right enough there. He wasn't the boy's natural father.' She glanced round, as if afraid of being overheard. 'You know who the father is, don't you? Mrs Buchan's husband.'

'I've heard talk,' Katie said, 'but it's not for us to judge, is it?'

Cook ignored her. 'I know Mrs Buchan is a hard mistress to serve, but no woman deserves to live with a man who can't keep his trousers on!'

Katie frowned. Cook was so blunt.

'And what about you, then? Have you see Bull Beynon today?' Cook's eyes were bright with curiosity. 'I know you and him have fallen out again but take my advice and make it up with him. You won't find a finer man.'

'But I saw Rhiannon coming out of his house early one morning, Cook. How can I trust Bull now?'

'Listen, my girl, you don't take no notice of women like Rhiannon. Mind, she's out to get Bull back whatever way she can—he's a good meal ticket, especially now he's been made up to manager.' She puffed out a breath. 'Those maids are taking an awful long time laying the table. Go and fetch them, Katie. They'll be loitering around like ladies of leisure. You'd better given them a hand or we'll never get done here.'

Supper-time at the big house was always busy and so it was tonight, even though Mr Morton-Edwards and his daughter were the only ones present. For a while Katie was too busy to think of Bull or Rhiannon, but as she served the food she

299

couldn't help hearing the conversation around the table.

'I'm so sorry for Llinos,' Mr Morton-Edwards said. 'She's bereft without Joe.'

'But she didn't stay true to him while he was alive, did she?'

'I don't condone what she did but in her heart she always loved Joe very deeply.'

'Then why did she go to my husband?' Jayne demanded.

Katie kept her eyes lowered. What the master and his daughter were saying was no business of hers.

She felt rather than saw the master shrug his shoulders. 'I've asked myself that a thousand times. It could be that she wanted to prove to herself she was still desirable.'

'Well, my husband thought so—he probably still does.' Jayne waved her napkin in an effort to cool the red flush that stained her cheeks.

'And Joe had taken a mistress, remember,' the master said. 'Anyway, she finished with Buchan long before he was married to you.'

'Well, I don't think she should be playing the part of the grieving widow, not when she's free to get another man into her clutches.' She glanced up at Katie, who made every effort to appear engrossed in her task of taking away the soup plates. 'I only hope you're not going to be stupid enough to fall into Llinos's arms now that she's alone, Father.'

'What I do is my business—and we will not talk about Llinos any more, we will only quarrel.'

Katie left the room. The gentry could make a mess of their lives just as poor folk did.

300

In the kitchen Cook was taking a rest. She looked up at Katie as she came in and said, 'Now, Katie Cullen, my advice to you is to talk to your man. Tell him all that you saw and let him explain. It's only fair to hear his side of it.'

'I know, Cook, but I can't get it out of my head that Rhiannon stayed with him in his house all night alone. What if she tempted him and . . . well, you know.'

Cook leaned forward. 'Listen to an old woman before you ruin your life with jealous thoughts. You know full well that Rhiannon walked out of here without thinking about a roof over her head. If she turned up on the man's doorstep with nowhere to lay her head, do you think Bull could turn her away?'

'I suppose not.' Cook's words confirmed what Katie had thought. 'You're right, Cook,' she said. 'I should give him a chance to explain. I'll go and see him tomorrow when I do the shopping.'

'Aye? Well, don't forget tomorrow's the opening of Swansea station. Crowds will be there to see this Mr Brunel person and I doubt you'll get a chance to talk to Bull till it's over.'

'All I can do is my best.' Katie felt more cheerful now. 'I'll try to see him early, before all the pomp and ceremony starts.'

Cook heaved herself out of her chair. 'Good. We'd better shift our legs now—we've got a lot to do before we can go to bed.'

Later, as Katie lay in her bed, her doubts returned. Rhiannon had seemed so triumphant, so positive that she'd get Bull back. 'Am I deceiving myself?' she whispered into the darkness.

'So, Dafydd, it's true that you've taken another mistress?' Jayne gazed at her husband with dislike. 'I think you might have told me yourself, instead of letting me learn about it from the gossips. Where did you meet her and when?'

'That is not your business, madam.'

'I think it is when every servant from here to Cardiff knows about it.'

'I'll keep up the pretence that I still care for you.'

'How kind.' Jayne's voice was heavy with sarcasm. 'And am I to know who she is?'

'She's younger than you, full of the joys of life, and besotted with me.'

'A younger woman? So the merry widow could not be tempted?'

'That is over and done with.'

'She told me she'd never bother with you again, and Llinos is a woman of her word.' Jayne frowned. 'It's more than that, though, isn't it? I expect you tried to persuade her but she would have nothing to do with you. You see, Dafydd? We all find out what you're really like. In the future I see you as an embittered old man.'

'And what about you, Jayne?' Dafydd said. 'I can take a dozen mistresses if I like and no one would turn a hair—but a respectable woman may not have a lover, may she?'

'I am aware of that,' Jayne replied. 'I've only to see how poor Llinos is treated because of you.'

'So you'll lead the life of a nun, will you?' Dafydd was taunting her, but Jayne smiled.

'I will live the life of a successful businesswoman

302

who can outshine her husband at every turn. Don't concern yourself about me. If love-making is what you gave me I will never miss it.'

Her barb had struck home for Dafydd blanched. 'I shall leave you for tonight, my dear wife,' he said. 'I'll go to the arms of a woman who knows how to love.'

'And knows how to spend your money, I dare say,' Jayne said. 'Mistresses don't come cheap—at least, not from what I've overheard of servants' gossip.'

Dafydd turned on his heel and left the room. Jayne felt no regret, only relief that the pretence was over.

She moved to the desk, unlocked the little drawer and took out her share certificates. The paper crackled in her fingers and she smiled. This meant more, far more, than all Dafydd's bedroom fumblings put together.

CHAPTER THIRTY-TWO

Llinos had never felt less like going out than she did today. Only a short time ago she had watched her husband laid in his grave and the pain was still sharp, but Sion was looking forward to seeing the train arriving in Swansea for the first time and she could not disappoint him.

'When is Uncle Eynon coming for us?' He stood in the window, barely able to contain his excitement. 'And will there be crowds of people on the *Western Princess*?'

'Is that what the train is called?' Llinos made

303

herself pay attention. 'You know more than I do about it, Sion.'

'There he is! Uncle Eynon's here.'

Eynon came into the house. 'All ready, then? I see our Sion is raring to go.' He stepped closer to Llinos. 'Have you heard from Lloyd? I know he missed the funeral but I thought he'd be home by now.'

'Lloyd is living a new life. I think he follows the American Indian belief that his father is gone to a hallowed place and the ceremony of burial as we know it here is not necessary.'

'Still, I think he should have come, if only to support you.'

Llinos thought so too, but she did not want to be disloyal to her son. 'You were there, Eynon, and you always are when I need you.'

'That's what friends are for, isn't it?'

'Where's Jayne? I thought she was coming with us?'

'She's going as a guest of the bank, and she's thrilled to bits about it. Now, the carriage is waiting. Come along, Sion, we'll try to get as near the front as we can—we might even see Mr Brunel himself, if we're lucky.' He looked down at Llinos. 'And afterwards we'll be celebrating with the public breakfast and we'll certainly meet him there.'

'Oh, good,' Llinos said, without enthusiasm. 'Where is it being held?' She had hoped to be back at home within the hour.

'Mr Edgington of London has provided an enormous tent,' Eynon replied. 'There's to be a great feast with dishes to tempt even the most jaded palate. Lamb and collard veal as well as beef will be served, not to mention lobster and oysters straight from Oystermouth village.'

'It sounds wonderful,' Llinos said absently, but she knew she would not be able to eat a thing.

The drive through Swansea would normally have left her gasping with pleasure: flags fluttered from rooftops, and streamers hung from upstairs windows giving the town a festive air. But without Joe to share it with her she felt numb.

'Look, Uncle Eynon.' Sion pointed to a group of bandsmen dressed in red jackets piped with white braid. 'Aren't they grand?'

Llinos could think of nothing but Joe. Her world was incomplete without him in it. Even when he had been far away in America, she'd known he was thinking about her, loving her.

Sion took her hand, and it was as if he sensed her grief. 'Papa would have wanted you to enjoy today,' he said gently. 'You know he's looking down at you, keeping you safe.'

'You're like an old man,' she said. 'You've got a wise head on young shoulders.' But the child's words comforted her and her spirits lightened. For his sake she would try at least to give the impression that she was enjoying herself. 'I'm glad you brought me out, Eynon,' she said brightly. 'I think I'm going to enjoy today, after all.'

*   *   *

Dafydd took Serena's arm and led her towards the tent where the festive breakfast was laid out. He was bored with her already, but she would do until something better came along.

He smiled thinly. His wife would not expect to see him there, and certainly not with his mistress.

305

That would take the smug look off her face. She had forgotten that, as an important businessman, Dafydd would have received an invitation and today, even though he was not a shareholder, he intended to make the most of the occasion to speak to some influential people. He would buy his way into the Great Western Railway, whatever it cost him.

'Oh dear,' his mistress moaned, 'do we really have to suffer the indignation of pushing through these crowds of common people?'

'Be quiet, Serena, or I'll begin to wish I hadn't bought you. We'll make our way round the back of the tents—it should be less crowded there.'

'But the ground is damp and my shoes will be ruined.'

'Oh, for heaven's sake!' He stared down at her. 'You're becoming a bore.'

She opened her mouth to reply but shut it again as three burly men barred their way.

'Can I help you, gentlemen?' Dafydd said mildly, but his shoulders were tense: he sensed that these men meant trouble. By heading off the main track he'd laid himself open to any footpad who happened to be waiting for good pickings. He glanced around him but there was no escape. He could hear the crowds that thronged the field— women's laughter, the shouts of children—but realized that no one would hear him if he called for help.

'What do you want?' he demanded, but no one spoke. The first blow felled him and he lay in the dust, trying to clear his head. 'What's this all about?' He wiped the blood from his mouth just as another blow caught him in the ribs.

'If it's money you want, take it.' He fumbled for his wallet but one of the men kicked it out of his hand.

'You bastards!' Dafydd said, feeling his lip swell to twice its normal size. 'Tell me what you want and I'll give it to you.' He tried to get up but his feet were kicked from under him and he fell heavily to the ground. He twisted and turned but the silent beating went on remorselessly until, at last, Dafydd gave up the unequal struggle.

He must have passed out because it was some time later when he opened his swollen eyes and peered round him. His attackers had gone and so had his mistress. He staggered to his feet, ignoring the curious looks that came his way, and slowly made his way home.

CHAPTER THIRTY-THREE

Katie stood at the edge of the crowd, straining to see if the train was coming into the terminus. Work on the Swansea station was not yet completed, but banners hung everywhere and some of the crowd were waving flags excitedly. She sensed someone beside her and looked round quickly. 'Oh, Rhiannon, it's you.'

'Hello, Katie. On your own, then?'

'Yes, I am, and you know why, don't you, Rhiannon?'

'Aye, 'spects I do. Lor', that Bull, he's a demon for getting up early, always has been.'

'I know you're doing your best to take him away from me,' Katie said, 'but I heard this morning from one of the maids that you're not living with Bull at all. You're working for Mr Cookson, the engineer.'

Rhiannon looked away sheepishly. 'Well, that don't stop me seeing Bull, does it? I think my boy's had a change of heart now, see. No fault of yours, mind, it's just that I know what pleases Bull.'

Katie felt a dragging sense of despair, but before she had time to say anything a man came rushing along the track shouting at the top of his voice: 'Accident! Up the line! A man and a boy are trapped! Someone come and help!'

He caught sight of Rhiannon and grabbed her arm. 'Come quickly, it's Bull,' he said. 'There's been a fall of earth between Landore and Swansea, and he's caught up in it.'

Katie froze. 'Is he all right?' she called over Rhiannon's shoulder, but the man ignored her. His sympathy was for Rhiannon, who had been Bull's woman for a long time.

'You'd better get up there, Rhiannon,' he said. 'The engine with the directors on board will be coming in about one o'clock and you'll never get past the crowd then.'

Katie had a sudden picture of Mrs Mainwaring at her husband's funeral. She saw again her drooping shoulders, and in that moment she was more frightened than she had ever been in her life.

'I'm coming with you,' Katie said. 'Don't try to stop me, Rhiannon, because I'm coming whatever you say.'

'Be quick, then.' Rhiannon began to run along the trackside pushing her way between the crowds. Katie followed in her wake, easily keeping pace, fear wrapping itself around her like a cloak and

308

sweat beading her brow. 'Please, God, let him be alive,' she murmured over and over again.

She gasped as the huge fall of earth came into sight. The navvies, dressed incongruously in their Sunday best, were digging feverishly. Seth O'Connor was among them, covered in earth, and she ran as close to him as she dared.

'Seth, what's happened?' she called, and the Irishman looked up sharply.

'Get away from here, Katie Cullen. God only knows what we're going to find.'

'Tell me what's happened, please, Seth.'

He came to her then, rubbing the sweat off his brow with his sleeve. His face was red and he was breathing heavily.

'A little boy was playing here,' he gasped. 'We saw the earth on the bank start to slide and Bull jumped forward to save him. The last we saw of him was half an hour ago when the earth covered them both. Put yourself in mind of it, Katie. The chances are that both the boy and Bull are goners.'

'No!' Katie scrabbled at the earth with her bare hands. Somehow she knew in her heart that Bull was nearby.

'Go back, Katie! 'Tisn't safe here, colleen.' Seth tried to drag her away. 'Stand over there with the other women—we'll get him out, I promise you.'

'Seth,' Katie looked at him, her eyes pleading with him to listen to her. 'Bull is under here, I just know in my bones he is. Please, Seth, will you dig this part of the earth for me?'

He nodded and carefully put his spade into the soft earth. 'If he's here I'll find him, don't you fret.'

After several agonizing minutes Katie heard the spade strike something metallic and Seth looked up at her. ' 'Tis a bit of piping. It might just be . . .' His words trailed away as an answering knock sounded on the pipe.

'Over here, boys!' Seth called excitedly. 'There's someone alive down here.' He glanced at Katie. 'Don't get your hopes up too high, love, it might just be the little boy.'

Slowly the men began to uncover the pipe. 'Look, boys,' Seth called. 'A man would get air to breathe through the pipe and some of the timbers under here are poking through the earth.' His voice rose. 'It looks as if Bull had a chance to save the boy before the earth covered him.'

Katie clasped her hands together. 'Mother Mary, keep Bull safe! I don't care what he's done or who he wants, just let him be alive and I'll never ask for another thing as long as I live.'

With painful slowness the pipe was uncovered. Seth grasped the end of a piece of timber and hesitated. 'We got to do this carefully, boys,' he said, 'or we could cause another fall of earth.'

Slowly the timbers were raised and a cheer went up from the men. Katie strained to see but the navvies crowded round, only too willing to help.

'Here's the child!' One of the navvies lifted the boy and wiped the earth from his face. He was passed carefully from man to man until he was in the arms of his weeping mother.

A loud cheer went up from the navvies, and Katie almost stopped breathing as Bull was pulled from the earth. He stood up, brushed the dirt from his face, and Katie felt as if her heart was melting inside her.

'Thank you, Mother Mary, thank you, thank you,' she whispered. Then she watched as

Rhiannon pushed forward. The crowd of men parted to let her get to Bull and he hugged her, but his eyes were scanning the crowds. When he saw Katie he put Rhiannon aside and came towards her, his arms outstretched. Beneath the earth that grimed his face and matted his hair, he was smiling.

'My little love,' he said. 'I knew you'd be here for me.' He put his arms around her and she closed her eyes, loving him so much it hurt.

'Thank God you're alive. I was so afraid I'd never see you again.'

'Oh, you can't get rid of Bull Beynon that easily,' he said. 'I had to live to make you my wife. You will marry me, won't you?'

Over his shoulder, Katie saw Rhiannon, head bent as she walked away, but her heart was so full of gladness that all she could think of was Bull, here in her arms, safe and well and needing her.

'Go on, Katie Cullen!' Seth shouted. 'Put the man out of his misery! Say you'll marry him.'

Katie's voice shook as she answered him: 'I'll marry you, Bull, my sweetheart. How could I say no when I love you so much?'

Seth O'Connor began to clap and the other navvies joined in. They crowded around Bull and Katie, slapping Bull on the back and heaping congratulations on them.

From the distance came the whistle of the train bringing the directors into Swansea. Bull looked up, his arm still round Katie's waist. 'Come on, boys, we're not going to miss the greatest spectacle of our lives, are we? Get down to the station and catch a look at the great man himself.'

He took Katie's hand and ran with her towards the station. As she struggled to keep up with him,

311

her heart sang with joy. Bull was alive, and he was hers for now and for always.

Breathless, she came to a stop beside him. She could see the colourful uniforms of the band, the mayor standing at the edge of a red carpet and, in the crowd of dignitaries on the platform, Mr Morton-Edwards with Mrs Mainwaring and her little boy. Then Jayne Buchan pushed forward, impeccably dressed as always. Katie looked down ruefully at her own earth-spattered skirts. But that didn't matter. She slipped her hand into Bull's and he squeezed it gently. 'Any minute now, Katie.' She knew by the excitement in his voice that he was happy to be here with her to see the majestic engine come into sight. She stood on tiptoe but then, laughing, Bull lifted her in his great arms so that she could see over the heads of the crowd.

Slowly, the gleaming engine came into view. Steam billowed from the funnel like a pale cloud in the sunshine and sparks fell like stars into the grass.

A great cheer went up from the crowd as the train ground to a halt. Men with tall hats stepped from the carriage, and the mayor of Swansea, his gold chain gleaming, was shaking the hand of one.

'That's Brunel himself,' Bull said, and Katie looked at the man who had made the Great Western Railway possible and saw that he was ordinary, stocky, broad-shouldered, not a patch on her Bull.

The band struck up, and Katie felt a catch in her throat as the procession moved away from the platform. Bull put her down and Katie curled into his arms. 'You must be very proud,' she said, looking up into his dirty face. 'You've been part of

312

all this from the start.'

'Katie, at this moment I'm a happier man than the great Isambard Kingdom Brunel himself. His dream has come true. He's brought the Great Western into Swansea. But my dream, from the first moment I met you, was to make you my wife.' He bent towards her and a shower of earth fell from his hair on to her face, but Katie didn't notice for Bull's lips were claiming hers, and her heart was singing because this was the happiest day of her life.